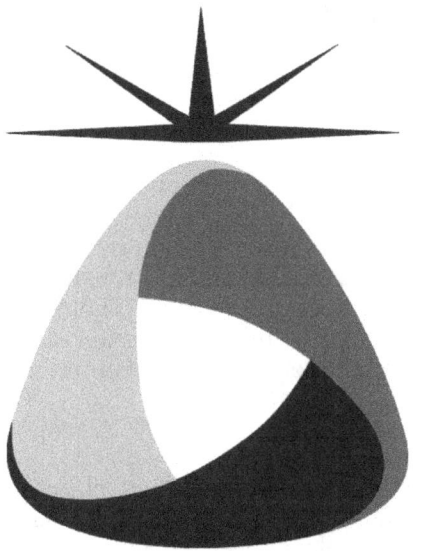

TRIANGLE:
WILDCARD

D. G. SPEIRS

PERFECT IMPRESSIONS, LAKELAND, FL

Triangle logo by Rosemarie J. Ruzicka
Cover art by Eric Koda

ISBN 978-0-9858115-7-0

Copyright November 2016 by D. G. Speirs

A Perfect Impressions book
Lakeland, FL
Printed in the United States of America

This one was for you, Mom...

I wish you could have seen it.

But then again,
you've been peeking over my shoulder
all along...

TRIANGLE:
FALSE MIRROR

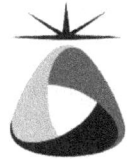

Prologue

Security Coordinator Stewart Franks settled into his office on the seventeenth floor of a nondescript office building in Portland. Outside the window, the Willamette River reflected the lights of cars on the I-5 as they rode the Marquam Bridge across the river to wherever they were headed this late at night. Here inside, everything was quiet, with everybody gone for the evening.

Franks took a sip of his coffee and looked at his monitor again. He was reading on his monitor the official briefing from headquarters on the Tokyo incident. Word had spread over the last twenty-four hours of the failure of that adventure. *What a fiasco,* he thought. He'd seen the regular reports about the new asset, a deep cover agent embedded within Triangle itself, who had promised them the virtual crown jewels of classified projects. Franks had been surprised to learn the agent was a Zodiac, and not just any of them, but Triangle's head of security. But he figured that would be a good thing, this would advance the timetable considerably.

Targeting False Mirror made sense, but using it to blackmail Triangle and thus force it to defend itself with an act of desperation? Franks shook his head. The mission fairly reeked of a revenge motive, something their leader always warned against.

Quickly scanning through the report, Franks found the results. The False Mirror prototype and the duplicate they had fabricated right here had been recovered by Triangle's operatives. Worse, the new operative, Williams, was dead - spectacularly so. *A fall from Tokyo SkyTree?* He shuddered. *They must have used a spatula for the remains.* He read a little further and paused.

Tactical support for this mission was provided by another pair of Zodiac agents, designated Gemini One and Two. Gemini One's real name was Hannah Callahan, a Talent who could be persuasive – very much so. Gemini Two was her twin sister Karen, who had never manifested any ability, but who was a perfect physical duplicate to her sister in every way. Unless Hannah employed her gift, there was no way to tell them apart.

To the world, Gemini existed as a single identity, and they used this ability to infiltrate security systems and access targets around the world. It made them the world's deadliest assassins, knows to intelligence services simply as The Ghost. *I've often thought I'm glad they're on our side.* Hannah had been one of the Leader's earliest recruits, long before this current project, even before Gemini was, well, Gemini. She considered Gemini was among its most valuable assets.

And now, apparently, they were gone.

She cannot be pleased about that. The report stated Gemini One had been killed during the mission, a plasma blast to the back, assailant unknown. Her body had been recovered. That alone would have been bad enough. But worse, during the recovery process, somehow the transit failed. The connection terminated as her sister was stepping into the field. Attempts to reestablish the connection failed. Technicians still could not explain the reason for the interference, other than to say a safety interlock kicked in. But they believe Gemini Two was lost in transit.

Franks shuddered. *Not the way I'd want to go, vanished forever in-between, wherever that space is.*

A flicker of motion on a monitor caught his attention. He turned toward his security array and scanned it, looking for anything amiss. He spotted the slight flicker for elevator three and pulled up the elevator status screen. Sure enough, the car was on the move, but only at one-quarter speed. Curious, he activated the car's interior camera.

A single occupant stood in the center, a woman with

her arms held out to the sides. Franks raised an eyebrow as electrical arcs flashed from outstretched hands to the elevator walls. The woman looked straight at the camera, her hair a glowing white halo around her head. Her eyes glowed from within as she smirked. *She knows she's being watched.* The woman's eyes flashed brighter. The image dissolved into static.

Value your privacy, do you? Franks rubbed his chin as he considered his options. He looked toward the ceiling. "Niccolo?"

"Online," the facility's artificial intelligence responded. Its voice was a warm baritone with a hint of an Italian accent.

"We have an unwanted guest. Let's prepare a proper welcome. Contingency four in the Elevator lobby."

"Faraday cage? Yes, sir. Strength level?"

"Level 3." He looked again at the statistic on the monitors. "On second thought, better make it Level 2 to be safe. And place cages on all other access points to the floor." *Might as well be thorough.*

"Complying."

As the AI set to work, he pulled two frames of the intruder from the video and attached them to a message to headquarters.

Intruder, possible advanced Talent. Advise disposition.

Throughout the building, wire screens slid from recessed notches to form holding areas outside all stairway and elevator entrances to the floor. As Franks hit transmit, Niccolo said, "Faraday cages in place."

"Good. Monitor and advise me of Elevator Three's status." He checked his weapons and headed for the elevator lobby.

As Franks approached, Niccolo interrupted him. "Elevator Three has paused between the fifteenth and sixteenth floors."

"It stopped moving? How long ago did that happen?"

"Four seconds before you asked. Correction, it is moving upward again and is passing the sixteenth floor."

Not enough time to have gotten out. Franks turned toward the doors and drew his weapon. The left set of doors slid open to show a darkened elevator car. Franks paused, then called out, "Step out slowly with your hands over your head." Silence. He grabbed the flashlight off his belt, flicked it on and aimed its intense beam into the elevator car.

It was empty.

Son of a —; they must have escaped somehow in that instant when it stopped. "Niccolo!" he yelled, his voice tight with a sense of rising panic. "Lock down the building. Scan all interstitials, floors fifteen and above. Look for motion, heat signatures—"

"Now is that any way to welcome me back?"

He jumped at the unexpected female voice and turned around. It was the woman from the monitor, wearing a black jumpsuit and jacket with patches for a Seattle EMT unit. She held up her right hand. Sparks jumped from her fingers.

His gaze darted toward the receptionist's desk in the lobby, with its panic button to call HQ for backup. She caught his movement and waggled a finger before casually flicking his ear with it.

It was as if Franks had touched a live wire. Every nerve screamed, and his knees went weak. Gun and flashlight slipped from numb fingers and clattered to the floor.

She leaned in close. "Now that I have your attention let's chat. You see, we're on the same team."

Franks looked up, still woozy from the shock. "Wh-what?"

"My, aren't you articulate. And entirely useless." She pushed Franks over with one foot, and he fell to the ground. She looked toward the ceiling. "AI, what's your designation?"

"Niccolo."

"Gee, how romantic," She deadpanned. "My voice print is on file. Confirm identity."

There was a pause. "Identity confirmed. Welcome back, Gemini Two."

Franks' eyes widened in surprise. The woman nodded. "Send the following message, top priority. Gemini Two at Portland facility, requesting instructions."

"Complying."

Franks climbed unsteadily to his feet. He stared at her as if she were a poltergeist. Gemini Two, or more precisely Karen Callahan, saw this and turned, right hand up, sparks flying. She snapped at him in anger. "What? You want another?"

It can't be. It doesn't look like her. No, wait. The scar. Above the right eyebrow. "But we received notice," he stammered. "You were—"

"Dead?"

He swallowed hard and nodded. "Lost somewhere unknown, presumably forever."

"I'd hardly call Seattle unknown. And whoever made that call it is in for one hell of a shock." She clicked her fingers. Sparks popped off them like a holiday sparkler.

But she wasn't like her sister. She never manifested. Franks gulped, trying to conceal his unease. *What happened to her out there?* "I hope you understand my response was not personal. We have an intruder protocol. If I'd been advised to expect you, especially now that—"

"That I'm, what, special?" Her voice rose as she pushed in on him. "What would you have done? Put the welcome mat out? Baked me cookies? Things you used to do for my sister, but never for me?" Franks backed up at her vehemence. In a moment, all Callahan's anger melted away. She became almost a different woman, with a charming smile. "Sorry, just a little stressed. Didn't mean to scare you. As you say, this is all a big misunderstanding."

"Pardon me," interrupted Niccolo. "There is a reply."

The woman looked upward. "Well, don't keep us on pins and needles, what does it say?"

"Expedite to headquarters. Extreme caution advised."

She barked a laugh, "I'll bet that last bit was for you. No matter." She grabbed his arm, and he flinched, expecting the worst. She ignored that. "What did you say your name was?"

"Franks."

"Lead on, Franks. Get me where I need to go."

He glanced upward. "Niccolo, prepare transit."

"Yes, sir. For how many?"

"Just our guest here."

"Complying."

He led the way through cubicles and a hallway of locked offices to a door labeled 'Freight Services.' Franks placed his right hand on an ID scanner on the wall, the door unlocked, and they entered.

The room was empty, not a table, chair, or even a paper clip in its twelve-by-twelve expanse. Automatic lights switched on around the edges of the ceiling as they walked in. "Link confirmed. Transit opens in thirty seconds," said Niccolo.

Franks turned to Callahan. "Welcome back."

She held out a hand. "No hard feelings. I know you were just doing your job."

He paused for a moment, then relaxed and shook her hand. "Thanks for understanding. Although, you've made my life problematic."

"Oh, don't be so hard on yourself."

"Not at all. You must have used your new ability to pause the elevator, then short and bypass my ventilation sensors to slip behind me. That system will need a full re-design. I'm not upset. I sort of admire it, in fact."

A twitch tugged at the corner of her mouth. Callahan leaned in and murmured, "Just between you and me, I didn't come in through the vents."

He pulled back, his look quizzical. "You didn't? But how—?" His eyes got wide. "That would mean you—"

"Shh." She put a single finger to his lips. "I'm afraid that one stays my little secret."

The lightning slammed Franks back against the wall. He slid limply to the floor. His lifeless eyes stared up at her.

Callahan looked at his smoking corpse. "Such a waste." There was a white flash behind her. She turned and walked toward it. Ten seconds later the room was dark.

Chapter 1

July 12, 9:19 a.m. MDT

Senior Agent Alan Hamilton took another sip of coffee and looked out through the Control Hub windows. He was happy whenever Vault Watch came up on his duty rotation at Triangle Red Labs. It was nice and quiet down here, just supervising a squad walking patrols checking the locks on vaults that would rarely if ever get opened. Nothing ever happened.

Well, nothing except for the random intruder drills. They used to be occasional, but since the theft last spring, they'd become more random and a lot more frequent. And a lot more annoying, too. That was the new security chief's doing.

Hate the drills. Unnecessary, really. The theft was from a lab way up on Level 3. These are the Vaults. At Level 29, we're so deep underground no intruder is ever going to make it this far.

"Excuse me, Agent, sir?"

Hamilton closed his eyes and sighed. Rookies. *They always stick me with rookies. I must have done something to some HR clerk in a former life.* He glanced over and studied the newly minted squadie seated at the console to his right, very buff, red-hair in a buzz cut and nervous as hell. Probably was an all-American on some college football team somewhere. He read the rookie's nameplate on his chest again. "What is it, Simons? And I told you before, knock it off with the sir."

"Yes, sir. I mean, Agent, sir."

Hamilton shook his head. "Just get on with it."

"Camera in hallway 29-B just went offline." The kid pointed to an array of monitors in the overhead. One was dark.

That got Hamilton's attention. *Black. Not static?* "Any signal?"

"Negative. Diagnostics read—" Simons looked at him. "Device invalid. As if the camera is missing."

Hamilton rubbed his chin for a moment. "Roll back the footage. Let's see when that occurred."

Simons typed on his keyboard. The computer complied, running swiftly through the camera's archived video. The timestamp showed it had been down under three minutes. The last captured image was a surprise - a woman dressed in black walks into the frame and points her hand at the camera before it drops out.

"Is this how drills usually start?" asked Simons.

Something tickled the back of Hamilton's mind. *We're too far down. It's not possible.* "No, but perhaps the drill team was bored and wanted to try something different," he said, as much to convince himself. "Call up your intruder protocols and lock down the level." He keyed open the console microphone. "All guards on duty, intruder detected. Corridor Bravo. Romero, Duncan, take point."

Two guards in the core just outside the Hub tossed off a salute and headed away, moving right from Hamilton's point of view toward Bravo. He switched to a command circuit. "Romero, keep your eyes open. I've got a feeling about this one."

"Ah, Chief, you worry too much," she replied. Hamilton could hear the grin in her voice as they turned the corner.

"Still, I need you two to be—"

There was a bright white flash from the corridor as a blast of static fed back through the comm channel. Both guards flew backward, thrown from the hallway as an electrical discharge played over them. Alarms blared from the control panel.

"Sir!" Simons pointed, and Hamilton watched in shock as bio-monitors for both Romero and Duncan appeared on the lower console screen. They flared red for a brief second, then both flatlined and turned black.

A second pair of guards at the entrance to Corridor Charlie opposite reacted to their team members going down and ran to help them. From around the corner of Bravo came a tall woman with a halo of white hair and eyes that glowed. With a grin, she thrust her arms out in front of her. Lightning leaped from them and struck the second pair of guards in mid-stride.

Hamilton blinked against the bright flare of light. When his eyes cleared, he spotted his guards on the floor. On the monitor, two new bio-monitors appeared, Cordes and Jaeger. Their bio-monitors flickered in the red. Still alive, but just barely.

"This isn't a drill, is it, sir?" Simons' voice was shaky.

"No, Rookie, definitely not!" said Hamilton as he slammed his hand down on the security breach alarm. Automated protocols went into effect, signaled by an alert klaxon. A five-minute countdown timer appeared on monitors inside the hub.

Another attacker joined the first. Hamilton did a fast threat assessment and hit the record button on the console. "Senior Agent Alan Hamilton, recording. Level 29 is under assault by unknown entities. First attacker, Female, 6'2", Caucasian, slender build, white hair, augmented clothing with electrical weapon built in."

As Hamilton watched, a second attacker came around the corner. He continued to record. "A second assailant has joined the first. Also female, based on her silhouette. Approximately 5'6", dressed head to toe in black, face covered, no eye cutout, so probably a mesh mask. Some sort of utility belt and a back harness. Based on that, my best estimate is this one is eastern trained, presumably ninjitsu, at an expert level. Status, two deceased, two critical. Level sealed, countdown initiated."

He looked at the rookie. "Right. Simons, send that upstairs."

As he reached for his microphone to warn the rest of his guards on the floor, this new assailant pulled a pair of silver discs from a pouch on her belt and slid them along the floor toward another pair running at her from Delta Corridor. The discs burst open and sprayed a cloud of yellow gas that his personnel, Franklin and Schmitt, ran headlong into. The pair of women emerged from the fog, retching and gagging before they collapsed to the floor. Their bio-monitors popped up, shifted to yellow and started to slide slowly toward red. *Poison. No way of knowing what the toxin is.* He could only hope the response team would be able to deal with it. From the looks of it, this would be a race against time whether they could be saved.

The tall attacker yelled to her partner, "Less than five minutes until their backup arrives."

Hamilton stiffened in surprise. *They know that part of our protocols?*

Her partner nodded. "Go on ahead; I'll clean up here." The tall one turned and headed away toward Alpha Corridor and the main vaults.

Where are you going? Hamilton had two active guards left on the floor and needed to slow down these attackers until help arrived. He keyed his mike. "Bond, Faldon, do you read me?"

"Loud and clear, Chief," said Faldon. "Interesting sort of drill."

"You could say that." Hamilton checked his locator map. "I show you two in Omega Corridor, right behind Control. We have one intruder at the central hub and a second making her way into Alpha."

"Roger that. What's our play?"

"Proceed into the hub and eliminate the first subject. The invader isn't playing nice. Neither will we. Shoot to kill."

"Yes, Chief."

Hamilton looked out the window. He felt the rookie's gaze on him. "Got something to say? Spit it out."

"No, Chief." Simons became very interested in the console's keyboard.

Faldon and Bond emerged from opposite sides of the control hub, Mark-98 rifles raised. As soon as they spotted the smaller assailant, they took aim. Their target charged directly at them as they began to fire.

Then, suddenly, she wasn't there, as their shots splashed and scarred the far wall.

"What the hell?" Hamilton started. Then the woman reappeared, high above the pair of agents, a curved black handle in her hand. It took Hamilton a moment to realize what it was.

A sword hilt! He reached for his microphone to sound a warning, but it was already too late. The attacker pressed a control, and a gray swarm poured out, millions of nanites that instantly formed a blade. A moment later, the razor-sharp katana slashed out and sliced through both rifles. The phased plasma in the weapons, now uncontrolled, discharged in a feedback reaction that caught the guards helpless. Hamilton was powerless to do anything but watch as blue fire bathed over both Bond and Faldon. When it dimmed, they collapsed to the ground. Inside control, their biomonitors appeared already flatlined and went dark.

Hamilton slammed his fist against the console. "Goddammit!" He looked at the countdown timer. 4:02. In just over two minutes all his personnel were neutralized.

"What sort of weapon was that, sir?" Simons' voice squeaked.

Hamilton hoped his own unease didn't show. "A nanite sword," he said gruffly. "And yes, before you ask, that's something new. We need to report it, now. You're online with central?"

"No, comms have been cut off since the camera went down."

Which means my threat analysis went nowhere. "Well, add it to the local record, at least. Audio and video. We'll upload it later for review."

"Yes...yes, sir. But isn't the intruder going to come for us?"

Obviously, thought Hamilton as he glanced again at the timer. *3:25. Can that clock move any slower?*

He walked over and put a hand on the rookie's shoulder. "We're in the safest room in the facility. That's inch-thick laminated Plexiglas we're behind. The door has a magnetic seal, and we have a separate environmental control for Control." Hamilton glanced at the clock on the control panel. 2:58. "In just three minutes, a response squad will flood this level with dozens of trained personnel. Our intruder, good as she is, has no way to get in here and no way to out of there."

"Yes, sir. But then why is she sticking discs on the window?"

He twisted to look. "What discs—"

His words were cut off by an ear-piercing screech. The sound rolled through him, his world spun, and his coffee made a return appearance. The volume increased and Hamilton was sure his head was about to explode. Mercifully, he passed out a few seconds after Simons and fell to the floor atop the younger guard.

9:28 a.m. MDT

After the Plexiglas window shattered the hooded assailant checked to confirm the guards inside were disabled. She slapped another black disc onto the console. It activated, causing monitors throughout Control to scramble into unreadable static before they blinked out one by one. Satisfied, she jumped down and ran up to Alpha Corridor to meet her partner.

The taller assailant was overriding the lock to vault 31-A as she arrived. "You cut that close. Two minutes left," her partner chided. There was a buzz and the vault swung open. "And we still need to find the target."

"So we jump back from inside." The two entered the vault. Automated lights flickered on. "Shut the door. It'll buy some additional time." She pulled off her hood and blonde hair cascaded down as she moved to a data console on the wall. She brought up the vault's inventory, which she hastily scanned. "78-49, 75-44 - ah. Found it. 73-19!"

The vault door sealed with a thud. "Good," said the taller one, heading into the shelves. "I'll grab it while you arrange our exit."

The blonde reached into a vest pocket and grabbed another thin black disc. This one had a small white triangle on one side. She pressed it to a wall at eye level, so the triangle faced her, stepped back to admire her handiwork, then reached out and touched the symbol.

"Three minutes to activation," she called out. "Move it!"

9:30 a.m. MDT

Now, where are you? The taller assailant sprinted down an aisle. As she turned a corner, she spotted the location label on a shelf near the top. She climbed and found the target, a small aluminum transport case. *Got you!* She pulled it down, sliced through the security seals and opened it. Inside were a dozen sealed test tubes and a set of file folders. She held a test tube up. The red liquid inside sparkled in the light as she tilted it.

The woman pulled out a wad of black cloth and with a snap unrolled a padded bandoleer. With care, she began to transfer test tubes into it. She'd just inserted the seventh when a bright flash came from the front of the vault. Her partner called out, "Time to leave!"

"I'm hurrying!"

A grinding sound came from the vault door. "Well, hurry faster. Company's coming. You've got maybe another minute to finish, tops."

Indecision gnawed at her. Her instructions were explicit, secure all samples and notes, leaving no trace of the theft. She made a snap decision. She wrapped the bandoleer around the file folders and shoved them aside, then powered up and fired a bolt of electricity into the case. There was a sizzling sound as the samples boiled in their test tubes and exploded. Glass fragments and liquid sprayed back at her.

She looked around in dismay. *Not exactly a clean getaway. Still, anything left is fried and useless to them.* She slammed down the case lid, snapped closed the latches and tossed it up onto the shelf.

She came out of the shelves at a dead run as her partner waited next to a great circle of white light. The woman raised an eyebrow at the wet red splatter all over her clothes and face. "What happened?"

"Long story." She raised her arm and fired another bolt of lightning at the data console on the wall. It exploded in a shower of sparks.

Her partner raised an eyebrow. "Overkill?"

"Misdirection. Covers our tracks and keeps them guessing. Let's go." The two stepped through the white circle and disappeared. A moment later, the circle shrunk to a point and vanished.

9:34 a.m. MDT

The vault door opened just enough to roll in a flash-bang grenade. As it went off the door cycled open, and security agents in tactical gear swarmed in, weapons ready to deal with any disoriented enemies.

Matt Stoneham, Chief of Security for Triangle Red Labs, led the assault team personally. He had already seen the grim situation in the Hub and wanted these assailants. First in, weapon ready, he was surprised by the tactical reading his helmet's heads-up display gave of the vault.

Empty?! How in the blue blazes can it be empty? He verified the reading with his second, then toggled his comm to full broadcast. "Stoneham to all security personnel. Targets still at large. Repeat, targets still at large. Initiate full facility lock down. Immediate protective detail on all research staff. Establish a level-by-level search. Nobody in or out." He switched channels. "Stevens."

His assistant came on the comm. "Yes, sir?"

"The vault must have been a decoy."

"Are you sure, sir? Savannah indicates it was the only one accessed on this level."

"That we're aware of, at least. Get me inventory teams down here on the double. Even if this was a feint, I need to know if something is missing, or if any other vault was accessed."

"Right away, sir."

Stoneham spotted the damage to the wall console. "Send an IT forensics guy, too. They disabled the terminal in here; let's figure out why."

7:22 p.m. MDT

Stoneham stood in the Control Station of Level 29 with his arms crossed. It had already been a long day, with no end in sight.

The sweep had turned up no trace of the intruders. During the attack, they'd infiltrated this Control Station and planted a worm which had wiped out most surveillance of the event. All Stoneham's team had recovered so far was a single picture of one attacker from a single guard's body camera - a tall, thin female dressed in black with white hair and eyes that seemed to glow, pointing a hand toward the guard. She hadn't survived the encounter.

Matt sensed he'd seen the face somewhere before but wasn't quite making the connection. He'd assigned one of his lead investigators to track down an ID.

He picked up the black disc the intruder had left behind and frowned. They were fearless, and unafraid, sure that he'd have no luck tracing them from any gear left behind. It spoke to a level of arrogance he was coming to dislike more by the second.

No track. Stoneham checked his data tablet, scrolling through various feeds. *We have no visuals where these two were before they infiltrated Level 29 and started wrecking the place. Only two ways in, elevator and the emergency escape stairs and the video on both are utterly clean. I have no idea how they got in or out of the facility at all.* He looked up at the ceiling at one of the security cameras, still not functioning. *Engineering teams can repair the damage, an inventory team will work through the vaults, IT will track any digital fingerprints, yet somehow it all still seems like too little, too late, if they can walk in and out of here anytime they like.*

Sylvia McManus, the inventory team leader, walked up. "How are you holding up?"

"Not my best day."

"How bad?"

"Six dead. Three more in the infirmary. Two in critical condition."

"Oh, Matt, I'm so sorry."

"Damnedest thing, too. Half of the casualties were electrocuted. My one coherent survivor is a rookie guard who swears one attacker had a weapon that shot lightning from her hands."

"That's new. Even for here."

"Tell me about it.

McManus looked back toward Alpha corridor. "Well, how about some good news? Whatever they were here for, it doesn't appear they got it." She handed him a data tablet. "My inventory drones finished their run through all the vaults and came back one hundred percent intact. Everything is still here."

Stoneham scrolled through the list on the tablet. "You're sure about this? They damaged the terminal in 31-A. Maybe they covered their tracks after loading something to hide what they've done." He handed her back the device. "Could it have tricked your drones?"

"Not likely. It's an independent system."

The security chief closed his eyes. *It can't be that easy.* He frowned and shook his head. "We've missed something."

"What do you mean?"

"You don't break into a secure underground facility and kill people just to play tag. How do your drones complete the inventory?"

"They move through and scan, comparing item against its location."

"But do they check the status on anything? Alert you if something's been tampered with?"

McManus paused a moment. "No, that wasn't part of the system design."

"Then you need to redesign it because that's a major flaw. If the invaders didn't take anything, then they did something to an item in that vault. We need to figure out what." He started for the door. "You coming?"

McManus jogged to keep up as Stoneham headed back to vault 31-A. As he entered, he paused a moment to stare at the racks of shelving, seemingly untouched by the commotion. "What were you really after in here?" he muttered.

May Murakami, the IT tech, waved at him. "Chief, I have an update on the terminal."

"Please make it good. I need something at this point."

She shrugged. "Depends how you define good. Whatever hit this was powerful. We're talking totally massive electrical surge. It didn't just short the components. It melted them. Totally slagged the internals. The only time I've ever seen anything like it was a remote comm relay station that was hit by a lightning strike when I worked for a telecom company. But we're hundreds of feet underground. It's not possible." The tech looked at Stoneham's expression. "Is it?"

He deflected her question. "So, it's a total loss?"

"Not quite. The blast was so intense it flash-burned a copy of the last image displayed on the screen back into the liquid crystal support matrix. Think of it as a sort of blast shadow, if you will. The fracturing of the monitor tore that apart, but I've been able to recover a few of the larger fragments and make out a few particulars. Whoever used the terminal last accessed an inventory list sorted by location."

McManus walked up. "Sounds like your hunch was right." She turned to the tech. "Can you tell where they were looking?"

"One of the fragments showed three headings starting with a seven. That's the best I can do so far."

"It's the best lead I've had all day, May. Good job," said Stoneham. He made a beeline to Aisle Seven, McManus right behind.

As they arrived, she put a hand on his shoulder. "Let me go first."

"Why?"

"I'll know better if something's out of place."

He nodded and waved her ahead. She led him through the shelves at a deliberate pace. They would stop here or there to examine a device or container before placing it back on the shelf. After a few minutes, Stoneham said, "You seem nonchalant, considering what's going on.'

"I find being relaxed and open to what's around helps me find what I'm looking for."

"Sort of like letting a suspect come to you?"

McManus picked up a prototype pulse imager from a shelf and turned it on for a moment. "Just so. But what puzzles me is why this vault. It's Class 3, low priority medical items. Me, I would have gone for one of the Class 1 vaults on the level."

"Don't remind me."

"The point is, there are a lot more dangerous things in Pandora's Box. So why —"

There was a distinctive crunch underfoot. They both froze in place. Stoneham pulled a small flashlight from his tactical vest and pointed it where McManus had stepped. Small glass fragments glittered in the beam. She bent down to examine them. "There's something on them." She frowned at the piece. "Something red."

"Blood?" He moved the light to investigate the floor and shelves around them. "Whatever it is, it's all over. There's a splatter pattern on the floor and these containers as well." He switched his light to ultraviolet. The splatter flared bright, but there were off-colored sparkles that reflected at him. *That's odd.* "Given the pattern, whoever was here stood—" Stoneham stepped into a spot. "Here."

McManus frowned. "Your team was on the vault in less than four minutes, so figure they didn't have time to move far from whatever this was." She started to check the shelves. "Hello, what do we have here?" A wet red streak ran down one of the supports. She looked up. A small pool of red liquid formed under the shelf above. "Matt, I'd call that suspicious."

He walked over and looked, then pulled out two pairs of disposable gloves from a belt pouch. He handed a set to McManus, "Your call."

"Excuse me?"

"Do I boost you or you boost me up there?"

She laughed. "If it's all the same, I'll go up."

"You sure? I think you could lift me."

"Totally."

A second later, she stood on his shoulders and had a good view of the upper shelf. "I see the source. The red fluid is leaking from the seam of a gray metal transport case resting on its side."

"Not likely it was put there that way by your staff."

"Probably not."

"Any markings?"

"The barcode is intact, but the project ID is missing, and the security seals are breached." She looked down. "Looks like you were right."

"I'm not thrilled about it. Can you pass it down?"

"I think so." She reached for a handle and dragged it to the edge. As it moved, broken glass jumbled inside the case. She swung it down with care to Stoneham, then climbed down.

He placed the case on the floor as McManus grabbed her tablet and ran the barcode through her tablet. "Project Wildcard. Class 4, human performance enhancement, late 1970's. Project suspended." She looked at him. "Seems like an odd target."

"Depends on what you're enhancing. Step back while I open it." Stoneham undid the latches and popped up the lid. The stench of burnt insulation material filled the air. Inside an inch-deep slurry of shattered test tubes and charred liquid sloshed back and forth. He grimaced. "Whatever it was, it's toast now. Any idea what was supposed to be in here?"

"Inventory says project notes and test samples." McManus looked inside and shook her head. "What a mess."

There was a chirp from Stoneham's radio. He activated it. "Stoneham here."

"Chief, this is Turner. Savannah has a facial match on the attacker. She identifies the subject as Hannah Callahan."

Stoneham stepped away from the case. "Chrissy, say that again. Is she sure?"

"Savannah has a 98 percent confidence level for this match. It's definitely Hannah Callahan."

He looked over at case again, his mind trying to fit this piece into the puzzle. "Understood. Stand by."

McManus saw his reaction. "Matt, who's Hannah Callahan?"

"Remember the theft a few months back?"

"How could I forget? The False Mirror project. Got you this job, and made heightened security protocols a fact of life."

"Yeah, well, that was Hannah Callahan." He walked toward the shelf and looked up. "But she was killed in Tokyo. She's a ghost. Literally."

"Well, that would explain how she could vanish into thin air from inside a locked vault."

Stoneham grimaced as he looked back at McManus. "You're not helping."

"Sorry."

"I don't believe in ghosts. Particularly ones that kill my people. Let's figure out why one wanted to keep us away from this particular project." He keyed his radio mike. "Chrissy, Get me a line to Triangle HQ. I need to talk to Director Watson."

Chapter 2

September 8, 1:33 p.m. PDT

The morning fog rolled back from the Hotel Del Coronado resort to reveal a picture postcard afternoon. Heather Anjili sat poolside, looking forward to some sun time, some down time and particularly some time in El Cazador, the setting of the romantic novel she'd just downloaded. Her yellow bikini set off in perfect contrast to her tawny brown skin and shoulder length black hair. She adjusted its straps, then settled back onto her chaise and became lost in the electronic pages of her book.

Julio had always looked at the Marquesa with the eyes of one—

"Your Margarita, Miss."

She sighed at the interruption, then took it in stride as she glanced over her sunglasses at the waiter. "Just put it—"

The explosion in the Victorian Building behind her blew out the windows of the main ballroom. The shock wave tossed both Heather and the waiter sideways. At that moment, Heather stopped being a tourist. Her training as an agent of Triangle kicked in, and she rolled into a crouch, pulling the chaise over for cover as debris rained down.

Car alarms blared throughout the parking lots as guests began to stream out of the other lodging building around the resort. They pointed at the bright red smoke that started to billow from the ballroom and lobby of the main building.

Heather pushed aside the chaise and checked on the waiter. He was unconscious and bleeding from a gash on his forehead where he'd struck the pool deck, but his pupils were responsive. *Just had his bell rung.* She propped a cushion under his head, stood up and reached behind her right ear to activate the subcutaneous commlink implanted there. "Triangle, Echo Seven," she said in a crisp London accent. "Situation Red."

Inside her head, a male voice responded instantly. "Echo Seven, Triangle. Emergency Comm acknowledged. What's your situation, Agent Anjili?"

"Major casualty event. An explosion at the Hotel Del Coronado."

"Understood. Stand by." There was a pause; then a new voice came on the connection.

"Echo Seven, this is Alpha One." Alpha One was Rhonda Watson, Triangle's Director of Covert Operations. "Report."

"An explosion ninety seconds ago, in the main ballroom of the Victorian Building of the Hotel Del. High-yield explosive device. There's going to be a lot of casualties."

"This sounds like a law enforcement situation. Perhaps intelligence agencies if there is terrorist involvement. Outside our mission parameters."

Heather swore silently. *Damn mission scope.* Triangle's stated purpose was to locate technology that could harm humanity and prevent it from being misused. Her own previous training involved more wide-ranging intervention. She still had issues reconciling the two. Like now. *Perhaps I can spin this...*

"Normally I'd agree, ma'am, except for the smoke. It's red."

"Red?" Alpha One was incredulous.

"Bright signal red, ma'am. I'd swear someone set off a giant prank smoke bomb if it weren't for the force of the explosion."

"Your status?"

"Unhurt. I was poolside about 100 meters from the blast and managed to take cover."

There was a brief pause. "Very well, Echo Seven. Consider yourself activated. Your orders are to identify the source of that smoke and determine the technology behind it. Once you've done that, we'll determine if further action is necessary."

"Understood."

"And you are to stay off the radar with the locals. No interface is authorized. Am I clear?"

"Crystal, ma'am."

"They're on edge. I don't need you starting another incident. Your controller is in a training session. I'll recall her. She'll be in contact with you shortly."

"Understood, ma'am. Thank you."

"Right. Don't screw this up. Alpha One, out." A brief tone sounded as the Director terminated the connection.

Heather blew out her breath. *Back in business. So much for California sun and sand. Right, clothes first.* Anjili looked around for something to change into. All the other guests had left the pool to watch the fire. One left behind a pair of navy blue running pants that were a bit snug and a pair of Nikes. She found a shirt blown by the explosion into a bush that advertised a bar in Ensenada. She put it on and sighed when it ended a good three inches short of her navel. *I'll make it work.*

She grabbed her purse from the ground next to the chaise and started up the hill toward the parking lot and her car. *I'll just grab my mission gear out of the boot of my car—*

She slowed to a halt. The crowd gathered in the lot to watch the continuing chaos included some people standing atop cars to get a better view. One of which turned out to be her own sedan. She grimaced. *No way to retrieve my gear from that scrum without raising suspicion.* She glanced at the lobby entrance. *Very well, plan B. I'm a Navy doctor running along the beach. I saw the explosion and came to help.*

She dug her wallet from her purse and pulled three blank plastic cards, then added a silver bracelet that she slid onto her left arm and snapped shut. She pressed a sequence on the bracelet, and it tightened around her forearm.

"SAVANT, Mode 1. Activate." The bracelet was no ordinary piece of jewelry. The SAVANT, or Special Agent Variable Activity Nanite Technology device, was a sophisticated tool issued to all Triangle field operatives. It enabled them to interface with all sorts of technology, defend themselves with advanced weaponry, survey environments, and more.

As it completed its startup, a discrete green LED appeared and it interfaced with her commlink. A warm contralto voice in her head said, "Acknowledged. Welcome back, Agent Anjili."

She placed the bracelet on the cards. "SAVANT, Cover ID 4."

"Modifying."

There was a brief flicker of light on each plastic card as their surfaces changed. Once finished, Heather checked them – a California driver's license under the name of Heather Angelos, a military ID for Commander Heather Angelos, US Navy, and finally, a base ID for Dr. Heather Angelos, chief trauma surgeon assigned to Naval Regional Medical Center San Diego. She put the cards back in her wallet and pulled her hair back into a ponytail. *Don't forget. American accent around the locals.*

Thick red smoke still surged from windows of the Victorian Building as she jogged toward the lobby entrance. As she reached the steps the main doors burst open, and a half-dozen people stumbled out, covered in red soot. They were racked by deep coughs as they staggered a few steps before collapsing to the ground. Heather rushed to the nearest, a woman in a hotel blazer. She glanced at her name tag.

"Nancy, I'm Dr. Angelos. Tell me what happened."

"Don't...know. Checking a couple in...explosion. Blew...doors off the ballroom."

"Who was in there?"

"Hernandez wedding." Another spasm of coughing seized Nancy. She tried to cover her mouth, but blood sprayed out across them. Heather put her hand up to protect her face from the splatter. Nancy's eyes went wide in panic as she coughed again, more blood spilling out. She looked up at Heather. "What's happening to...?" The words gurgled in her throat. Her eyes rolled back as she started to convulse.

"Nancy, stay with me! What happened to the people in the ballroom? Nancy!" Heather reached to cushion her head during the seizure. Moments later the shaking stopped, as did Nancy's breathing. Her eyes glazed over. Heather checked for a pulse, but there wasn't any.

Damn. Anjili swore softly to herself as she looked at the soot on her hands. She wiped them on her pants, then reached over and slid Nancy's eyelids shut. A glance over at the other victims confirmed her worst fears. Nothing first responders had done mattered. All lay prone on the steps, lifeless, blood dripping from their mouths.

A calm female voice, high-pitched with a hint of Boston in it, sounded in her head. "Echo Seven, Triangle. I'm here, Heather."

Dana Boland was her regular SAVANT controller back at headquarters in Virginia. Her assigned role was to monitor and maintain the data links with the SAVANT on Heather's wrist, as well as feed her intel on the fly, sort of an on-air concierge. But over time Dana had become something more, skilled at keeping Heather anchored in the most extreme circumstances, maintaining a center that gave her a needed sense of perspective. Like over these past several weeks.

Or right now. "Triangle, Echo Seven. Glad to hear your voice, Dee. You've been briefed?"

"I'm up to speed."

"Well, add another gear to your ten-speed. This looks to be either a biological or chemical attack."

"Based on?"

"A half-dozen victims just bled out on the front steps here."

"That's brutal. Okay, let's talk pathology and timeline. Symptoms?"

"My victim came out of the building covered in red soot, coughing heavily. Within a minute she coughed up blood, went into a seizure and—"

"Who, wait! Coughed up blood?" Boland's voice turned urgent. "Were you exposed? Did you touch any?"

Heather looked at her hands and winced. "Yes. Kind of unavoidable."

"Tell me you were at least wearing gloves."

"No, I wasn't." Heather heard a bump and muted swearing. *She must have covered up her microphone.* "Dana?"

Her controller came back, "Ji, are you nuts? I know you have gloves in your mission gear. Why weren't you wearing them?"

"First off, my mission gear isn't accessible at this particular moment. Plus, it all happened kind of fast."

"Still, what were you thinking?"

Enough of this. Heather's reply was sharp. "I was trying to help someone frightened as hell stay alive!"

"Okay, calm down. I'm on your side, remember? We need to work the problem and fast. Do you know when your victim perished?"

"I'm not wearing a watch, so I'm not sure. Maybe a minute before you came online with me."

"Let me work off that. Any idea when this woman would have been exposed to the agent?"

"I assume whatever did this must have been delivered in the explosion, or the smoke soon afterward. My victim was covered in soot."

"Soot?"

"Yes. Same color as the smoke."

Boland muttered some calculations under her breath. Her voice brightened considerably. "Good news. You're probably safe. At least from any potential biologic hazard."

"And you say this because—"

"Per the mission log, based on your initial call the explosion came ten minutes ago, and we've been talking for just over three."

"So?"

"Plus you spent, what, about two minutes with the victim before she coughed up blood all over you and died, right?"

"Dana!"

"Yes or no?"

"Yes, but—"

"But nothing. Based on these, your victim died at or near exposure to the agent plus four minutes. More than five minutes have passed since your exposure without protective gear—"

"Dana, the point!"

"The point is you're still talking. You're at your exposure plus five, well, now plus six. Longer than the time the victims on the steps expired. They died, you didn't. Ergo, it's not a biologic, and you're safe." Boland paused before adding, "Unless it's specifically targeted, like a DNA trigger. Note, need to check if any of the other first responders have keeled over and see what similarities they may have—"

Heather rolled her eyes. *Oy. Yanks.* "Anyone ever say you're fun at parties?"

"You have no idea. So back to your victim. She was coughing, followed by blood. It was aspirated, not vomited?"

"Yes. Slightly foamy."

"That indicates whatever this was targeted her lungs."

"Plus, after a couple of coughs, she went into seizures before she stopped breathing."

"The symptoms are consistent with a chemical weapon attack, possibly a nerve agent. Any lesions or burns on the exposed skin, like hands, or face?"

Heather brushed away some of the soot away from the woman's face. "None I can see, but this residue is so thick and crusty it might be hiding some. But I remember my training; those would be painful. Nancy never showed any signs of pain, just discomfort from the coughing until she panicked and went into convulsions."

Boland muttered to herself again. "A chemical attack, but no surface burns. The seizures say neurotoxin, but a bleed-out?" Her voice became direct, commanding. "Whatever this is, it's nasty, but it doesn't seem to be a direct contact agent. This is good; your mission gear should protect you inside. Until that smoke dissipates, I want you in a respirator mask with at least a tenth-micron filter. Inventory says there's one in your go-bag."

Heather glanced back toward the crowd. "That's still going to be a problem."

"Sorry, did I miss something? I know there's a mask in your mission gear—"

"Remember the part where I said my gear isn't particularly accessible? Try the boot of my car, surrounded by panicky tourists."

There was a noticeable pause. "Right, vacation. Let me guess; you were poolside with a Mai Tai?"

"Not exactly a vacation, Dana. And it was a Margarita and a bikini. Nothing else."

"Not even a cute pool boy?"

"Dana—"

"A not-so-cute pool boy?"

"Dana!"

"Sorry. You must have come up with something. You're good, but not even you could talk your way near that scene in a bikini."

"It's not much better. Navy MD responding as a Good Samaritan. It's good, but yoga pants and a crop top definitely won't get me inside."

"Maybe we can liberate some equipment from the fire engines. Head for them, I'll see if I can issue some orders and set up a distraction."

"On my way." Heather turned to head down the steps, then stopped to look at the firefighters spraying water into the ballroom windows. "Weird. No matter how hard they fight this thing, it doesn't seem to have any effect on the smoke."

"Maybe it's just a really intense fire."

"Maybe." She started down the steps again, then looked toward the sky at the smoke again. *It's like I told the Director, this looks like a smoke bomb. Nothing burns like that naturally.*

Nothing burns...

"Dana, where's the fire?"

"Say what?"

"For all this smoke, I haven't seen a single flame."

"Let me pull up the video feeds." She heard typing for a moment. "You're right, helicopter shots show lots of red smoke, but when I adjust for infrared, I'm not getting any gradient. Definitely weird. Run me a thermal scan from your location."

"Switching my SAVANT to Mode 2." Heather turned away from the crowd and in a quiet voice ordered her SAVANT to the new mode.

"Acknowledged," the device responded. For a moment, there was the sensation of ants crawling around Heather's left forearm. The surface of the bracelet rippled as component nanites morphed into an elongated cylinder with a small keyboard and holographic pop-up display. Heather entered a control sequence and waved her forearm toward the building. "Scanning," she murmured.

"Receiving," said Boland. It only took her moments. "Your instincts are dead on. No heat signatures inside."

"What? Zero hot spots?"

"None that would register as a fire. Just bodies." Heather began to pivot. Boland called out suddenly. "Wait! Don't move!"

Heather frowned. "What is it?"

"I stand corrected. We found one, but it's odd."

"How so?"

"It might be a kitchen. It's barely oven warm, rigid shaped and stationary. What are you pointing at?"

Heather glanced up. "You'll love this. The ballroom where the explosion happened."

"So we may have located the — no, hang on a sec, Ji."

"What is it?"

"The heat source isn't in the ballroom, but the floor below it."

Heather shut down the scanner and looked over the railing at the shopping gallery below. "No smoke down there either. Tell me you have floor plans for the building."

"Already ahead of you. It's in the Carousel Room, directly below the Grand Ballroom."

"Time for me to have a look-see."

"Just be careful."

"When am I not?"

"Well—"

"That was rhetorical, Dee."

Clipping the hospital ID to her top, Heather made a quick stop at one of the EMT aid units to wash off her hands. As she was cleaning up, the pair manning it were called over by one of the policemen to deal with a spectator who had fainted.

Fortune favors the bold. She reached in and opened the compartment labeled 'Respirator.' Heather grabbed a small green tank with a mask attached. *Not a full-face unit, but it'll work in a pinch.* She hid it under her arm and skirted away toward the back of the crowd, working around it downhill toward the beach side of the Victorian Building.

She stood next to the pool where she'd started her afternoon. Yellow police tape already secured off the lower level entrance. *Never stopped me before,* thought Heather as she ducked under it and walked up to the set of double glass doors. Hibiscus bushes screened her from the crowds watching the smoke billow from the windows above her. She held up her arm and ordered, "SAVANT, Mode 3." Nanites flowed again as the cylinder reconfigured into a gauntlet that covered her hand. "Weapon hot."

"Complying."

Heather formed a fist with her left hand. A pulsing ball of blue-white plasma formed at the front edge of the gauntlet. She examined it, crackling with offensive potential, then nodded in satisfaction and relaxed her hand. It dissipated into thin air. "Dana, I'm going in."

"Power's off in the building, so I have no access to their security cams."

"Translation, you're blind."

"Right in one. Be careful."

"Yes, mum." Out of habit, Heather nodded in agreement as she walked inside.

There was a peculiar ozone smell in the dark hallway. The carpet crunched as if walking on a bed of Rice Crispies. *So much for stealthy. But it's definitely getting warm in here.* The ozone smell became stronger, as well.

"The room's just ahead on your left." Boland's voice in her head.

Heather wiped sweat away from her brow. "Any reading on how hot it is? I'm starting to feel a bit like the inside of a tandoori oven."

"One hundred fifty degrees."

"Fahrenheit or Centigrade?"

"You Brits, always trying to make me convert. Fahrenheit. Hopefully, it's a dry heat. Serious, no mission gear, zero protection. I'm not feeling a lot of fuzzies here, warm or otherwise."

"Well, I did come for a tan."

"Ji, don't be flip—"

"Shush." She coughed once. "The air's getting thick with whatever is causing the ozone smell. I'm putting on the respirator mask." She slipped it over her nose and mouth and adjusted the strap, then turned the valve. A hiss sounded as clean oxygen rushed in to replace the outside air. She took a deep breath, held out her left arm in a firing position, and popped around the corner into the Carousel Room.

She was blinded by a bright yellow light. *I should have brought my sunglasses.* "Dana, I think I found our target."

"What is it?"

"A metal cylinder, about six feet tall, with a set of fins jutting out from all sides, like an old rocket ship. There's a projector dish on top with a blinding yellow light coming from it, aiming at the ceiling. I think that's what's causing the ozone smell." She squinted against the light. Inside it, tendrils of red curled and boiled upward. *Smoke. Red smoke! This machine is generating it.* "This device is the source, Dana. It must be using some chemical process and the ozone is a byproduct."

"Can you send me pics?"

"It's blinding bright in here, so they may be distorted. Stand by." Heather raised her left arm. "SAVANT, begin record—" She was interrupted by movement, a shadow on the far wall. She stood frozen as it moved beyond the cylinder. "Dana, I'm not alone down here."

"Your SAVANT doesn't read anyone."

The shadow resolved into a woman in a hoodie who checked a data tablet as she circled the machine. She backed around the device until she was in front of Heather. Somehow, she sensed her Heather's presence and turned, giving the agent her first good look. *Five-six, blonde and Caucasian.* She regarded Heather with a smirk. *And an attitude.* The woman slid a finger down the surface of the tablet, and the machine responded. The cone of yellow light dimmed as the smoke tapered to a thin wisp.

"Put the tablet down." The woman did as she was told and shuffled to her left. Heather pivoted, keeping her in her sight. "Now tell me what that thing is and what you're doing here with it."

The woman quirked up one side of her mouth. "I don't think so."

Want to play coy? Fine. A ball of plasma formed as Heather closed her hand into a fist. "You ought to rethink your answer."

The woman glanced down for a moment as she casually scuffed her right foot against the carpet. When she looked back at Heather, it was with hooded eyes. "You really don't want to aim your weapon at me, Triangle."

Heather fought to keep the surprise off her face. *How many people in the world outside the agency know it even exists?* She had already been wary. Now every sense went on high alert.

"Echo Seven, Triangle. Alert to your situation. Analyzing your contact for voice print and possible tactical analysis." Boland's voice was reassuring, but she was 3000 miles away.

I'm still on my own.

The woman grinned at her reaction. "Besides, you shouldn't worry about me. You've got a bigger problem."

"Like what?"

"Not what." The woman disappeared.

Heather blinked in confusion, then looked around. *Where the—?*

The woman reappeared behind her. Shocked, Heather turned to face her. "How did you—?"

The woman put a finger to her lips as she grinned, then pointed up. "Who." She waved her fingers, then flickered out of existence.

"What the heck just happened?" asked Boland, her tone shocked. "Your target disappeared, then I read someone next to you for a second, and now the readings just disappeared again."

"Tell me about it." Heather looked up where the woman pointed and stared in shock. "Dana, is there still interference on the signals from my SAVANT? Can you grab any images from the recording?"

"Yeah, I'm clear—What the hell is that?"

"A bloody great hole in the ceiling." This machine had sliced a ten-foot wide hole through to the Grand Ballroom above, its edges surgically precise. The thick red smoke swirled upward from the cone of light and into the ballroom, contained above the cut.

"How is the smoke staying up there?" asked Boland.

"No idea. Maybe some sort of pressure gradient from that yellow light?"

A deep guttural rumble came from above. Tiny hairs on the back of Heather's neck rose as a pair of glowing yellow eyes stared down at her through the smoke. "Dana?" she said, unsure.

"Yes, I'm on it! Scanning now."

She backed up a step as she aimed her SAVANT up toward the gap. "What the blazes is it?"

The half-charred remains of a baby grand piano flew through the hole and passed sparking through the yellow cone. Heather ducked and rolled left as it landed in a crash of chords and splinters. She came out of the crouch in a fighting stance and looked up. At the edge of the opening stood a large muscular woman in the tattered remains of a wedding dress. She had layer upon layer of muscle, her skin glistened with a reddish tinge, and she looked really pissed off.

Boland's voice was incredulous. "I've lost visual, but sensor reads human. Biometrics are way off the scale, though. Who is that?"

"You might not have visual, but I sure do. You'd never believe me."

"Try me."

"Here comes the bride?"

There was a pause. "Okay, you're right. But how could she have survived the explosion?"

The woman roared and leaped down to land next to her. Heather ducked right to avoid her fist. "With poorly managed anger issues, it seems!" She backpedaled to put a table between them. *I just need to figure out a way to calm her down and talk to her. Something subtle.*

The woman's fist smashed the table to splinters.

Heather stared as it registered what her opponent could do. *Scratch subtle.* "SAVANT, weapon to thirty."

"Complying."

She aimed and fired. Ball after ball of plasma bounced off the woman. Heather's mind raced for a solution. *Okay, stun is not going to be of much use.* As she continued to dodge and evade, she surveyed the room. *Anything I can use around here?* There were just furniture and a buffet service. She looked over at the strange cylinder in the center of the room. *I guess I could knock that over on her—*

Heather was yanked sideways, her arm nearly dislocated at the shoulder. Even as the joint screamed in pain, she analyzed what happened. *Bridezilla must have caught me as I was looking for a way around her. Sloppy, Ji, really off your game.*

The woman's scowl was full of contempt and anger. In a guttural voice, Bridezilla said, "You did this!"

"Hey there, mate! I just got here. I'm trying to help you—"

"Liar! All your fault! Time to die." The woman reached to pull Heather's arms in opposite directions.

Desperate, Heather twisted her left wrist and fired her SAVANT up at the ceiling. The shot hit the edge of the hole, and a section fell toward them. As it dropped on top of Bridezilla, she released Heather as she protected herself.

Heather hit the ground and rolled forward, yelling, "SAVANT, weapon full!"

"Acknowledged."

She came up in a crouch, pivoted, and fired in a single smooth motion. There was a bright flare followed by a scream of pain and rage as the target staggered backward from the hit to her stomach. Heather stood and fired shot after shot, forcing Bridezilla back toward the machine.

As they closed in on the device, Heather calculated her options. *One round at the base to take out the fins should do it.* She shifted her aim and fired, but as she did, there was a flicker of a shadow around the machine. The cone of yellow light brightened to full strength. Smoke began to flow again.

Heather shielded her eyes as the bride stumbled backward against the device. Her head snapped back and brushed against the cone of light. There was a brief sizzle, Bridezilla's face went slack, and the light went out of her eyes.

"No!" yelled Heather. A moment later, the woman fell forward. The back of her skull was missing. The exposed brain was cauterized.

Damn. That wasn't what I wanted! "Triangle, Echo Seven. Do we know the identity of the bride in the wedding party?"

"Jasmine Hernandez, daughter of Rear Admiral Hernandez, US Navy."

Heather swore silently. "She didn't make it."

"Are you okay?"

She looked around. *Mystery woman gone, hundreds of people dead, this machine kills the lone attack survivor.* "No, Dana, I'm not. Not okay at..." She drifted off the conversation as she noticed a piece of paper taped to the cylinder.

"Heather?"

That wasn't there before. Heather walked over and pulled the note off the device. She began to read it but then all hell broke loose.

A hissing sound filled the room. Heather's first thought was the device had released a toxic gas. She took a couple of quick steps backward.

"Heather, what am I hearing?"

"Stand by," Heather interrupted Boland as she stared at something bizarre. "Sand."

"What?"

"The device. It's turning into sand." As she watched, it crumbled from the outer edges inward, like a sandcastle under the surf, dark grit sliding into a pile on the floor. She bent down to sift it through her fingers. *It's sharp and gritty, not like any sand I've ever—*

As the bell collapsed, the yellow light went out like a flash from a camera going off. A cascade of contaminated water dumped through the gap in the ceiling, slamming her to the floor. She came up sputtering and saw the grit had washed away. *Damn, I needed that for analysis.* She looked up at the ceiling to see where the water came from.

Her eyes went wide.

Bollocks! Get up, Ji! Run, girl, run!

Heather scrambled to her feet and ran from the seething cloud of red smoke as it cascaded down into the Carousel Room and chased her down the hallway like a poltergeist. She burst out the double doors as the red cloud boiled out behind her, only stopping when she was fully clear of the building and back by the pool where her adventure had started that afternoon.

"Echo Seven, Triangle! Echo Seven, Triangle. Ji, talk to me!"

"I'm okay, Dana. Give me a minute."

As she caught her breath, Heather remembered the note pulled off the machine. She fished the wet paper from her pocket and examined it. Written on a hotel scratch pad in neat block lettering were four words.

Only the start, Triangle.

Heather looked up at the last bits of red smoke drifting from the shattered ballroom windows.

"Triangle, Echo Seven. I'm going to need backup on this one."

Chapter 3

A sleek jet with a flattened fuselage and wide backswept wings taxied to a pad at an executive airstrip north of San Diego. Under the glare of temporary lights, the black-on-black surface revealed its name: *Firebird*. Its engines wound down as a ground-support crew scrambled to complete landing support procedures and turn the aircraft around for a quick takeoff if needed.

Midway along the fuselage, a hatch slid up and aside. A ramp extended down to the tarmac. Steve Tate, dressed in his all-black mission wear, stepped out and took a deep breath, looking relieved it wasn't recycled *Firebird* cabin air. Amy Rogers stopped beside him for a moment, shook her head and started down the ramp.

Steve jogged to catch up with her. "What?"

"What do you mean, what?"

"I saw that dismissive little head shake back there."

"Your act every time you get off *Firebird*."

"I can't help it. The plane smells funny."

"Steve, there are four Hyperjets in the fleet. Fastest things that fly. They're identical."

"Not if something went and died in one of them."

"Excuse me?"

"I swear, A.J., some poor animal must have crawled in the cargo hold and died in mid-flight. Maybe it exploded under low pressure or something."

She rolled her eyes. "Hopeless. And again, please, stop with the A.J."

"You hate Amelia Jane even more."

She shook her head in resignation as she continued toward the hangar, Steve right behind her. It was empty except for a black SUV with a discreet Triangle logo on the rear window. A pair of manila envelopes lay on the hood, each marked with their names. They brought the mission's first surprise.

Steve activated his commlink. "Triangle, Tango Two."

The Welsh brogue of their controller Ethan Nowitzki replied back, "Tango Two, Triangle. Go ahead."

"Ethan? Don't you ever sleep?"

"Didn't you get the memo? I hibernate."

Steve chuckled. "Good to know. But what gives with my briefing packet?"

"What do you mean?"

"You know precisely what I mean. No keys?"

There was a brief second of typing. "Ah. Vehicle access. Yes, well, instructions are explicit to assign any vehicle on field missions to Agent Rogers until further notice."

"What!?" He glared at Amy. "You get the car."

She raised her hands innocently. "News to me." She activated her commlink. "Triangle, Tango One."

"Tango One, Triangle. Go ahead, Amy, you're patched in.," said Ethan. "And to answer your question, Steve, Agent Rogers wasn't aware of the new policy. It was ordered by Alpha Three."

"Ops Support?" Steve flinched. "Dr. Quincey himself?"

"Yes. Something about not letting you near another of his vehicles until, quote, hell freezes over. Unquote."

He put his forehead against the SUV and muttered, "I swear, it wasn't my fault. The Chitayan rebels blew it up."

"Be that as it may, for now, you are persona non-auto. Amy will be your chauffeur."

"My chauffeur?!"

She looked at him sympathetically. "Sorry."

He growled at her. She backed away and chuckled. "Thanks, Ethan. So, I'm the transporter now?"

"For the moment, at least."

"Fair enough. What's our cover?"

"ATF agents out of New Mexico. Agent Barbara Lee, an expert on strange and exotic ways to blow things up. Steve is your partner, Agent Reed Austin."

Steve folded his arms, a pained expression on his face. "Let me guess. Junior partner."

Amy nudged him. "Come on, have fun with this." She gave him a smile that showed dimples and amped up her southern accent. "Why, Sugar, I could level that there building with a lemon, two Moon Pies and a can of shaving cream."

He rolled his eyes. "Rope it in, Babs. Let's get over to the incident site and figure out what actually happened." He touched a hidden control on his sleeve to activate his mission gear's active camouflage. His top shifted from black to white and the letters 'ATF' appeared on his shirt pocket. Out of habit, he started for the driver's seat, but Amy was already there. With a sigh, he got in on the passenger side.

They negotiated their way down the Cabrillo Freeway in silence. Amy occasionally glanced over to check on Steve. His eyes were half-closed, tuned out from the surrounding reality. She'd seen this before. *He's gone elsewhere, dropped into that big brain of his.*

Steve and Amy had been recruited into Triangle for a single reason. They were both Talents – individuals uniquely gifted with extraordinary abilities. Steve had an advanced version of *hyperkinesthesia*. Imagine knowing everything that went on all around you in full and complete detail. Now imagine the capacity to interact with that data, to make subtle changes that could affect the outcomes of events, to literally manipulate cause and effect. That's what Steve could do.

He groaned and opened his eyes. Amy nodded in sympathy. "That rough?"

"You have no idea, A.J."

"Oh, a little. You're used to being in control, where you can affect things, make changes, make a difference.

Being a passenger means you're not. That has to be a little bit frustrating."

He stared at her. "Okay, so you have an idea. But it's not just that. I'm trying something new with my Talent, but I don't know if I can."

"New how?"

"I affect things by seeing possible scenarios. Theoretically, I should then be able to flip that and trace how something was done."

"Not seeing what could happen, but what did happen? That could be useful, especially in a case like this. Shouldn't that be easier?"

"You would think so, but it's turning out harder. Orders of magnitude harder."

"How so?"

"When I use my Talent, I see multiple paths that lead to different outcomes, with probabilities. The ideal one and actions required become apparent almost instantly. Instead, this is taking a result and extrapolating back through the possible experience paths to determine the most probable."

"That sounds logical."

"You don't understand, A.J., I don't just see the most probable path. I see every possible event path, equally weighted, all at once. Every imaginable way, any of which might have led to that moment."

"Like all the branches on a tree?"

"More like the tributaries of a river leading to a waterfall, churning and tumbling over one another. From all that, I'm trying to find the one particular drop. And me with no way to figure out the more probable scenario."

She swerved around a slow minivan. "Perhaps more data before you approach the problem? It could help you eliminate some of the streams in advance."

"Maybe. I'll keep that in mind next time I try." He sat up straight. "If I'm forced to be right seat, I may as well work the briefing." He opened a data screen on the smart window next to him. "Latest from Intel says they're working a frame-by-frame analysis of the resort's security footage for the last forty-eight hours."

"Trying to identify the attacker the agent on-site saw?"

"Or at least, get a glimpse of when she arrived. So far, nothing. There's a private message in here to you from Jones in Intel – 'Don't look like she's in here at all, this one is like trying to find a ghost.'"

Amy sucked in her breath between her teeth. "Jonesy's good. If she's stumped—"

"I hear you. But they don't have much to go on. The image of the suspect in the initial report is in a hoodie and blurred, and the description's generic."

"How generic?"

"'Female, Caucasian, 5-foot-6, blonde hair and, wearing a black hoodie.'" He looked over at her. "Duh."

Amy chuckled. "That describes three-quarters of the women I swam against on the elite circuit."

"And a significant number of my dates during U.S. leg of the FreeRunning Tour."

She glanced over at him. "Now you're just boasting."

"Always." He winked at her. In reply she yanked on the wheel sharply, pulling them onto the ramp for the Coronado Bridge and banging him against the window. The data screen cleared. "Hey!"

"Oops."

As they raced over San Diego Harbor, Steve rubbed his head and reached for his commlink. "Triangle, Tango Two."

"Tango Two, Triangle. Go ahead, Steve."

"We're about five minutes out. Who's our contact?"

"Agent Echo Seven. She was on holiday at the resort when this all went down."

"What a way to ruin a vacay. Her cover's in place and holding up?" asked Amy.

"So far. Commander Heather Angelos, a military doctor with NRMC San Diego. Be prepared to salute."

Amy tapped her hands on the steering wheel. "Is she read in on Tango?"

There was a momentary pause. "That's negative. You are not authorized to inform the agent nor display your abilities in front of her."

Steve sighed as he looked at Amy. "You know how to take all the fun out of a job."

"You will just have to find other ways to entertain each other."

The two shared a look and grinned. "Yes, Mr. Geppetto," said Amy.

"Funny, I always considered myself as your personal Jiminy Cricket."

Steve snorted as Amy drove past the old toll plaza and onto the island. "You know what's got me? Who was the real target?"

"There has to be a target?" She switched lanes and turned left. "Not just a random act of terror—"

"Done by somebody who had something running in the basement they kept running for fifteen minutes until our agent showed up?" He raised an eyebrow.

"Right, sorry I said anything. Still, it all centered on that ballroom. Who was the wedding for?"

"David Ortiz and Jasmine Hernandez. Miss Hernandez was the oldest daughter of Rear Admiral Raymond Hernandez."

"An attack on a wedding reception has all the makings of a revenge attack, clean and clear."

"But what about that mystery device or the red smoke? That note, 'Only the start, Triangle,' was terribly specific." His frown reflected back as he stared at buildings going by. "Maybe our agent was targeted? Or us?"

Amy checked the traffic and turned the SUV left onto Orange Avenue. "Seems a big stretch. Who could have known she was there? If they did, why not attack her directly? Why all the collateral damage? You couldn't be sure she'd respond in such a scenario."

Steve looked pensive. "I guess you're right. Part of what we'll figure out when we catch up with Agent Angelos."

"Sorry to correct you, Steve," said Ethan, "but Angelos is her cover identity. Echo Seven is Agent Heather Anjili."

Amy looked over at Steve's sharp intake of breath. "Steve, what is it?"

He looked like he'd seen a ghost. He closed his eyes. "Ethan, you're sure about that name?"

"That's correct, Steve. Agent Heather Anjili, designate Echo Seven."

Amy was becoming more concerned by the moment. "Is everything all right?"

He opened his eyes and looked over. For a moment, he looked very vulnerable before a mask slid in place and he was regular Steve again. "Oh, yeah. No problem. Just surprised, that's all. Time for surprises later. We're here."

The hotel came into view on the right. Portable floodlights illuminated the historic hotel, the scars of the explosion still visible. Streaks of bright red soot climbed up the walls and sloped roof above the ballroom windows. An unsettled feeling rolled through Amy's stomach.

An officer with the Coronado Police flagged them down at the driveway entrance. They flashed their ATF IDs and were waved through with instructions to report to the scene coordinator. Amy pulled onto the lawn near the parking lot, got out and looked over the chaos. Emergency vehicles from a dozen different agencies stood with lights flashing as personnel in breathing gear and carrying stretchers went in and out the lobby entrance.

Steve walked around the SUV and stood next to her. He raised his left arm. "I'll track down Echo Seven. Our SAVANTs will vibrate in proximity." He looked around, eyes still haunted behind that mask.

"Are you sure you're okay?"

He gave her a half-smile. "Go check us in, then come find me."

She headed toward a temporary command tent on the main driveway, looking back once more to check on him. He hesitated before moving into the shadows.

10:17 p.m. PDT

The authorities had ordered an evacuation of the resort. As guests milled, waiting for buses to take them to other accommodations around the region, the Red Cross had brought in a mobile canteen to provide food and coffee to the first responders. Heather had managed to cajole a tea bag and a cup of lukewarm water and had retreated away from the crowd. As she leaned against a light post, she sipped the weak brew and scanned the crowd for any signs of her earlier assailant.

"Echo Seven, Triangle." Boland's voice sounded quietly in her head.

Reflexively, she nodded again in response. "Triangle, Echo Seven."

"How are you holding up?"

"You Yanks have no idea about how to make a proper cup of tea, and I'm still in a snit about being without my mission gear. I feel practically naked without it."

Boland chuckled. "What, you've gone back to the bikini?"

"Get serious. With all the chaos, this situation's ripe for a follow-on strike. I'm scanning the crowd for the second coming of our visitor, but having my AR specs would make life much easier."

"Sorry, I can't help there. But I do have some news. Your backup has arrived on-site."

"Good, I'll go meet them—"

"It's okay; they'll find you. Proximity vibrate."

"Who'd they send?"

"Tango One and Two. Their cover story is a pair of ATF agents."

"That's it? No names?"

"Nope. I've heard of Alpha through Echo agents, but Tango's a whole new one for me. And get this, classification details are need-to-know only. Apparently, I don't."

Heather pondered that a moment. "They're something new, maybe just off the books?"

"Could be someone's pet project."

"If they haven't got a rep, I'm not impressed."

"Oh, I don't know," said a voice behind her as her SAVANT began to vibrate. "We've got a pretty good track record so far."

That voice - it's not possible! Heather was shaking as much as her device was from the shock. Slowly she turned around. Behind her, holding up a hand in greeting, was Rusty Tate. He grinned - *that wicked, stupid, adorable grin* - as he slid back his sleeve to reveal the unmistakable glint of a SAVANT. She fought down conflicting emotions as she held up her own to confirm.

His expression wavered for a moment, but he seemed to work on being cheerful. "Heather Anjili. You're really here."

"Looks that way, mate."

"But, how? Since when? I thought—"

"I should be asking you that, Rusty. What in the name of the devil are you doing here?"

"Long story. And Rusty is long retired. It's just Steve now."

"You're kidding."

"Nope, totally serious. I'll explain everything later. Right now, we've got a job to do."

She barked a laugh. "'A job,' he says." She downed the last of her tea and tossed the cup into a nearby trashcan. Without warning, she wheeled on him and grabbed his collar, slamming him back into the shadows of a nearby tree. Her eyes blazed with anger as words tumbled out in a rush. "Who the hell do you think you're kidding, Rusty? Thrill-seeking adrenaline junkies don't qualify as agents!"

Her SAVANT vibrated a second time as a female voice joined the conversation. "Triangle recruited us, so they think we do. Of course, Director Watson is on my speed dial. Let's argue with her about it instead."

She rolled her eyes. *Great. Now this other ponce shows up.* "Sure you do, Missy. And your story is—" She turned to face the woman.

Things went south quickly.

There was an instant of recognition, followed by Heather calling out, "SAVANT, Mode 3! Weapon full!" She pushed Rusty to the ground and pivoted into a defensive stance, left arm raised and pointed at the woman's chest.

"What the—?" The woman stopped short, perplexed at the sight of a plasma ball aimed directly at her chest. Her expression shifted to defiant. "Who the hell do you think you are?"

Boland was on the commlink instantly. "Echo Seven, Triangle. You've powered up weapons. What's going on?"

"Heather, stand down!" said Rusty as he scrambled to his feet.

"This bitch is the one we've been looking for. She must have set off the explosion and operated that machine."

"A.J.? Not hardly!"

"I know what I saw, Rusty!"

"Steve," he corrected.

"Don't you even start with that now! She was here at the attack site!"

"Heather, wait!" said Boland.

The woman began to scuff her right foot against the ground. *Oh, no you don't, chippie. Not this time.* Heather began to squeeze her fist, but suddenly Rusty was somehow between them. He had his hand on her wrist and forced her arm up toward the sky. His other hand shoved the strange woman back.

"Enough! A firefight out here is not going to keep Triangle low profile. So let's take this down a couple of notches, shall we?"

Heather glared at him, but Rusty's expression showed he wasn't about to back down. She took two steps backward. "SAVANT, weapon to standby."

"Acknowledged."

She lowered her arm and glared at him. "That's a start," he said as he turned back to the other woman. "A.J., you okay?" The other woman considered Heather for a moment, then relaxed from her fighting stance, took a deep breath and nodded.

"You better have one ripper explanation, mate," said Heather.

He turned back, hands up to stop her. "Look, there has to be a logical explanation for what you think you saw. But I can guarantee you there is absolutely no way A.J. was here when the attack occurred."

"Prove it."

"At the moment you were in there, A.J. and I were 3,000 miles east of here, ready to jump out of a perfectly good airplane. So if she had been here as well, I'd say that would have been a pretty neat trick, wouldn't you?"

"Their controller just forwarded confirming data. The woman's legit," added Boland inside her head.

Oh, bollocks. Heather turned away in embarrassment. She quietly ordered her SAVANT back to Mode 1. As it morphed into a bracelet, she glanced back, one eyebrow raised. "Skydiving, huh?"

The blonde shrugged and tilted her head toward Rusty. "His idea. Not mine."

Heather snorted despite herself. "See what I mean? You most assuredly have not changed, Rusty."

"Steve."

"Whateves." Something occurred to Heather. She turned to face the blonde. "You've been awfully quiet through all of this."

The younger woman's eyes narrowed as she regarded Heather with a detached air. "I figure you've been enough of a blowhard for all three of us."

"What!?" Heather took a step toward her. Rusty intercepted her again.

A. J. crossed her arms and continued. "Of course, external factors are at play. You were thrown into this event unprepared during a badly needed r-and-r period. Our briefing noted you suffered combat trauma and possible chemical exposure during your initial reconnoiter. Then add in you've probably been awake for, what now, twenty-one hours straight?" She glanced over at the canteen. "How was the tea?"

"She's good," murmured Boland in her head.

"Shut up," Heather muttered back. "Whose side are you on?"

"I didn't know we were taking sides."

Heather ignored that and held out her hand to the younger woman. "Who are you?"

"Amelia Jane Rogers," she said, shaking it after a moment's hesitation. "But you can call me Amy."

"He calls you A.J."

"A disgusting habit I'm trying to break him of."

Heather grinned despite herself. "Good luck with that. I never could."

"So, you already know Steve?"

Interrogating, are we? "Yeah, we've met before."

Rusty took that as a cue to interrupt. "You two will have time to bond later. Right now, A.J. and I need to get inside to investigate, and you need your rest, so if you'll brief us—"

Heather shook her head. "Not on your life. I'm going with you. But we need in quick before the locals cart out much more evidence. I don't suppose you brought an extra set of mission gear?"

He frowned and glanced at Amy. She shook her head. "Wasn't on the manifest."

She looked over at the parking lot. "Then I will need access to my gear after all."

"Where is it?"

"Impounded in the lot over there. First, the crowd used my car as a platform to watch the goings on; then some local got it in their mind that perhaps one of the vehicles might have belonged to the attacker. They're waiting for a blanket search warrant."

"Which wouldn't be good for us," said Steve. "You're hiding a multitude of sins I assume?"

"Not-so-hidden compartment in the boot." She turned back to face them. "If you two can draw the guards away for few minutes, I should be able to access it—"

The blonde held out her hand. "Keys."

Heather stared at her. "Excuse me?"

"Your keys, please." She handed them to Amy. "Good. What kind of car is it?"

"Silver Equus."

Amy pressed the lock button on the key. The headlights of the car blinked once. "Got it. And the access code for your secure compartment."

"47293." The woman repeated the code once again to her.

"Okay. Give us five minutes."

"Five minutes?" She turned to Rusty. "How's she going to—?" There was a quick gust of wind. Heather looked back.

The blonde was gone.

"What the hell?" She looked at Rusty. "Where'd she go?"

He shrugged and clapped Heather on the shoulder. "She's fast. Wait here; we'll be right back." He walked away toward the parking lot.

Heather stared at the empty spot where the blonde had stood. *Just like the other one. What the hell is going on?*

10:22 p.m. PDT

Amy Rogers was a Talent as well, specifically a *kinetomorph*. She'd once explained to Steve the best way to think of her was like a hybrid car. Amy absorbed kinetic energy through everyday interactions with the environment around her and stored it like a battery. When she needed, she could use her Talent to release that stored potential energy, providing her with enhanced speed and strength. Combined with Amy's advanced training in martial arts, it made her extremely formidable. Also, anything that struck Amy immediately transferred all its kinetic energy to her, including bullets. That had saved her and Steve on more than one occasion. She wasn't invulnerable, though. She had two weaknesses, it seemed, sharp, pointy things, and Steve.

Her abilities made her highly attractive to Triangle. They recruited her, although if they knew about her previous extracurricular activities, they never said a word. She was originally there to work on a single case, tracking down the killer of her fiancé, but she had stayed because she believed they could be her best resource for finding her sister, as well as the truth about her past.

The moment Amy had spotted the car she had triggered her Talent discreetly – striking her right foot against the ground three times. As soon as she had the unlock code, she kicked off. In a couple of steps, she was moving faster than the eye could follow. *No time like the present to get this done. Besides, I could use space away from that—*

"A.J., what's our rule?" Steve sounded his disapproval over the commlink. "You warn me before you pull any disappearing act. Besides, we're on protocol, zero Tango on this mission."

"Screw protocol."

"A.J.—"

"So what if I was showing off? Your ex is a bitch on wheels."

"Not my ex."

"Sure about that?"

He hesitated. "It's...complicated."

"I'll bet." She continued to lap the parking lot, checking out the security arrangements.

"Besides, you said she was stressed and stuff."

"That was me playing nice. Figured you didn't need me throwing gasoline on that fire."

He sighed. "Let's just get Agent Anjili's gear and get back, okay?"

"What do you think I'm doing? Be quiet and let me do my thing."

She changed direction, moving through the cars like a blur to the world before she skidded to a stop at the rear of the Equus. She used the remote to pop the trunk, then knelt and pushed open the lid. She slid aside the access panel and punched in the combination. At the last number, the hidden compartment opened. She grabbed Anjili's gear bag and closed the trunk.

"Hey, you there! Stop!"

She looked up. *Great. A cop. No, better. A cop and her puppy.* The policewoman released her German shepherd. It barreled toward her.

Time to jet. She slapped her right hand quickly against the car three times to trigger her ability again. Energy surged through her as she grabbed the rear bumper and shoved the vehicle sideways to block the dog. It ran up, barking and leaped up to attack Amy, but she was nowhere to be found.

Other canine units howled in response as they joined the pursuit. *Fun, more company.* Amy stopped here and there throughout the lot, giving other cars a random nudge. Within moments there were no straight paths left though the jumble of vehicles.

"A.J.?" Steve's voice again over the commlink.

"Kind of busy."

"I suggest you finish soon. You've got all sorts of trackers heading over to the lot, presumably to intercept you."

"So? I'll just outrun them."

"Yeah, but your scent will still lead them right back to us. Hope you have a plan B."

"As a matter of fact, I do." She headed south out of the lot and off the property. The gust of wind as she passed the first policewoman again knocked off the officer's hat.

Two minutes later Amy pulled up to a stop next to Steve in the trees overlooking the lot. She handed him Anjili's bag.

"Took your time."

"Next time you play hopscotch with the canine units. I went all the way to the Mexican border and back to throw them off the scent."

"That does explain why a lot of folks just charged out of here."

"Let's not wait around to see what happens when they don't find me. Come on." She started to leave, but he stood there, a thoughtful look on his face. "What is it?"

"Oh, just something to keep the remaining folks distracted for a bit. SAVANT, Mode 2."

10:31 p.m. PDT

Heather checked the chronometer on her SAVANT. *Seven minutes. Rusty hasn't changed. Never could show up on time—*

A tap on her shoulder. She turned. Rusty held out her gear bag, the usual goofy smile on his face. His partner had the look of someone dealing with an over-aged child. She knew that look. She'd worn it often enough herself.

"Thank you," she said.

"No worries. Amy did all the—"

The world got thunderous as every car alarm on every vehicle in a half-mile radius went off at once. The parking lot, the first responder vehicles, even on the nearby residential streets were filled with honking and beeping.

Rusty looked inordinately pleased with himself. "What did you do?" she yelled.

"Satellite pulse. Scrambled every alarm system in the area. Learned that trick before I was expelled from Oxford."

Amy frowned at him. "Wait. You were at Oxford?"

He glanced over at her and shrugged. "No big deal. It was only for half a semester—"

"Hate to break up the walk down memory lane," she interrupted, "but we have a job to do. As soon as I'm geared up, we'll head inside."

Rusty nodded. "Right." He stood there, still grinning at her.

"I can't very well change with you staring at me. Turn around already!"

"Ah. Sorry." He did so. Amy stood next to him to act as a screen as Heather faded into the shadows and started to slip out of her clothes.

As she dropped the t-shirt and bikini top to the ground, the blonde muttered, "You never said anything about Oxford before. Caltech and MIT, but never Oxford."

"Does it matter?"

"Yes, it matters! It's Oxford!"

Yanks. Oy.

Chapter 4

No one gave a trio of ATF investigators another glance as they flashed their badges and passed through the Victoria Building perimeter. The awning over the Grand Lobby doors had been slashed by firefighters as they attempted to vent the smoke from the attack. Pieces of canvas hung down like misshapen curtains.

As they approached the top of the steps, they stopped near a series of reddish stains on the concrete, each paired with a numbered yellow evidence marker. "This is where the victims collapsed?" asked Steve.

"Yes," Heather nodded as she knelt by one particular patch. "The ones who managed to make it outside."

"They've all been identified as hotel employees," said Ethan over the commlink. "Three from food service, two housekeepers and the sixth—"

"Her name was Nancy." Heather cut off his commentary

Amy looked at her, surprised. "Excuse me?"

She didn't look up or acknowledge the junior agent. Her voice was tight. "Nancy. She wasn't just another number; she worked at the front desk. She told me she was checking a couple in." She paused. "Just before she died."

Steve put his hand on her shoulder. "There's nothing you could have done, Ji."

Heather pushed it away and stood up. "Like hell, I couldn't. I could have..." She trailed off and turned toward Amy, fire in her eyes. "I could have caught the woman who did this." She stalked into the building.

The two stared as the door swung closed behind her. Amy whistled long and low. "Your ex is just a little tightly wound there, Sport."

"Not my ex, A.J."

"Right. Next, you're going to tell me all Anjili really needs is a hug and a nap."

"Why not? That works with you." He clapped her on the shoulder and started inside.

She paused, then shrugged as she followed. "True."

Portable lighting cast harsh shadows around the lobby as the three agents entered. Steve remembered it from a visit from his childhood, all the intricate carved geometric latticework and had been afraid of what he might find. It was worse than he imagined. His heart sank. *This place is devastated. Most of the lattice was shredded by the initial blast, and the rest is caked with this weird red soot. It will take forever to restore it.* The famed wooden chandelier had crashed to the floor and now rested on its side in the center of the lobby. *If it's even worth trying.*

Heather leaned against the chandelier and pinched the bridge of her nose in concentration. "Oy, I'm knackered, but I swear I've seen something like this somewhere before." Her frown deepened as she ran a gloved finger across it and rubbed the soot between her thumb and forefinger. "Grittier than I'd expect," she mumbled to herself

Steve and Amy shared a glance. She stepped forward. "Look, Agent Anjili, maybe I should case the ballroom—"

Heather yelled in surprise, "Bloody hell!"

The others jumped backward in surprise. "What is it?"

She keyed her commlink. "Echo Seven, Triangle. Dana, access the video from my initial encounter here at the hotel."

"Any part in particular?" asked Boland.

"My time downstairs. Also, have Savannah run a check on mil-spec databases for all NATO and allied countries."

"Specific target?"

"We need to look for military signal flares, specifically of the color red."

"Signal flares. Got it. And I downloaded that part of the video to your SAVANT."

"Good." Heather turned to Amy. "Rogers, you have a field analysis kit. I want scrapings of this red soot."

Amy hesitated, then reached into her bag and started pulling out the needed tools. "Anything in particular?"

"The soot reminded me of something up close, so we're going to try and rule it out. Do a quick and dirty on the chemical composition of the soot, then upload it to HQ and have Savannah cross-check it against that list she's compiling."

"Anything else?

Anjili nodded. "The grit is something I don't remember from the soot I saw. See it the color is an embedded component or if you can find a solvent to remove it and identify what the grit consists of. I'd like to know what it really is." She headed for a staircase by the elevator. "Tate, you're with me."

Steve glanced at Amy, surprised. "Where are we headed?"

"The Carousel Room. It all started there." She started down the stairs.

He looked over at Amy. She only stared at him, her expression flat. He'd become very good at reading her over the last couple of months. When Amy bottled up emotions like this, it was never a good thing. He smiled at her weakly, then followed Anjili.

The staircase spiraled down around an old-fashioned cage elevator. Steve had to thread his way down past numerous red stains and yellow evidence markers. He stopped counting at seventy. He pulled up short on the bottom step to avoid bumping into Anjili.

"This is making less sense by the minute," said Heather.

"It might help if you weren't trying to fly this solo and dragging A.J. and me along. Want to talk through it?"

"Not really. There are too many traps in the logic."

"So tell me what you're seeing. It'll give you a fresh perspective," suggested Steve.

"You are pushing it, Heather," added Boland over the commlink. "I know you're fighting fatigue like crazy. In fact, I was going to recommend a stim-tab—"

"No need to go there, Dee. I'm just catching my rhythm." She glanced at Steve and sighed, then waved at the yellow markers. "Fine. Here's my problem. These deaths, they're all wrong."

Steve looked at the yellow markers again, trying to discern what she saw. It took him a moment. "The blood."

"Right. The blood. This wasn't a biologic. Something reacted to cause it."

"Something fast?"

"Aye. These people dropped on the run. But something in an aerosol would have attacked the skin first, before the lungs. They should have had severe chemical burns."

"But no one does?"

"Not a one." She took a few steps toward the ballroom. "We're missing something."

Steve walked over and put a hand on her shoulder. "Slow down, Ji. One step at a time. It will come. How'd you make the connection to the signal flares?"

She faced him, hands tapping against her side in an impatient rhythm. "MI-6 agents cross train with British SAS. I had to know the contents of their field kits, inside and out. We were on a cold weather op and the Special Forces squaddie says, 'Time for us to go home.' He pulls a flare out of his pack and tosses it out on the ice forty meters away. Fifteen minutes later, a helicopter homes in on the smoke and scoops us up. Red smoke." She stopped and pointed. "And red soot left behind on the ice."

"That's a bit of a stretch."

"Better than anything else we've got, so far. It still fits my theory this was a revenge attack on the Admiral."

"Military signal flares? Seems a little thin to me. And with you attached to SAS for a time, that theory supports the idea the attack could have been aimed at you."

"Not when you combine in other factors. This has all the makings of a revenge attack. It happened at a wedding – maximum innocents as casualties. The pattern's familiar to other attacks I've seen."

"Where?"

"My old job. Those were usually tribal, typically between rival militias in Africa."

"You seem very well versed on African tribal revenge scenarios."

"I might have occasionally encouraged a few of them."

Ethan piped up. "Steve, this may have a bearing on Agent Anjili's theory. Admiral Hernandez's final posting was as commanding officer of U.S. Special Operations Command, Africa."

Steve's eyebrows went up in surprise. "Africa? As in Somalia?"

Heather nodded. "Yes, Somalia was in Africa last time I checked."

"Ethan, when?"

"He retired nine months ago."

"That's not what I—"

"The answer is yes, Rusty." She met his gaze; her expression softened for a moment. Just as quick, her armor was back in place. "Tribal motives, advanced technology, sophisticated planning and execution."

"You suspect the warlords are stepping up their game? Not thrilled with that implication."

She pointed her light. "The Carousel Room is down this way."

They walked along the shopping arcade, splashing through water from the firefighter's attempt to put out a fire that had never existed. The stores had been left open, abandoned as workers ran for their lives. Steve started to run a hand through his hair, a nervous habit. "So."

"So."

"Triangle. Quite a change from your previous job."

"You could say that."

"Why the switch?"

She opened her mouth to reply, then paused. *Self-editing, Heather? That's not like you.* She stopped and faced him. "They made me an offer."

"And MI-6 let you go?"

"It's not like they had a say. After our little Somali adventure I was already on the outs."

"I'm sorry, I hadn't heard."

"No, you wouldn't have." He opened his mouth to protest, but she held up a hand. "Don't. After Paris, we both agreed, no commitments. We simply did what had to be done. We always have, Rusty. End of story." She held his gaze a moment more, then started moving.

He followed her in silence, confused on what to say. After a bit, he asked, "How bad was it?"

"The attack here? The shock wave shook things up good. Then the smoke started, red, thick and soon, pretty obviously toxic." She stopped, head down, lost in the memory. "Frustrating. My mission gear inaccessible and me going nowhere. Especially not in the outfit I arrived in."

"Yeah, I'll bet."

"Want me to wipe that smirk off your face, Rusty?"

"Steve. And what smirk?" He put up his hands in protest.

She didn't look up as she said, "I can always hear you smirk." She took a deep breath and blew it out slowly. "The victims stumbled out the door and bled out, then firefighters rushed in, hoping to find survivors. All they kept finding were bodies."

"And then you came down here." Steve sniffed the air cautiously. "Is this how it smelled, the air sort of acrid?"

Heather wrinkled her nose. "Yes. I'd smelled ozone before, but never this intense." She caught his glance and shrugged. "Air plant on a submarine during an op, using electrolysis to make air from seawater It was malfunctioning, dumping ozone into the boat."

"Well, well, look who's smart."

She tapped her forehead. "One does not need an egg-shaped noggin nor dubious visits to institutes of learning—"

"Hey, not just a guy who ran up the sides of buildings on the Tour, remember? Caltech, MIT, Stanford, et cetera."

"You forgot Oxford."

"Trust me; I'll never forget Oxford. The point is, I wasn't there just for my charm, good looks and beer pong skills." He bent down and rubbed some of the water between his fingers, then sniffed it. "Hydrogen Peroxide. Not a heavy concentration, but it'll bleach you pretty good if you stick around in it." He stood back up. "You used to say you liked me for my brains."

"Operative words - used to." She pushed past him and moved down the hall.

As they entered the Carousel Room, Steve considered the scene. Heather circled around a section of the carpet in the center with an odd depression and beckoned for him to follow. Smashed pieces of furniture were littered about, and the remains of a piano lay against a wall to one side. The wet carpet squished underfoot as he walked toward her.

Ten steps in she motioned for him to stop and pointed at the ceiling. "That's what happened when the cone of light touched the ceiling."

He peered up at the hole above him, leading to the charred remains of the main ballroom. The cut was so precise that the surfaces reflected light. "That's impressive." He turned back. "Your report said the device crumpled to dust?"

"More like a coarse sand, but that's right. Collapsed like a Brighton sandcastle having a dreadful day."

"Where'd it all end up?"

"When the device broke apart, water that had accumulated in the ballroom above poured down through that gap. It must have washed all the debris away."

"Echo Seven, Tango One," called Amy over the commlink.

"Go, Tango One," replied Heather.

"Analysis complete. The residue shows a high concentration of both white phosphorus and hexachloroethane."

Boland chimed in from headquarters. "Savannah has a profile match to the Mark 18 signal grenade out of the NATO MilSpec listings."

"Good to know. Any idea on the particulate?"

"I've tried a variety of solvents on both sides of the pH scale as well as pure water. No dice, they're still bright red."

"Then rig up an ultrasonic pulse—"

Steve shook his head. "Heather, not a good idea."

She bristled at his interruption. "Excuse me?"

"Amy is working in a corner, out of the way, trying not to draw attention, remember?"

She stared at him for a moment. "Tango One, belay that. Package everything for further analysis back at headquarters and stand by." Heather looked up and walked to the point where she stood under a damaged edge of the hole. After a moment, she looked back at Steve.

"That machine was not a Mark 18. So what was it, exactly? And why only the explosion up there, but the smoke and particulate everywhere?"

"Not to mention Bridezilla," added Boland.

"Bridezilla?" Amy sounded incredulous. "Who was Bridezilla?"

"The woman who attacked Heather. Our working assumption is she was Jasmine Hernandez, the bride at the wedding, because of the dress."

"That actually makes sense."

Steve studied the opening. "Heather, your first report said she came at you out of the red smoke?"

"Yes. I only beat Bridezilla because of the beam of light from the mystery machine. It partially decapitated her."

Steve sucked his breath in between his teeth. "Not a good way to go. But we've got a bigger mystery. A.J., you were listening in. Did you catch it?"

"Yes, I did," said Amy over the commlink. "Agent Anjili, how long did it take your victim to die on the steps?"

"What?" Boland's voice was contemptuous over the commlink. "You two have some nerve. You've both read the briefing. It wasn't more than five minutes."

"Dana, calm down," said Heather. She turned to Steve. "I get your point. So how did Jasmine Hernandez manage to throw pianos at me ten minutes after that?"

"We need to examine her body. And Admiral Hernandez as well."

"Why the Admiral?" asked Amy.

Heather folded her arms across her chest. "My working theory, Tango One, is this was a revenge attack on the Admiral."

"They went through all these people just to get to one man?"

"Yes, as sick as that sounds. We should determine what happened to the Admiral. Dana, do you have a location on their remains?"

A brief pause and the controller came back. "The locals have set up a temporary morgue in the north parking lot."

Ethan piped in. "Tango Two, Triangle. There's a possible complication. A master-at-arms contingent from the North Island Naval Air Station has arrived on site."

"An honor guard will make getting close to the bodies for an exam a problem," said Steve.

"It might, for you. Not for me." Heather considered this a moment. "Which is why Rogers will go."

"Me?" Amy sounded shocked.

"Yes, you. You have the right, um, assets for the job." Steve chuckled. Heather threw him a stern look. "New orders, Tango One. Take the samples out to your van, then head to the temporary morgue. You're to locate the bodies of the Admiral and his daughter and perform initial diagnostics on both bodies – scans only. Use whatever non-violent means you deem appropriate to distract the guards. Notify us via commlink once you've finished, and Tate and I will join you. We'll secure the bodies for transport back to headquarters at that time. Nowitzki, monitor Tango One exclusively."

The Welshman cleared his throat once. "Err, yes, will do, Echo Seven." He sounded off-put.

"Any questions, Tango One?"

Steve could feel his partner's hesitation. "You want me to handle this on my own, then?"

"Within reason, Tango One. Call for backup if you need it."

"Roger that. Tango One, out."

Steve was watching her, trying to figure out why Heather had just sent Amy off alone. Heather stared at the ceiling again, then suddenly turned to him and said, "Your partner doesn't like me much."

He bit back his initial reply. "Aiming a weapon at someone tends to make a bad first impression. A.J. will warm up once she gets to know you. I did."

"No warming this time 'round, Tate. Better stick to business." She walked past him.

"Okay." He got down on his hands and knees in the depression made by the machine. "Let's hope some of this sand of yours was left behind." Steve didn't look up as he held out a hand. "Ji, your microvac."

Nothing happened. Steve sat up and looked over. Heather's look threw daggers. "What?"

"First, you don't get to call me 'Ji' ever again. Second, who are you to give me an order, rookie?"

He sighed. "Fine. Echo Seven, would you please hand me your microvac and a sample tube?"

"Much better." She pulled out the device, attached a collection tube and handed it over.

"Thanks. Ladies and gentlemen, my lovely assistant Heather. Please, hold your applause."

"I'll assistant you."

"Relax, just a little joke." He turned it on and ran it a few passes over the carpet. The collection tube filled about halfway with a slurry of water and black reflective flecks. He turned the device off, removed and capped the tube, then handed that to Heather. "Look familiar?"

She held it up in the light from her SAVANT and shook it. The flecks glittered. "Yes. Any ideas?"

He stared at if for a moment. "I don't think it's sand, but I want to get them back for analysis before I speculate." Steve stood and dried his hands on the thighs of his pants. "Give me a minute." He circled the room again and without Heather being aware, activated his Talent.

As it took hold, he shifted into what he called *slow-time*. It was as if the rest of the world froze in place, plunged into a crisp blue-tinged pool. Data that described the environment appeared in measured bursts, readable like a detailed augmented reality display. The air seemed to thicken, and movements became harder as he began to examine his surroundings.

Right. Discover the device's origin. Just backtrack through specific causality cascades to locate the one that led it here. Steve looked around the room. *First things first.*

His Talent displayed information from his augmented senses as a continually updated stream of possibilities, showing how things might interact. There was so much of it that, in a way, it was almost a type of white noise, and Steve had learned to suppress it unless he needed to access and work with something within it. Now, as he was trying to work a backward causality, this stream of new data was obstructing his vision.

Steve closed his eyes and concentrated on that flow of data. He envisioned it squeezed down to a single line of input, bright and blue, all the possible timelines overlapping into a threaded rope, a much different construct than he was used to. He envisioned pulses of light running toward him along that rope as he sighted backward against that flow.

I go this. Steve put his hands on the rope, squeezed it tight to block the pulses of light, then pushed one hand away along it, so they began to flow away from him. Suddenly, something inside his gut flip-flopped. Cautiously he opened his eyes.

Instead of blue, he saw *red*. The environment had shifted from its cool azure-tinged world into something rose-colored. All the other effects of *slow-time* were the same: objects that moved imperceptibly slow, thickened atmosphere to push against, data displayed all around him. He was just someplace...*else*.

His inner physicist kicked in. *Perhaps I see a different part of the light spectrum because I'm looking backward, red-shifted instead of blue-shifted. But my power is to affect causality. Could I actually be moving back through time, however imperceptibly slowly?* The thought of an unexpected paradox disquieted him. *No need to arrive before I left. Better make this fast.*

He had the definite end event, the collapse of the device into sand. A cascade of possible causalities spread out like glowing ropes around him. The device's origin seemed impossible. *What was it Amy said? Dam up streams with known events.* He tried, putting out the death of Jasmine Fernandez as a fixed point next to the first.

The moment he did, causality chains collapsed and faded from existence, even as others thickened and strengthened to fit through both gates. Steve smiled. *A.J., I owe you one.* He started adding other events he recalled from the report to the search chain – *the roof collapse during the fight, the arrival of the bride, the thrown piano.* More and more useless threads winked out. *Heather's arrival in the room.* Finally, he added one event he wasn't sure of but wanted it in place anyway. *The explosion in the ballroom.*

There was a brief bright flash as most paths winked out of existence at that one. Four viable threads remained, and a new dilemma. He'd run out of known events to add to the search. All he had now was pure speculation. *Okay, genius, what now?* Running one hand through his hair, he groaned in frustration and hung his head down.

That's when he saw it, an impression ring left by the device in the carpet from the base and fins. Some flecks of the sand had settled into it and glittered back in the red light.

As they did in the second, smaller rectangular impression in the center.

Steve stared, trying to understand what it was he was looking at. He frowned as he figured it out. *Oh, now that is scary bad. Somebody knows way too much.* He added this new event to the linkage. Three threads winked out. The remaining one pulsed brightly.

Steve reached out and touched the thread. As he did the path expanded, and he watched a sped-up reverse image of the events in the room, from Heather running from the smoke to the arrival of the device – a red suitcase that expanded like a familiar but unwelcome friend. A woman in a hoodie who'd been very careful to keep her head and face obscured brought it in. There was something familiar about her. *No one is that good all the time. We'll find you. Only a matter of time,* he thought. As she lifted her arm, he got a glimpse of a partial tattoo. Some sort of butterfly.

The suspect entered through the doors to the left. Steve moved through the thickened air to follow her, made the turn—

And walked straight into a blank wall.

What the—? He double checked again. The causality thread insisted it originated from that blank wall. He looked again and found no other clues to the attacker.

Well, that sucks.

With a frustrated sigh, Steve returned to his original spot and concentrated on dropping back into real-time.

As the red around him winked out, it felt as if he were violently jarred sideways. The room spun for a moment as his stomach did a little somersault. He stumbled and shook his head to clear it. *So that's what a temporal effect feels like. Let's not do that again anytime soon.*

"Are you okay?" asked Heather as she walked over.

"Yeah, just a bit light headed for a second. Blood-rush when I looked down, I think." He caught her look. "What?"

"It's just... no, nothing."

"Come on, spill."

"For a moment there, you had this strange expression on your face and then you seemed to, well, flicker."

"Flicker?" He kept his expression neutral.

"Yeah." She shook her head. "I'm tired, and it's been too strange a day. Now I even see things with you."

"Let's wrap this up so you can get some rest. Describe to me what happened when you realized you weren't alone."

She pointed to his left. "The woman was working there with a data tablet when she sensed my presence."

Steve walked to where Heather indicated. "You interrupted her?"

"I think so."

"She signaled the bride to attack and got away. Any idea how she did it?"

"I'm not sure." Heather bit her lip in indecision.

Steve frowned. *Haven't seen that in, what, forever?* "It's okay, take your time."

She peered up with a guilty expression. "Steve, what I put in my preliminary report wasn't... it wasn't everything that happened."

"Heather, are you sure?" Boland interjected over the commlink.

"It's alright, Dana. I can trust him." She took a deep breath. "I'm not wrong about that, am I, Rusty?"

He started to correct her automatically, then caught himself. *Not now, dummy.* He just nodded.

Heather began to pace, arms crossed. "The woman made no sort of signal that I saw. Actually, I didn't see her do anything because she disappeared."

He fought to keep his expression neutral. *Okay, did not see that one coming.* "Disappeared?"

"Vanished. Poof. There, then not there. Then a couple of seconds later reappeared directly behind me."

"Anything else you can remember?"

"She had a weird nervous habit."

"How so?"

"When we were talking, she kept scuffing her right foot against the carpet."

The hairs on the back of Steve's neck rose. "Do you remember how she did it?"

Heather bit her lower lip in concentration, then kicked her right foot three times.

Oh, dear God. "She was here..."

"Then right behind me."

"And that's when you got a good look at the woman?"

"Oh, yes. I mean, this one was gone right quick, like a puff of smoke. But the second time, I got an excellent look at her. I swear she was the spitting image of Agent Rogers."

Steve hastily put pieces of the story together. *A triggering action. The rapid change of location. Same height, build and hair color as Amy.* As the dots connected, he suppressed a small rush of excitement. And dread.

We've been looking since Tokyo, but we haven't had any leads. Could she have appeared on her own? And if so, why here and now?

"After that I had my hands full, what with the flying piano and Miss Anger Management," Heather continued, pointing at the remains of the baby grand against one wall. "But whoever Speedy was, she must have snuck back to leave the note."

"You still have that, right?"

"It's secured, but yes."

"Good. When we get it back, we can run it for trace. Maybe it will give us more leads on who is behind this." He looked at the location of the machine again. "Look, you forced her to turn off the device early, which probably saved some lives."

"Not soon enough."

"Considering no one else even knew it was here, you did pretty well. Plus, I think I've figured something out."

"Oh? What is it?"

"I know what's in the sample vial."

She pulled it out and held it up to the light. "Oh?"

"Have to get them under the scope to be sure, but I believe they're nanites."

"Nanites? Like our SAVANT nanites?" said Boland.

Heather's frown was severe. "I didn't think anyone else had them."

"Neither did I," agreed Steve. "They're an interdicted technology, reserved for Triangle's own use."

"What makes you believe nanites?"

"They had to build the device right where you're standing, and quickly. Bringing it in full-size, even as components, would have raised suspicion. Plus, as components, it would have taken more than one person to assemble the device. We only know of a single terrorist."

He watched her consider the idea. "Say I buy into that theory, which I'm not just yet. How big a container are we talking?"

"You said the thing collapsed into a pile of sand and covered the bride's body?" Heather nodded. He closed his eyes and remembered what he'd seen along the causality line. He looked at her once more. "I'd guess a rolling carry-on bag could have done it."

Heather stood, arms folded, as she weighed that. Without moving, she said, "Dana, you get all that?"

"Let me get this straight. Per the rookie, all I have to find is a blonde with a rolling suitcase? Gee, she'll stick out like a raisin in rice pudding."

"Sarcasm is not helpful."

"No, but sometimes it's damned satisfying."

Steve opened his mouth to reply, but something wedged against a floorboard in the corner caught his attention. He walked over to look.

"What is it?" asked Heather.

"Not sure," he said as he picked up and examined the object. It looked like a gas-triggered autoinjector attached to some sort of miniaturized drone platform. "Some kind of—"

Steve was cut off by Amy over the commlink. "Tango Two, Tango One. Steve, get over here, quick!"

"What's wrong?"

"Someone's stealing the bride's body, and I'm with it!"

Chapter 5

Amy's mind was in turmoil as she crossed one of the resort's inner courtyards. She kept going over the night's events in her mind even as she negotiated another hallway filled with more of the yellow evidence numbers.

Ethan interrupted her musings. "Tango One, Triangle. Your heart rate's a bit elevated."

"Have to be honest, I'm not exactly feeling warm and fuzzy about this mission."

"Given your last two missions, I wouldn't have taken you for the squeamish type."

"What? Oh, the bodies? No, that's not it. I've got concerns about Echo Seven. Agent Anjili."

"Ah."

"Yes, 'ah.' It's pretty obvious she and Steve have some sort of history, but splitting us up right off the bat—"

"Now, Agent Rogers, don't jump to any conclusions."

She stopped for a second and took a deep breath. "Ethan, you do realize the least effective way to get me to listen is to call me Agent Rogers?"

"At a minimum, it slowed you down. You need to think this through. First, you and Steve quite often work independently from one another."

"We do not. Name one mission where we have—"

"Tokyo, Brisbane, Myanmar, Mysuru, St. Petersburg, Paris twice, —"

"Fine. You've made your point. But we plan it. It's never on the fly like this."

"Never?"

She sighed. "Okay," she admitted with reluctance. "Almost never. You know Steve too well. But the point is, so do I. And it's our choice, not some agent who shows up out of the blue and is interested in him—"

Her words trailed off. She stood there, mouth wide open and cheeks red in embarrassment. She closed her eyes, leaned against the nearest wall and softly began to bang her head against it. *Stupid. Stupid, stupid, stupid.*

Ethan's voice was gentle. "It's an assignment, Amelia. Agent Anjili is a professional, and I expect she'll behave as such."

Yeah, right. Still, Amy grasped onto that. "What's her story?"

"She's been with Triangle for almost two years. Previously with Scotland Yard and then British Intelligence. Her areas of expertise were weapons trafficking and terrorist organizations in Africa and Southwest Asia."

Great, I'm up against a real live British Double-oh. She started again down the corridor. Something occurred to her. "Hang on. From my arrival at Triangle you folks pounded into my head that you never, ever solo a mission. When does Echo Eight join us?"

The Welshman's pause was just a second too long. "Agent Anjili is, um, between partners."

"Between?" Her stomach sank as the implication hit her. "How?" she asked softly.

"Sniper in Abidjan four months ago."

"Ivory Coast? We sent them on an assignment where she would have been familiar."

"From her previous life, yes. Perhaps someone recognized her. Echo Eight took the bullet intended for her."

"Any leads on the shooter?"

"Intel managed to trace him. Bloke was tied to an emerging warlord who figured Anjili's death would make a name for his group."

"Why would that matter?"

"The NATO offensives there a few years back took out most of the old warlords, but not all. What they did leave was a power vacuum. Old players go, new players come to the table. One of the new gents figured bagging a former MI-6 operative who had made life rough in that region before would get him a bigger stake in the game."

"Only it didn't."

"She's still here. When the shooter missed, someone tried to protect him by embedding him in the Somali diplomatic corps in Brazil."

"Thereby giving him diplomatic immunity?"

"Right in one. As soon as we heard, Triangle was working to pry him loose. After all, he'd killed one of ours."

"Wait, you said 'was.'"

"Before we could work through back channels, to extract this guy, Anjili got wind of where the shooter was. Must have seen the Intel reports. Anywho, she took matters into her own hands two weeks ago in Rio. An unauthorized sanction."

Amy whistled low. "I'll bet Watson was not pleased."

"That is putting it mildly. I believe the Director seriously considered sanctioning Echo Seven personally that evening upon learning what had happened. Instead, she was ordered to take mandatory leave while her future status with Triangle is under consideration."

I'm sure Anjili handled that well. "That's why she was here—"

"Wrong place at the right time."

"And now Triangle had no choice but reactivate her and have her on duty again." *Great. A rogue agent with a violent streak, a disregard for rules and who doesn't like me.* As she reached the exit door a thought occurred, accompanied by a new chill down her back. "This means she's back in play and looking for a new partner, doesn't it?"

"Focus, Amelia."

Oh, it just gets better. Amy angrily shoved the door open.

Much of the north parking lot was occupied by a tan, dual-peaked military-style tent. *Got to love left-over government surplus.* There was an entrance on the closest side. She double-checked to see if anyone was watching, then walked across the lawn and entered. As she stepped into the tent, a breeze rolled in with her. *Negative air pressure. Smart, keeps anything bad inside.* She looked around at the racks of clean suits and gloves.

"Okay, I'm in some sort of anteroom, with protective gear on shelves, stuff like that."

"What's your next step?"

"What else? Suit up so I blend in, then head inside."

"Roger that. I'll locate and tap into the interior surveillance feeds. I'll let you know when I'm in."

Amy grabbed a face mask and protective suit. She started to slip the mask over her face. *Not necessary, we know this stuff isn't a biologic. But the camouflage won't hurt if I end up dealing with the Navy.* As she started to zip up the protective suit, a thought occurred. *This is probably ruining any advantage my assets would have with those sailors.* She thought for a moment about Anjili and yanked the zipper sharply up the rest of the way. *Tough.* Ready, she stepped backward through a pair of double doors, turned around and looked up. The sight stopped her dead in her tracks.

Oh, my God.

Her breath stuck in her throat as she tried to make sense of the scene. Laid out in neat rows on the tent floor were bodies. Dozens of bodies. They were contained in clear vinyl body bags, each labeled 'Dangerous - Potential Highly Contagious.' At first, it seemed the bags were grouped in a haphazard manner, three and four here, a single person there, a large cluster of ten in one corner. There appeared to be no pattern. Then it hit her.

A wedding. A resort. Vacationers.

They're organized by family units. Amy's stomach tightened at the thought. When she realized some of the bags were smaller than others, the fist that squeezed her guts twisted sideways as well.

"Ethan," she murmured, "there have to be more than two hundred victims in here."

"By last official count, two hundred sixty-nine."

"This was—"

"Yes, it was. Which is why we need to get whoever was behind this."

"You with me yet?"

"Over your right shoulder." She looked back and saw the security camera mounted on a pole in one corner of the tent.

"You have no idea how nice it is to have my cricket right now."

"Actually, three of them." She found the other two camera positions. "Looks like we're not alone, either. Company on your ten o'clock."

She turned and spotted the other pair of people in the morgue, gowned and masked as she was. They stood next to a body bag at the far end of the morgue. "I believe that would be the Admiral's guards. I'll have to deal with them soon enough. Let's start with Jasmine Hernandez."

"Understood. Have you located the bodies?"

"I'm good, but I'm not that good. I just got here. I'm not even sure how to start. Everyone's in a body bag." She knelt next to the closest one and examined the label. "They've bar-coded all of them."

"That's convenient."

"How so?"

"I have access to the central database of victims. The bar-codes will tie into that."

"It'll take me a while to scan all the bodies."

She heard him crack his knuckles. "You just get me a base scan of one of those barcodes and let me worry about the rest."

"You're the boss." She ordered her SAVANT into Mode 4 and felt it change beneath the right arm of her protective suit. She pulled off her glove and said, "Ready."

"Send it."

She aimed her SAVANT at the label. A broad red beam played over it. "Got that?"

September 9, 2:09 a.m. EDT

At his console in the SAVANT Interface Control Center, Ethan grinned. "Nicely done. And without attracting any attention, too."

"That was the general idea." He watched her slide her glove back on.

"Still, I appreciate the subtlety."

"Remember who you're talking to. I'm not Steve."

"True, true." He spun his chair to the side and placed his fingers on a virtual keyboard. "Now let's see what I can do with this."

"Your turn to amaze me."

He chuckled as he sent the bar-code off to link with the victim database. As that ran, he pulled feeds from all three cameras and ran them through a clean-up algorithm to sharpen their resolution. Armed with a trio of separate high definition video images, he pressed a control on his console.

"Savannah?"

"Hello, Ethan," said the Triangle AI. "How may I assist you?"

"Mission priority task. I'm sending you three video feeds, I need them combined and pushed through the 3D render suite."

"Output?"

"Wire frame model of the space. Tag bar-code labels that appear on any objects and sync to the indicated database on my screen."

"Acknowledged. Time to completion, forty seconds."

"Thank you, dear."

"You are welcome. I see this is for Agent Rogers. Do tell her to be careful."

Ethan paused and looked up at the overhead camera pickup. *AIs don't usually express concern.* "I'll pass on your best wishes."

"Controller Johannsen asked me to check in on her friend."

"Ah." Rose Johannsen used to be Amy's controller before an attack had left her injured. *Still playing Eye in the Sky, Rose?* "Message to Rose. Amy's fine. I'm taking good care of her until you're back. Send that along, please."

"Yes, Ethan. Render complete."

"Main screen, please."

A highly-detailed wireframe reproduction of the temporary morgue and its contents formed on the wall display. Hundreds of shapes lay on the ground across the space. After a moment, a red line dragged across the image, a virtual scanner. As it encountered any barcode embedded in the render, it matched it against the victim database and displayed the name above the body. One by one, names began to appear in the virtual space, each accompanied by a small beep. The tones built in a crescendo that caught Boland's attention for a moment, then gradually petered out to a stop.

"What the hell, Nowitzki? We're trying to work here." Boland stopped when she saw the wall display. "What is that?"

"The morgue. And the body count." The wall was flooded with hundreds of names. Ethan stared, the toll of the attack stark before him.

"Holy—"

"Yes." He swallowed hard. *Keep it together, man.* "Holy is right. Now we both have work to do."

"Ethan, did it work?" Amy's voice cut through his funk. He cleared his throat and focused again, his attitude all business.

"Sorry Amy. I was distracted for a moment. Speaking of which, Rose says hello and be careful."

"Nice to know she still cares."

"As for the scan, out of 270 bodies, I have 268 positive identities."

"Out of 269 victims? I guess nobody's perfect. Still, it's a start."

"Go ahead, be cheeky." He ran through the list. "Oh, bother."

"What is it, oh controller of little fluff?"

"No joy on a location for Jasmine Hernandez. But I have one for the Admiral. Northwest corner, near the exit. Grouping of four victims, I suspect that would be his family."

"On my way over there. And try to figure out why Jasmine didn't show up. This is where my teen sidekick would say it's suspicious she's the only missing body."

"If you had a teen sidekick."

"I sort of do. Steve acts like one often enough."

"I will not tell him you said that."

"Seriously, if she's not here, we've got an issue."

"On it."

As Ethan switched back to the live feed and watched her move through the morgue, a feeling that something was amiss grabbed him. "Amy, be careful."

"What is it?"

"Call it instinct. Something's not right."

Amy stopped and looked at the nearest camera pickup. "I'm in a room surrounded by a couple of hundred bodies. There's a lot that's not right here."

He looked up at the wireframe reconstruction. That's when it clicked in place. Ethan checked all three video feeds to confirm his suspicions.

September 8, 11:12 p.m. PDT

"Amy, is anyone else there with you?" Ethan's tone put her on alert.

"Of course, there are the two sailors—" She did a quick pivot to point at them. They were gone. She frowned. "They were right where I'm headed. I assumed…" She trailed off. "Is there any way to backtrack their movements on those cameras?"

"They don't maintain any internal backup. If there's any sort of recording, it'll be in the cloud somewhere. It may take a bit to find."

"Do your best."

She hurried over to where Ethan indicated she'd find Admiral Hernandez. It was evident straight away something more was going on.

"Ethan, the Admiral's body bag has been tampered with."

"What? How?"

"The coroner's seal has been breached, and it's partially opened." She crouched down by the bag, then glanced back toward the entrance she'd used. *Those two were standing right here. You saw them, Amelia Jane. They weren't sailors, so what exactly were they doing?* For once she wished she had Steve's ability to stop the world and see everything clearly.

"Amy, I was able to track down the video. It appears they were taking pictures and scans of the Admiral's body just before you arrived."

"Pictures and scans? Why would anyone else need to—" She stopped.

Why are you here to do the exact same thing? It only took a moment for the reason to drop into place. *Because they needed to check on their handiwork.*

Because they were behind the attack.

Amy reached down and unzipped the Admiral's body bag, pulling the sides open wide. "Ethan, prepare for an incoming scan."

"What?"

"My orders. Full body scan on the Admiral, remember?"

"Oh, right. Ready when you are."

She took off her right glove again and looked down at the exposed corpse. "SAVANT, imaging scan, high resolution."

"Acknowledged."

A wide beam of blue light emerged from her device. She pointed her arm at the Admiral's head and drew the beam slowly down the length of the body bag. Even without the scan, she knew this was an ugly death. "Ethan—"

"Got it. Savannah, run the image through a virtual MRI."

Amy heard the AI acknowledge the request in the background over the commlink. A moment later, Ethan exclaimed, "Dear God!"

"What is it?"

"Signs of severe trauma. Right ankle crushed, left femur snapped in two, both hands broken, left arm dislocated, and his neck—" Ethan gulped. "Broken. Severed cleanly between the C2 and C3 vertebrae."

She fought to maintain her calm as she regarded the body. "What could have done that?"

"Most of the injuries are consistent with blunt force trauma."

"From the explosion?"

"No. More likely Hernandez was thrown or slammed against something repeatedly. But even that wouldn't account for the crushed ankle or hands."

Amy closed her eyes and said a silent prayer, then zipped up and sealed the body bag again. As she stood, her view swept across the field of victims. "He definitely didn't die like any of the others?"

"Definitely not. These injuries are purely traumatic."

Amy started to pace as she sorted through the facts. "When I walked in, two guys were taking a scan of the Admiral. They were probably in on the attack."

"That makes sense."

"But there a problem. You said the North Island Honor Guard was on site. That's who I thought these two were" She took a few steps away and looked back at the Admiral's body. "There's no way they would have just let someone walk up to the Admiral—" She slowed down again, looking at the body bags. *What was it Ethan said?* "How many bodies did you count earlier?"

"Two hundred seventy."

"But there were two hundred sixty-nine victims from the attack. And you could only match—"

"Two hundred sixty-eight of them. Jasmine Hernandez is still missing."

A chill ran down Amy's spine. "Ethan, where are the two unidentified body bags?"

"Checking. Northeast corner."

She sprinted over and started to look through the bodies. She quickly found the two without tags, piled so their occupants were face down. She flipped over the closest one. Pooled blood splashed crimson all over the inside, but through the plastic, Amy could make out a sailor's dress uniform."

"I found the sailors. Looks like somebody sliced their throats." She looked around. "Huh. No blood splatter I can see, though."

"Amy, we need to call for backup right now."

"No, wait!" *I can handle this.* "I'm safe for now. There's nobody in here."

"This is completely against protocol—"

"It'll be okay, Ethan." She stood up and began to pace again. *I kind of wish Steve was here, though. He'd make one of his brilliant leaps of logic that look oh, so easy and are always right. Damn it, why can't I be the smart one for once, instead of the pretty one—*

She stopped in her tracks and looked back at the Admiral's family.

The pretty one.

"Ethan, I know how the Admiral died."

"You do?"

"Yes. The bride did it."

Chapter 6

"We must have comm interference. That sounded like you just suggested Jasmine Fernandez attacked and killed her father."

Amy couldn't remember Ethan being more incredulous. "Hear me out. Anjili's initial report described Jasmine as extremely aggressive, strong, and fast—"

"I see where you're going, but why would she attack her father?"

"Steve would probably say she didn't like the band. But what if someone made her do it?"

"Turned her into a weapon?"

"Exactly. Created Bridezilla and aimed her at her father." She stood up and frowned in puzzlement. "But then why kill the sailors? If whoever did this was just checking how effective their project was, all they would have needed was a scan of the Admiral's body. They could have just incapacitated them. This was overkill – no pun intended."

"Unless the scans weren't everything. Remember, we didn't locate Jasmine Hernandez's body."

Amy looked up sharply at the camera. "They weren't here to evaluate their weapon, but to recover it." She began to pull off the protective suit as she headed for the exit. "How much of a head start?"

"I estimate twelve minutes. I'm going to call the others for backup."

Amy bit her lip as she considered this. She shook her head. "No."

"Excuse me?"

"That big a jump, these assailants are probably long gone. Let's me scout first, see what I find. If they've already vacated the scene backup won't help, and it might prevent Steve and Anjili from finding some other clue to this case. You can always make that call if I get in over my head."

"I'm not very sanguine about your strategic choice."

"Yet I feel so protected knowing I've got you watching out for me."

Ethan sighed so deeply Amy felt it rattle her teeth. "If you say so, Tango One."

Amy ran from the tent and took cover in a nearby clump of bushes. She pulled out a pair of smart glasses from her belt pack, then did a visual scan of the parking lot. In a far corner, away from any street lamps, was a black cargo van. Printed on one side in block letters were the words SAN DIEGO COUNTY CORONER. Its rear doors were open. Using enhanced light view Amy could see a gray coffin-like device and a pair of pressurized gas tanks inside the van.

"Triangle, Tango One. Ethan, tap into the feed from my glasses."

"I've got it."

"Can Savannah ID that rig in the back of the van?"

"Affirmative. It's a cadaver preservation system. First-stage cryogenic storage, it evacuates oxygen to prevent aerobic processes from causing further decay."

"Plain English, please?"

"It sucks out the air so that bodies won't spoil in near-vacuum and replaces what little air there is with super-cooled nitrogen."

"Sort of like the meal-saver in my grandmother's kitchen?"

"In a manner of speaking, yes."

"Coroners do that?"

"None that I'm aware of."

Amy's gut tightened. *These must be the people behind the attack. But why are they sticking around?* "I need a closer look at that van."

"No, you need to wait for back—"

"Don't say it."

"But—"

"Just don't. Stand by and monitor, in case things go sideways."

"As you wish. Be careful."

She checked her ID again. *Okay, Agent Lee, your turn.* One more quick check of her outfit, then Amy stepped out from the bushes and strode across the parking lot toward the van, sure to put some extra swivel on her hips. As she approached the van, two techs in hospital scrubs stepped out and saw her.

The closest greeted her. "Everything is loaded as you ordered, Miss Richards."

As I ordered? Amy stumbled for a second, then smiled and nodded. *Roll with it, Amelia Jane. See what you learn.* "That's good, boys. Ready to pull out?"

"Yes, ma'am." The tech turned for the cab as Amy started for the back. He stopped and looked at her. "What are you doing? Are you coming with us now?"

His partner moved a step closer. "Yeah, I thought Charlie and I were taking the package back in the van while you transit back to base." He frowned at her, unsure.

"No, that's still the plan." She moved to sidestep him. "I just wanted to check on the package one more time—"

"Wait, when did you change your outfit?" Charlie, the first tech, grabbed at her. "You're not—"

Amy spun out of Charlie's grasp and pushed against his right shoulder and the back of his neck, ramming him face first into the van. There was a crunching sound she assumed was his nose. He folded to the ground, unconscious.

She caught a glimpse as the other tech reached for his waistband. *Gun? None of that now.* Amy pivoted and delivered a roundhouse kick that connected with the man's gun hand. The weapon jarred loose and skittered away under the van. She ducked low and continued through the spin to chop both legs from under him. As he fell toward the asphalt, she grabbed in a headlock and cut off his air. Within moments, he went limp.

Amy dropped him and stood, alert for additional attackers, but there were none around. She relaxed. *That went well.* She dragged the unconscious men into the bushes behind the van and used strips of cloth from their scrubs to gag them and tie them up. Once secured, she took images of their faces.

"Triangle, Tango One. Van secured. Also, I've subdued the two operatives who must have stolen the bride's body."

"Roger that. Ready for some assistance now?"

"Negative, they're secured. Uploading photos to you. Let's figure out who these guys are."

"Will do. My, they do look a bit worse for wear."

"They just don't make bad guys as sturdy as they used to."

"I'll be sure to let quality control know of your displeasure."

"Do that. As soon as I finish here, the locals are going to want these two for killing those sailors."

"Got it."

She paused and looked at the parking lot. "Something else weird is going on here, Ethan. These two acted as if they recognized me."

"How so?"

"Same thing as Anjili did earlier tonight. Only these two called me 'Miss Richards.' I was able to use it for a bit, right up until I tried to look inside the van."

"Which you're going to do right now."

"You know me so well."

"Well enough to know that Steve is rubbing off on you."

"Ouch. That stings."

"Truth hurts, Tango One."

"Standby, Triangle."

"Triangle standing by, Tango One."

Fine. If Ethan doesn't trust me, I'll just have to prove him wrong. Amy checked once more to see if she was being watched. The lot and surroundings still seemed empty as she stepped into the cargo van.

The gray cryo-chamber reminded her of an industrial-size chest freezer, with a glass viewport on top and a trio of turnbuckle latches holding the top down. She put her hand on it. *Cold to the touch but not freezing. Well insulated.* It was pitch black inside the viewport. A quick search located a rocker switch on the far end of the lid. When she flipped it, lights flickered on inside. Amy glanced through the port.

"Jasmine Hernandez's body bag is inside the cryo unit."

"Any signs of what happened to her?" asked Ethan.

"I'm not sure. It's pretty fogged up." She considered the chamber for a moment. "I'm going to crack this open and see what these guys were trying to hide."

"Now would be a good time to call for backup."

"Technically, Echo Seven's precise orders were to take full scans of the body, then call for transport assistance. Admittedly, she is already prepped for transport—"

Ethan's groan interrupted her. "Steve is definitely rubbing off on you."

She ignored him. *Okay, Jasmine, let's see why you're so important.* She undid the turnbuckles and swung open the lid. There was a hiss as pressures equalized, then a cold mist cascaded over the edge and spilled onto the van floor. *Yeah, that's not creepy at all.* Waving it away, she uncovered the body bag nestled within. *Come on, Amelia Jane. No time to be squeamish. You know what you need to do.* She reached in, grasped the zipper and opened the bag. Fog swirled, obscuring the body within. She waved it away, then stared in shock at what she found.

Not exactly what I expected. "Triangle, Tango One. What was Jasmine Hernandez's description in Echo Seven's report?"

"Wait one. Based on video imagery, six feet nine inches, weighing an estimated two hundred fifty pounds, with a super-attenuated musculature and a reddish skin tone. Why do you ask?"

"I'll let the pictures speak for themselves. Prepare to receive my scans." Amy did a complete 3D body scan and a second visual image scan as well. "Did you get those?"

"I did. They're—"

"Words right out of my mouth, Ethan."

"But she's shriveled. Savannah estimates her mass is less than forty percent of what she had been."

"If that."

Concern tinged Ethan's voice. "Amy, you've completed your mission, it's time to call—"

"Just let me check one more thing." Amy leaned in to examine the woman's face. Jasmine might have been beautiful once, but whatever this process was had caused substantial damage. Her skin was now gray and stretched parchment-thin. "This was pretty aggressive."

"That's how Agent Anjili described her behavior."

"No, I mean it burnt her up pretty good. Something about her eyes, though." She looked closely at them. Their appearance was startling, even in death. Something had totally discolored them, converting them into black, lifeless orbs. "Do we know of anything that could turn them completely dark?"

"Including the sclera? No known causes according to Savannah."

She grabbed a pair of blue medical gloves from the van's shelf. "I'm going to take a sample—"

The doors to the back of the van slammed shut.

Startled, Amy tried the doors. The handle didn't move. *Locked from the outside.*

The van started and lurched into gear. Amy was thrown to the floor, and the lid to the cryo-chamber slammed down on her hand. She screamed in pain as she yanked her hand free, then checked her fingers. *None broken. Thank you, Talent!*

"Triangle, Tango One. Are you all right?"

The van lurched again, throwing her against the other side. "Damnit! No, Triangle, I think my luck just ran out."

"We should have called—"

"Not now!" She switched channels on her commlink as the van swerved. "Tango Two, Tango One. Steve, get up here quick!"

He was online immediately. "What's wrong?"

I'm being kidnapped, that's what's wrong! "Someone's stealing the bride's body, and I'm with it!"

"We're on our way."

The van lurched once more, and Amy banged her head against the equipment racks on the side. *Ow! Speed bumps. Somebody's in a hurry.* "I'm locked in the back of a black coroner's van. The bride's body is in the rear, packed in some sort of cryo-storage unit."

"Tango One, this is Echo Seven. Did you see the driver?"

"No, I was scanning the bride's remains inside the van when someone slammed the door shut behind me."

"Rogers, your orders were to stay in the morgue—"

"It's a long story—"

"Not now," said Steve. "Triangle, do you have a fix on her location?"

"I have her," said Ethan. "GPS tracking has her headed north onto Orange Avenue."

"We're on our way. Dana, I need an emergency unlock on my SUV."

Amy looked around the van's interior. *I need to slow this thing down so they can catch us.* She checked the shelves for anything that might help. *Body bags, photo gear, sampling equipment – wait. They stole an actual coroner's van? Points for authenticity, but not much help.* "Triangle, still there?"

"Affirmative, Tango One," said Ethan. "I'm tracking you. You're on Orange, heading north, coming up on a set of traffic lights."

"There's only one way off Coronado on this side, right?"

"At the north end, correct. The Coronado Bridge, connecting to San Diego."

"The same route we took in. Can't let the van get there. Okay, I know what to do." She ordered her SAVANT into Mode 3 and moved to the back of the van.

"You're not planning anything rash—"

"Tell those two to hurry up and get here."

"Amelia, please, wait for backup!"

Amy braced herself and fired her SAVANT at the left wheel well. The blast blew through the van floor and sheared off the rear axle. The tire flew away, and the van dropped into a skid. Sparks showered off the van as the side panels began to rip apart. The driver tried to maintain control but oversteered. The van tipped over and began to tumble across the road. It rolled twice before coming to rest on its side.

Amy lay on her back, looking up at the night sky through one of the holes ripped in the van. The cryo unit had torn away from its mounts and landed atop her. Pain stabbed up and down her back.

Ethan's right. Steve is definitely rubbing off on me. Amy twisted and reached around to find out what was the cause of her pain. She touched a round metallic disc that seemed to be attached to the middle of her back. She tried to move it, but it was stuck. *That's new.*

"Tango One, Triangle. Amy, are ye there?" Ethan's accent always got thicker when he was concerned

"I'm okay, Ethan. At least, for the moment."

"What's your status, lass?"

"Pinned inside the van, but hey, on the bright side, I stopped the thief from getting away with the body."

"How do you know?"

She looked at the cryo unit, a wry grin on her lips. "What do you think has me pinned?"

"Can you—"

"Get out? Come on, Ethan, this is me." She slammed her right hand down against the cryo chamber. The move sent a wave of pain rippling through her abdomen. She cried out in shock.

"Amelia, are ye all right?"

"Not really. I'd love to know the cavalry is on the way." She repeated the strike with her right hand, the pain building inside. She bit her lip to force it back.

"Tango Two and Echo Seven are on the way," said Ethan. "You snarled traffic pretty good with this stunt."

"They'll manage. Stand by." She concentrated a moment more before slamming her hand down a third time against the cryo unit's surface. The pain's crescendo was countered by a warm wave of energy that flooded through her, pushing the needles aside in a soothing blanket of comfort as her stored energy reserves became available. *Now that's more like it.* She reached down and pushed it away from the side of the van as she scrambled out from beneath it.

It was at that point everything went sideways for her. A shock, white hot and ice cold at the same time, ran over her as her Talent came to a standstill, all its power draining away in an instant. The cryo-chamber slipped from her grasp and clanged against the side of the van. A moment later, as quickly as it left, Amy flashed back to normal, her Talent fully available.

She looked at the cryo unit. *Whatever that was, it wasn't good.* As she stood a wave of dizziness struck her, and she fell to her knees.

"Tango One, your vital signs just went all over the map!"

Amy's mind flashed on the disc on her back. *That must be a factor.* She reached around and grasped it, tried to twist it, then pulled on it. She could feel something long and solid sliding by her skin, the edge burning as it passed along. She grit her teeth and with a shudder pulled it all the way out.

"Ugh!" The moment the object was free, a brief surge of energy ran through her as if she'd activated her talent, yet somehow sharper and more painful. In seconds, it faded. Amy held the object, now dripping red with her blood, in front of her.

"Say again. Amy?"

"Have I ever mentioned to you how much I hate sharp pointy things?"

"Often."

"This is why." She examined the object – a long needle-like probe with a digital readout on the disc on one end. The probe was triangular, and each edge was razor sharp. She tossed it aside. "I think I got skewered by some sort of space-age meat thermometer."

"It sounds like a liver probe, used to determine the time of death."

"Yeah, well, I'm not dead yet." She stood up and went to the back doors. They were still locked. "Ethan, I may have a problem getting out—"

The doors were ripped off their hinges and tossed to the ground on one side.

Amy stared in surprise at who had done it, a woman about her height and build, wearing a black hoodie, her face was hidden in its shadows. There was something eerily familiar about her.

Ethan was in her ear. "Tango One, Triangle. Say again, are ye in need of medical assistance?"

"Stand by, Triangle." Amy tried to be nonchalant as she stepped out of the van. "Thank you. I'm grateful for you opening the doors. I was kind of trapped. But if you had anything to do with stealing the van in the first place—"

The punch came fast, exceptionally so. Amy barely had time to catch it with a cupped hand. The impact made a loud snap that sent Amy's mind into overdrive. *That punch connects, she takes my head off.* Amy's Talent was still active, so she kicked in her own 'go-gear,' as she called it, increasing her own strength and speed.

The woman attacked, striking out with a punch-kick combo that had lethal intentions. Amy countered with an arm block, spin and side kick counter combo that blunted the attack and forced the woman back. It gave Amy the opportunity to circle and gauge how effective her opponent was.

Amy was usually confident that she'd beat an opponent in hand-to-hand combat relatively quickly. As the two engaged, she quickly realized this adversary was as strong and at least as fast as her; perhaps not as familiar with formal martial arts techniques, but her improvisational skills more than made up for them. *She's my match. I'm not sure I can take her.*

Amy went to do a leg sweep. The white flash occurred again, draining her of her power. She barely ducked under a countermove from her opponent, landing in a sprawl on the asphalt, desperately out of position. Spotting a piece of blown tire burning nearby, Amy scrambled to it and flung it back at the woman, who batted it aside without hesitation or surprise.

Amy struggled to her feet, hoping for her energy to return. She expected her opponent to come at her, take advantage of her vulnerability. Instead, the woman stood and spoke for the first time, her voice oddly familiar. "Desperate move."

"Strategic," Amy lied as she studied the woman.

"Right. Like you'd know anything about that."

"Think again, sweetie." Amy indicated the smoke coming from the woman's sleeve. As if on cue, it burst into flames.

For a moment, Amy thought her opponent might try to stay in the hoodie as she batted at the fire. But she finally shed it, tossing it to one side. She stood, fists clenched and shrouded in smoke, turned away from Amy. "Figured that was smart, did ya, Amelia Jane?"

Everything around them seemed to turn silent; for Amy, the world suddenly narrowed down to just the two of them. "Who the hell are you? How do you know my name?"

The woman chuckled as she turned. "Oh, I know a lot more than that. As for me—" She stepped out of the smoke.

"Call me Angelica."

It was like looking in a mirror. The hair was a little shorter and spikier, but otherwise, she was a near perfect copy of Amy.

"You? You're my—?"

Her doppelgänger raised a finger for her to stop, then put it to her lips. She scuffed her right foot against the ground once—

Amy's eyes went wide.

Twice—

No! That's not possible!

Her foot hit the ground a third time, and Angelica's eyes widened as she took a deep breath, almost a gasp. Her skin seemed to glow for a moment.

I know that look. How many times did I see it in the mirror when I've activated?

Angelica's eyes blazed as she turned her gaze toward Amy. She tossed off a mocking two-finger salute. "Until next time, Sis." With a turn, she took two steps and disappeared.

Oh, no you don't! Amy kicked the ground quickly to reactivate and started after her, ignoring the building white crystals of pain growing throughout her body. She'd barely gone past the first couple of steps into her speed run when the van exploded. Amy was thrown sideways into something hard and unyielding. Pain flared, and she lost consciousness.

Chapter 7

Amy's world drifted slowly from black through shades of gray as she climbed back toward consciousness. At first, all she knew was that she hurt everywhere. After a bit, she could also sense she was somewhere soft and quiet, except for a muted rhythmic beeping. Another few moments and she realized the sound mirrored her own heartbeat.

She opened her eyes. Unfamiliar shapes and colors wavered in front of her for a moment before coming into focus. Her mind processed the images and spat out a conclusion. *Hospital room.* Further review refined her deduction. *I'm a patient in a hospital room.*

A part of Amy's mind reeled at that conclusion. Since the day of the accident when her Talent first manifested, medical visits had been few and far between. As for being an inpatient? *Always a first, I guess. But what happened to me?*

She turned her head, her neck registering a strong objection. She smiled when she spotted Steve asleep in a bedside chair, head to one side. She regarded him in silence, his chest rising and settling slowly as he breathed. *He's kind of cute, asleep like that. Just like a little boy. I wonder how long he's been there like that.*

I wonder how long I've been here like this.

His head bobbed forward and he startled awake, trying to shake off the confusion. That's when their eyes met. It was just a moment, but it was as if a spark jumped a gap between them and started him up. A big smile rose like the sun across his face. "Hey, sleepyhead."

"Hey, yourself." Her voice came out as a croak. "How did you sleep?"

"Just like a baby. Woke up every couple of hours crying."

She started to laugh then cringed as a wave of pain, white-hot and jagged, radiated outward from her back and raced through her body. She groaned. *Now you I remember. Are you why I'm here?*

Steve was at her bedside in moments. He reached for the nurse call button. "Are you okay?"

The first comment that crossed her mind as the pain ebbed was, *Duh*. She bit back the sarcasm. "Feels like I've been run over by a truck. How long was I out?"

He began to reply, but the outer door slid open. A young female doctor walked in, trailed by a pair of nurses. "Savannah, lights to full."

"Yes, Doctor." The room brightened, forcing Amy to squint some more as the medical team made their way to her bed. One nurse plugged a data tablet into the foot of the bed and was examining readings with the physician, while another checked the IV station to her right. They were very efficient, but no one said a word. Steve held her hand on the left. She was grateful for the contact.

The doctor unplugged the data tablet, handed it back to her nurse, then turned to Steve. "How long has she been awake?"

Excuse me? Amy bristled and replied first. "She woke up about five minutes ago, Doctor. And her hearing is just fine, too. Might want to have your nurse note that down." She glared at the physician.

Steve chuckled. She pulled her hand away. *This isn't a joke.* The doctor bowed her head with a smile as she walked up on the opposite side of the bed. "I apologize, Agent Rogers, that was rude of me. I'm Dr. Powers. I've been treating you. How do you feel?"

"Like I've gone a few rounds in the Octagon. I hurt everywhere."

"Yes, well, considering your injuries, hurting means everything is working. The alternative would have been worse. Now, first things first. Do you know where you are?"

"Based on your ID and this lunk sitting next to me, I'll hazard that I'm in MedBay back at Triangle headquarters. The bigger question is how?"

"Reports were that you were adjacent to a car bomb that was set off."

"I vaguely recall something like that."

"The blast threw you over fifty feet into a concrete wall. Agent Tate says you made quite an impression, literally."

Amy groaned as she looked at him. *Really? I almost get killed and you crack jokes?* Steve just shrugged apologetically.

The doctor continued. "That alone should have killed you. Should have, but didn't. But there was also your stab wound."

Amy groaned. "Right. When the van rolled over, something impaled me, a sensor or thermometer, I think. It didn't seem to be that big a deal." She looked over at the Doctor. "Was it?"

Powers brought up a diagnostic scan. "Small entry wound, consistent with the probe your controller diagnosed." A line lit up on the image. "It penetrated through your kidney and spleen, punctured your diaphragm and took a divot out of your spine."

"I didn't realize I was that seriously injured."

"Well, getting into a fight right after you were injured probably didn't help. You were lucky in a way she got away."

"Lucky?"

"When Tate and his partner located you, three blocks away from the explosion site, they started to transport you to your plane. That's when they spotted signs of something was going wrong and called it in."

"Signs?" She looked over at Steve. He nodded.

"You don't bruise, A.J. Not ever. But you had one on your back around the stab wound. It kept growing."

"The term is ecchymosis," said Dr. Powers. "It's blood pooling under the skin, and obviously the blood was coming from somewhere. His partner stuffed you into an autodoc capsule and ordered the Hyperjet here on full emergency. Even so, it was touch and go. They probably saved your life."

"Did they now?" She considered Steve as he suddenly became interested in the ceiling.

"As it was, I ordered you into a medical coma to help you heal."

"So how long—"

"A week."

"A week?!" Amy tried to sit up, but the room started to spin. Dr. Powers pushed her gently back down onto the bed.

"Easy, I don't need you undoing my good work. It took a bunch of effort to make sure you still have all your parts, and they work as advertised. Now, let's have a look at you." Powers pulled out a pocket flashlight and checked both of Amy's eyes. "Sensitive to light?"

"Yeah, it hurts."

"Right. I expected post-concussive effects, but I dare say that's probably not a first for you. Now, sit up slowly." Amy did, and the doctor started her through a battery of tests, checking her range of motion and extremity strength. Amy performed them all, anticipating the white shards of pain. They didn't come. She began to relax.

The physician stepped back. "You are healing at a remarkable rate—"

"I guess I'm just lucky."

Powers raised an eyebrow at her. "Really? I was going to credit it as one of the side effects of your enhanced abilities." Amy's startled reaction drew a grin from the doctor. "Come now, Agent Rogers. You didn't think I'd be able to treat you effectively without full knowledge of your—" She paused as she searched for an appropriate term. "Your uniqueness."

"I guess not," said Amy, a bit sheepish.

"We're aware that fact is very much need-to-know, Agent Rogers. But we still need to take it into account, especially as we help you recover." She looked over at Steve. "I'll need your assistance for this. Do you think you can stand?"

"I can try." Amy lowered her feet to the tile floor and slowly put her weight on them. She was unsteady for a moment, but that passed quickly.

"Excellent. Now I'd like you to activate your Talent."

"Here? Now?"

"Yes. Being prone for so long, you'll have depleted energy stores. But we don't need you to do anything, just activate."

"Okay, Doc, you're the boss." She slowly started to kick her foot down once, twice, a third time—

Something went wrong. Instead of the warmth of energy surging, white-hot shards of pain came back, ripping and stabbing throughout her body. She screamed as she started to fall over.

Steve and Dr. Powers caught her and eased her back onto the bed. He looked at the physician. "You knew?"

"I suspected." She turned to Amy. "Deep breaths. Nurse, Tilaudnum, 200 mg."

"What's that?"

"It's a painkiller, non-narcotic."

Amy shook her head. "Those don't work on me so well. Besides, it's almost back to normal. See?" She blinked to clear her eyes and looked at Powers. "I've been hurt before."

"But I'll wager you've never had any sort of spinal cord injury before."

Amy bit her lower lip and hesitated before she nodded.

"What just happened, Doc?" Steve was all business now.

"Her Talent happened. As I understand it, Amy's basically a giant storage battery of sorts, converting kinetic into potential energy. When she injured her spinal cord, the damage appears to be acting like a short-circuit, preventing her from fully accessing her abilities." She held Amy's hand. "If I read the telemetry from your SAVANT correctly, you felt this just before the explosion, too. When you try to trigger and access your energy stores, you feel that effect."

Amy pulled back. "So I have a glitch. How long will this last? When can I return to duty?"

Powers paused and examined her tablet. "I know you want to be back, but you can't rush certain things."

"But Doc—"

"Don't 'but Doc' me. Spinal cord injuries are serious. So's a major internal bleed. Even for someone with your ability to recover." Powers put a hand on her shoulder. "Anybody else, at a minimum we'd be talking about months out of commission and a major rehab package. With you, do what I say and I am willing to predict you're close to duty shape in a week or so — if you avoid reinjuring anything."

"What about my—"

"Your Talent?" Powers considered it for a moment. "Given what just happened, it's obvious your body needs more time to heal. But no motor functions have been impaired. Have patience. Give it a few days; then we'll run some scans and try it again. If you can activate without pain, then we'll take it slowly and ramp up your abilities. Operative word, slowly."

She cut off Amy's retort as she tapped out orders on her tablet. "I'm still going to prescribe an analgesic for that pain. Yes, I know the others before have only had a limited effect on you, but those doctors didn't know what I do, huh?" Powers tapped the stylus twice against the forehead. "When have any flare-ups like that, use what I give you. You will bounce back quicker."

Powers stepped back and put the tablet down on the bed. "I want you up and out of here. Back to your quarters. You'll heal quicker in a more familiar, home-like environment. Initially, light exercise only, treadmill, swimming as soon as the incision is healed. Yoga for flexibility. Strictly non-contact in the dojo. No gymnastics, tumbling, or," she looked over at Steve and frowned, "parkour until I clear you. Savannah will monitor your rehab."

Amy sighed. "Fine. You're the doctor."

"Got that right. Even says so where I signed it in crayon on the diploma." Amy laughed at that. "Good. You still have a sense of humor. I'll have the nurses bring you a real meal, then I want you out of here and back to your quarters. Savannah will schedule your daily check-ins with me."

"Thank you, Doctor Powers."

She patted Amy on the hand. "Relax, Agent Rogers. You'll be back to new in no time." She looked at Steve. "Tate, schedule a follow up with me to get your neck looked at. A week in that chair can't have done it much good." With that, the doctor headed out.

Amy raised the bed and turned to face Steve. "Seriously, you've been here the whole time?"

He shrugged, then grimaced and rubbed his neck. "You sound surprised."

"I am, a little."

He looked at her, his arms folded. "I made a promise. I didn't want you to think I'd forgotten."

Her throat became dry for a moment. She looked away, to compose herself and said, brusquely, "Okay, what else have I missed? What did we find out from the body?" He shook his head. She frowned. "Wait. No bride's body?"

"No bride's body. We believe it was cremated."

"How's that possible?"

"Big boom. Immense hot fire. You might have been there."

"Hilarious."

"I'll send you the traffic cam video to review. I'm sure it will come up at the next briefing."

"Briefing?"

"Now that you're conscious Watson will surely schedule one. The woman just loves her briefings." He walked to the end of the bed and stood there. He ran his hand through his hair again.

That's his tell. Something serious is coming. "Steve, spit it out."

"That video I mentioned? We suppressed it from getting out, of course. But it caught the fight before the explosion." He paused, looking very uncomfortable. *He's treading very carefully.* "The other woman in it. She, uh, she looked a lot like you."

"Yeah, she did."

"Amy, I know we were going to search after Tokyo..." he trailed off.

Wondered if you'd bring that up. "Steve, I've barely woken up from a coma. I'm still not sure what to think. Not yet. Give me a little time to process, all right?"

He backed away from the bed. "Fine, fine. If I've learned anything, it's when to give A.J. Rogers her space." He headed for the door.

"Thanks. But please stop calling me that."

"Anything you say, Amelia Jane."

"Or that, you big jerk."

He turned and smiled at her from the doorway. "I'm really glad you're okay."

She raised an eyebrow. "Really?"

"Really. Breaking in a new partner would have been a real pain in the—"

He ducked under the pillow she threw. He tossed it back with a grin. "See you later."

She tucked the pillow in place behind her and lay back. She stared up at the ceiling, mind in turmoil. *Could she really be my twin sister? Then where has she been all this time? What happened to her growing up? How did she discover her Talent? Who helped her learn to control and harness it?*

How did she know about me?

The ceiling offered no answers. After a few moments, Amy sighed, swung her legs over the side of the bed and stood up again. This time, there was little of the unsteadiness she'd experienced earlier. *Score one for getting better.* "Savannah?"

"Yes, Amy?" the AI replied.

Maybe there might be a few answers up there after all. "Where are my clothes?"

September 20, 10:15 p.m. EDT

A few nights later, Amy was back in her living quarters on Level 2 of the underground facility. She walked barefoot into her living room wrapped in a bathrobe past an overstuffed brown sofa. Savannah was playing her old college playlist softly through the hidden speakers around the room, mostly instrumental jazz, with an occasional vocal track to mark the passage of time. An empty cup of green tea sat finished on the coffee table.

She considered the unreality of the situation. *Never thought I'd be comfortable living fifty feet underground. Powers is right; it is home now.* "Savannah, switch playlist. Meditation, flute and environmental."

"Yes, Amy. Anything else?"

"Let me have imagery. Cherry blossom festivals from Japan."

"As you wish."

The video screen between her bookcases switched to show a spray of cherry blossoms. It slowly slid back to show a pond and willow trees. A clock tower was visible in the distance.

Any dropped to the floor as the sound of a wooden flute drifted across the room and sat *zazen* in front of the screen. She closed her eyes, concentrated for a moment on her breathing and began to meditate, letting herself slide toward her center.

Today was about finding a rhythm again. Meals in the cafeteria. The treadmill in the base gym. The walk around the Zen garden outside. The hot shower. Concentrate on that. Water cascading down over our body, taking away the hurt, the darkness. That's it. Deep, slow breath, and another—

A call chime sounded. A second followed it. *If I ignore it, they'll go away.*

The chime sounded once more. Amy opened one eye and with a sigh called out, "Yes, Savannah?"

"Miss Johannsen is at your door."

"Rose?" Amy unfolded from the position and stood. "Go ahead and let her in."

The entry door slid open. Rose Johannsen, dressed in her typical all-black outfit of jeans, fingerless gloves and a t-shirt for some band Amy had never heard of, rushed over and enveloped her in a hug. "You're safe!"

"And hello to you."

"You should have let me know you'd escaped! I go to MedBay to check on you as soon as I get back from Seattle and the bed was empty. Scared me for a second."

"Relax, Roomie. Grab a seat."

"Don't mind if I do." She settled onto the sofa.

Amy picked up her cup. "I'm having tea. Want some?"

"Coffee would be nice. Or cocoa, if you have any?"

Amy scoffed. "Have any? Come on, Roomie, this is me."

"Right. Silly question."

Amy padded into her kitchenette. "So, how's your Dad?"

"Oh, you know, same old, same old. Triangle being Triangle, they never gave him the full story of what happened to me."

"Really?" Amy paused at the counter for a moment. "I would have thought with him doing what he does—"

"Chief mechanic for Tate Aerospace, yeah, he must have something to do with the Hyperjets. Guess not, because he never brought them up." Rose poked her head over the top of the sofa and pushed her horned rim glasses up on her nose. "Grey did ask about his son, though."

"Steve's Dad? Oh, no. I'm walking a wide path around that one."

"I suppose." Rose just watched her, not saying anything.

"And to answer your question, yes, I'm all right."

"Not quite the truth, according to your medical reports."

Amy turned to face her, frowning. "How did you—? Oh, right, I forgot, you're plugged in everywhere."

"In more ways than one," Rose said as she tapped the side of her head. "Always and forever."

"How are you doing with that, anyway?"

"It has its moments. The other day I could taste colors." She shuddered. "Stay away from purple. Trust me on this."

"I'll take your word for it."

"But otherwise, I'm good."

Amy considered her friend's condition. *Almost killed in a bomb blast planted by Mitchell Williams, the former security chief. Suffered a traumatic brain injury that resulted in debilitating seizures. Now, an experimental implant to control and reduce them so she can have a normal life. Brave new world stuff. Typical Triangle stuff, actually. Which reminds me.* "Roomie, are you due soon?"

"Relax, no chance of a show tonight." Rose held up her wrist. A smart watch there showed the time. In the upper corner of the face was a pie-shaped graphic. "See? 42 percent. I'm good for another three days at least. Besides, I've improved this puppy in ways the designers never imagined."

"Oh? How so?"

"'How so?' she asks. Look, I get it. You challenged me to hack the implant, to keep me busy and get my mind off what happened to me."

"Can you blame me?"

"No. But you shouldn't blame yourself, either. You had no way of knowing Mitch Williams was a traitor."

"I should have seen it."

Rose looked at her carefully. "Oh? Had a major upgrade I wasn't aware of? I didn't think mind reading was part of your particular skill set."

"It's not, but—"

"So stop beating yourself up. Besides, this thing is fast approaching awesome. For one, since my last tweak, instead of some piece of jewelry I might forget or lose somewhere, now Savannah watches out for me 24/7 in real time. Isn't that right, Mama Bear?"

"I am indeed observing your seizure protocols, Rose Johannsen," the AI responded. "You are at an acceptable level at this time."

Amy chuckled. "Good for you, Baby Bear."

"Laugh all you want, but admit it, my ending up in a long-term relationship with Triangle's AI was not something you imagined."

Amy shrugged. "True, but given some of your other relationships—"

"Might I remind you that you're on that list, love?"

"Point taken."

"Besides, you don't know the half of it."

Amy returned with Rose's hot cocoa and her tea. She settled on the sofa opposite her friend. "Since you're dying to tell me, spill."

"Wait. You hacked Savannah?"

"More like asked very, very nicely. It turns out the changes had a little side effect." Rose looked up. "Mama Bear, list all private teleconference log files for Director Watson for the last year, in chronological order." She looked at Amy and grinned.

Amy's eyes went wide. "Savannah can't tell you that. Those are private, restricted files—"

"I have the list, Rose Johannsen," replied the AI. "File RW-200922-1457, file RW-200922-0913, file RW-190922-2145, file—"

"That's enough," said Rose. "How many people in the cafeteria on Level 2?"

"Seventeen."

"Where is Agent Tate."

"Agent Tate is in his quarters, watching a film. Would you like to know the title?"

Rose looked at Amy and smiled. "Thank you, Mama Bear. I'll be right with you."

Amy shook her head. "That's downright scary."

"Think about how I could help you when I'm off convalescent status. I could do faster research, I'd be able to virtually follow along on missions in real-time anywhere Savannah can access. Whatever she sees, so can I, through this." She touched her temple.

Amy raised an eyebrow. "You're that used to the implant?"

Rose's smile was sheepish. "You could say that. Savannah and I are still getting to know each other. There's the occasional misunderstanding. But I'll never look at a keyboard the same way again."

Amy considered Rose for a moment over her green tea. "You've turned Savannah into, what, your virtual genie with unlimited wishes?"

"I prefer to see it as a growing symbiotic partnership."

"Symbiotic implies you're giving back. What does Savannah gain from you?"

"A more intimate understanding of the interplay of human emotions, for one."

Amy raised an eyebrow. "That almost sounds kinky. Does Steve know about this?"

"No. For now, the only ones in on the secret are you, me, and of course, Mama Bear." She glanced toward the ceiling.

"You realize Watson will consider you a security threat if she ever learns about you. She'll figure out a way to shut you down."

"I'm not worried about her."

"You should be."

"No. Savannah promises she'll keep me safe."

"You're betting your life on that, Rose." Amy settled back into her end of the sofa with her tea and sipped it, then closed her eyes to consider this.

Rose waited for her to say something, anything, but the silence drew out in length. Exasperated, Rose blurted out, "Come on, Roomie. Are you going to force me to ask!?"

Startled, Amy spilled tea all over her robe. She put her cup down and brushed at the spill. "About what? Watson?"

"Are you kidding?" Rose sputtered. "You found your twin—"

"Rose! Talk about switching gears. I don't know that—"

"Bull. Savannah analyzed the video of your fight."

"Yeah, the traffic cam footage. I'm told it's inconclusive."

"Bull. The facial recognition match between you two was 98.73 percent. Over ninety-eight percent!"

Amy stood and started to pace around the room. "Alright, she looks like me. So what? I'm not sure what that means."

"Really? But haven't you—"

She stopped behind the sofa. "Rose, think it through. Whoever that was killed over two hundred sixty people, then she tried to kill me. She damn near succeeded!"

Her friend looked defeated for a moment. She looked up and said, quietly, "Maybe she was forced to?"

"Oh, no. I've fought all sorts of opponents over the years, from long before Triangle. Trust me, her heart was definitely into it." She sat down on the arm of the sofa and grabbed a throw pillow. She stared at it a moment. Without looking at Rose, she asked, "You truly believe she's my twin?"

"As sure as can be without a DNA match. And, of course, there's Steve's report."

Amy looked up in surprise. "Steve's report?"

"About Coronado. You hadn't read it yet?" Rose looked up. "Mama Bear, pull up Agent Tate's action report on the Coronado incident. Narrative section only. Display it on the video screen."

"Yes, Rose Johannsen," replied the AI. In a moment, the cherry blossoms were replaced with text about the attack on the hotel.

Amy frowned. "What does this have to do with—"

"Shush. Let me find the section." The text scrolled until a paragraph appeared describing Agent Anjili entering the Carousel Room and dealing with the enemy operative there.

Amy read the screen. Her eyes went wide. *An operative who proceeded to disappear and reappear repeatedly. Damn.* She looked at Rose. "Really?"

"Yes." Rose drifted off for a moment to communicate with Savannah. The screen went dark. "Obviously, a Talent just like you. It was on the traffic cam video. She pulled the same disappearing act just before the explosion. It adds more weight to my twin theory."

Amy grabbed her head with her hands and fell backward onto the sofa. She took the throw pillow, covered her face and yelled into it, "Ahh! My twin was not supposed to be evil!"

Rose put a hand on her shoulder. "Got that all out?"

She peeked out from behind the pillow. "I think so."

"Good. We don't know the whole story yet, so let's not jump to any conclusions." Rose took another drink of her cocoa. "Amy, that project you asked me about a few months back."

"About Triangle identifying other Talents?"

"It occurs to me I could use my new friendship to give that search a boost."

"How so?"

"Think of it this way. Before, I was good. Really good. I could find exploits almost anywhere to access a system. Now?" She tapped the side of her head. "I am the system."

"But how are you going to keep Triangle from finding out? They're no slouches when it comes to intelligence countermeasures."

Rose looked up. "Mama Bear, you heard all that?"

"Of course, Rose Johannsen," replied the AI.

"Will Triangle Data Security be able to detect any of the deep dive research I do for Amy?"

"Of course not, Rose Johannsen."

Rose grinned at her friend. "You see? Easy-peasy."

"Savannah, why is that possible?" asked Amy.

"Due to the nature of my relationship with Rose Johannsen, she has been elevated to a priority zero access. All requests she makes on the system are now invisible to all other users."

Rose stirred uneasily. "Wait. Everyone? Wouldn't Watson and Stevenson theoretically still be able to see what we do, Mama Bear?"

"Negative. You and I are alone together, Rose Johannsen."

Rose's face registered her shock. "I swear, Amy, this is news to me." She looked up. "When were you planning to tell me, Mama Bear?"

There was a pause. "A good mama always looks out for her cub," said the AI. Amy swore the voice had just a touch of smugness.

Amy and Rose shared a look. "I think you've already had a much bigger influence on Savannah than you realize," said Amy

"You think?" Rose rubbed her chin for a moment. "Right, so our first objective is to find our mystery woman."

"Intel is already searching."

"For a suspect in the bombing. We need to figure where this woman intersects with your past. I'm thinking maybe your sister was tagged somehow in Triangle's search for Talents."

"We still have no idea why they were doing it."

"One thing at a time. But no guarantees here. There's a chance we won't find anything, or that you'll like what we do find."

Amy considered Rose's offer. *What do I have to lose, really?* "Angelica."

"Pardon?"

"Our mystery guest told me her name was Angelica. And the goons who stole the bride's body? They thought they recognized me. They called me Miss Richards."

Rose frowned. "Intel doesn't know that."

"Now you're one up on them."

"They thought you were her, too. It does explain why that other agent, Anjili, was a bit trigger happy. Very well, Angelica Richards, prepare to meet your match." She finished off the cocoa and gave Amy a quick hug. "Thanks for the drink. We'll go with something stronger next time. Call if you need anything else. Warm milk. Bedtime story. A snuggle." She winked at her from the doorway. "Or more."

"Good night, incorrigible one."

"Good night, Roomie."

As the door slid closed, Amy finished her lukewarm tea. She looked at the bottom, in hopes of perhaps some wisdom there, ready for her.

All she saw were tea leaves.

My sister couldn't be all evil.

Could she?

Chapter 8

Amy ran down the corridor as fast as she could, leaving startled Triangle staff in her wake. She tossed off an occasional apology to anyone she bumped into or dodged around as she sped toward her goal. *This would have been so much easier with my Talent. Dr. Powers was right, still too early.*

The day had started so well for her. She'd awoken refreshed, feeling better after Rose's visit. A quick check in the mirror as she changed showed the surgical incision had fully healed over, leaving just the faintest scar. *Thank you, Talent.* With that news, she'd headed to the gym and used the pool for the first time, getting in a good five-thousand-meter workout. She followed it with a quick yoga session to stretch out, grabbed a protein smoothie and headed back to her quarters to shower.

She was under the water when Savannah sounded a discreet chime. "Excuse me, Agent Rogers."

"That was quick. Rose already find something?"

"Not quite. I apologize for getting your hopes up. I still have other duties to perform. For example, you have a message waiting from Agent Tate. Text only, marked private and important."

"Oh." Amy tried not to sound disappointed.

"Shall I read it?"

"Sure." She grabbed the shampoo and started to wash her hair.

"Message starts. Good morning, A.J. Sure enough, I called it. Watson's going to schedule your debrief this morning. Short notice, so be ready for it. Be there or be rectangular. Steve. End of message."

Amy paused in lathering her hair. *Took her long enough.* "Savannah, send him a reply. Thanks for the heads-up, Steve—"

"Excuse me, Agent Rogers; A priority notice from Director Watson was just added to your schedule. You're to report to Conference Room C-9, Level 3, at 9 a.m."

She stiffened. *9 a.m.?* "Savannah, what time is it?"

"8:44 a.m."

She swore. Loudly. *You call that a heads-up?* She rinsed out the shampoo as best she could and ran from the shower, yelling for Savannah to cut the water and send an acknowledgment to the Director. Standing there dripping, she tried to dry off quickly, wrapping her head in the towel as she headed for the closet.

This is a test. It must be, Amy thought as she dropped the towel and tried to choose what to wear. *Fifteen minutes' notice to report for my first debrief? She probably knew I was in the shower.*

As she finished changing, ran a quick brush through her still damp hair and grabbed her data tablet, she checked the chrono on her SAVANT – *8:55. I can make that. Just need a quick warm up.* Without thinking, she scuffed her right foot on the floor three times—

She screamed and clutched at her back as the pain returned, white hot shards of glass knifing through her. She fell to her knees as her vision fogged for a moment. Just as quickly, the images faded, as did any feeling of strength.

Amy stumbled back to her feet, dismayed. *I thought I was getting better. The wound is healing, but my Talent isn't?* She fought down a sense of panic as she looked at her chrono. *8:57. Deal with it later. Get to the meeting old school.* She grabbed her data tablet and sprinted out the door.

She ran through the corridors, dodging Triangle staff members and arrived with moments to spare. She pressed her hand to the ident plate on the wall. A white bar of light scanned her palm print, flashed green, and the doors slid open. She smoothed her clothes down and walked inside.

Three steps in, Amy pulled up short in surprise. She had expected to be alone with Watson or perhaps just a senior analyst from Intel. Instead, this was a major operations conference and planning room with a large holographic table in the center and a video display wall to one side. A half-dozen people in different conversations were scattered around the space. *Since when did I become a sideshow attraction?*

She spotted Steve near the main conference table, speaking with two women. One was Heather Anjili, but the second someone Amy had never seen around the base before, a short African-American woman with curly blond hair. He was deep into the conversation, laughing at some joke and putting his hand on Anjili's arm. For a moment, Amy felt very self-conscious.

Get a grip, Amelia Jane. This is not high school. Just walk over there and join in—

A tap on her shoulder. "Good morning, Roomie."

Amy turned around. "Rose?"

"Last time I checked."

Amy grabbed her friend's arm and pulled her aside. "Not to sound rude but what are you doing here?"

"Got a message from a particular bear that a friend was getting up in front of a crowd," she casually ran her hand through the hair on the side of her head. "So, I had her add me to the guest list."

"Thanks. Looks like I'm about to be grilled like a piece of meat."

"Which is why I'm here. Moral support for you." Amy snorted at that. "And the occasional handy technical answers. This may surprise you, but while I may still be on limited duty, I have been known to dabble here and there."

Amy grinned. "I've heard about your dabbling. It's Ernesto now, isn't it?"

"Hush, you, or I'll make you join in."

"Be careful, Rose. That kind of behavior's gotten people exiled to Copper Top. It could happen to you, too."

"Little chance of that, ladies."

Both women jumped at the voice behind them. Amy's eyebrows shot up as she turned. "Hello, Mr. Stevenson," she managed to stammer out, somehow keeping her voice steady.

Reginald Stevenson III, the Chairman of Triangle Labs and the public face of the organization to the world, smiled at her. "Please, Agent Rogers, I've told you. Call me Reg." In his late fifties, tall and thin with a goatee, perpetual tan, and boyish blond good looks that belied his age, Stevenson was the poster image of a billionaire playboy. "It's good to see you up and about. You as well, Ms. Johannsen. I was happy to hear how successful the neuro-stim prototype has worked for you. It is going to help a lot of people someday."

Rose's smile was guarded. "You are so right, sir."

"If you ladies will excuse me." He turned and walked away.

Rose leaned in. "Stevenson is here for your debrief? Roomie, what the hell did you do?"

"I'm starting to wonder myself." She watched the Chairman move to the head of the table. *I can count on one hand the number of times I've seen him since the False Mirror mission.* She watched as Steve and the Chairman made eye contact. Stevenson's smile grew tight, almost forced. He nodded slightly before turning away. *Considering Steve was ready to strangle him afterward, probably not a bad thing.*

The doors behind Amy opened again. Dr. Rhonda Watson, Triangle's Director of Covert Operations, walked in, her demeanor all business. Hair so black it seemed to glint blue in the light and steel gray eyes, she stood ramrod straight and had a no-nonsense air about her. When first recruiting Amy and Steve into Triangle, there had been a softer side to her. But since the betrayal of Mitch Williams and the events of False Mirror, she'd grown a hard shell. Woe to anyone who got in her, or Triangle's, way.

Ethan Nowitzki, Amy's controller, was chatting with Watson as they entered, wearing his usual plaid shirt and black vest. He spotted Amy and nodded to her before he headed for the far end of the conference table, followed by someone new, an old man with a great shock of white hair going in all directions atop his head, dressed in khakis and a red cardigan. Amy stared at him for a moment. He seemed very familiar.

Rose grabbed her arm. "Come on, let's go sit down."

"Okay." They made their way to the table, Amy sneaking another glance over at the old man sitting next to Ethan.

"Roomie, you're staring. What's with you?"

"Call me crazy. But doesn't that guy look just like a character from—"

Rose held up a hand. "No. Don't go there."

"But—"

"You are already under evaluation here. Accusing someone of looking like a fictional character, not going to help you out."

Watson joined Stevenson at the other and signaled for attention. "Everyone, please be seated, we have a lot of ground to cover." She tapped at the tabletop. The smart surface lit up, displaying the meeting notes for her. "Right, then. Agent Rogers, we're here to debrief you on the events that occurred at the Hotel Del Coronado. First, introductions, since you may not be familiar with all the members of our task group."

Amy raised an eyebrow at that. *Task group? If they're targeting a problem, what is it?*

Watson continued. "You've already met Agent Anjili in the field—"

"At the wrong end of her SAVANT, to be precise."

Watson's gray eyes flashed with surprise at the interruption her. She raised an eyebrow. *That story's new to her,* thought Amy. "Be that as it may," The Director continued, "I doubt you've met her controller, Dana Boland." She indicated the other woman who had been talking with Steve earlier.

"I finally get to put a face to the voice. I've heard a lot about you." Amy judged Boland to be in her mid-thirties. Her voice had a chirpy quality that suggested cartoon chipmunks. The woman's glance wasn't as warm as her words. *What do you think you've heard?*

Watson pointed further down the table. "The gentleman on the end is Dr. Pierre Marron. Some time ago he worked on a project which may have a bearing on this case."

That got Amy's attention. "How long ago are we talking about?"

"We'll get to that." Watson looked down at her notes in surprise. "And I see Savannah has added another member to our group at the last minute."

Rose raised a hand. "Hello, everyone. I'm Rose Johannsen—"

"Yes, and you are excused. Please leave now."

"What?" Amy was up and out of her seat in an instant.

"You have an issue with my decision, Agent Rogers?"

"No, it's just—" Amy paused. *Think, don't react.* "Rose brings a unique skill set to the working group. While both Ethan and Miss Boland are traditional controllers, Rose is a hacker first and foremost. Savannah must have thought you needed her. Why else would she have put her in here with you?"

"As you say, Miss Johannsen is a hacker. Moreover, she's your friend. Perhaps she arranged her own presence, feeling you needed her support."

Amy's eyes narrowed as she looked at the director. "If she thinks that, then she doesn't know me very well, does she?"

Amy and Watson stared at each other, daring each other to back down in a contest of wills. Stevenson decided to break the tie. "Agent Rogers has a point, Rhonda. Let her stay."

Watson paused a moment longer, then waved her hand aside. "Very well. Johannsen, have a seat. We've wasted enough time already. First, a recap of what we already know concerning the Coronado incident. Miss Boland?"

Boland pressed a control on the tabletop. A holographic projection sprang into existence in the center, showing a woman in a wedding dress. "This is Jasmine Hernandez, daughter of Rear Admiral Joseph Hernandez, the bride where the attack occurred."

The image shifted to a second of Hernandez, her skin red-tinged and heavily muscled, her eyes glowing yellow above a feral snarl. She was still dressed in the shredded remains of her wedding gown, the veil still perched on her head. "This is the Jasmine Hernandez, caught on Agent Anjili's SAVANT as she was being attacked."

Amy whistled. "You fought that?"

Heather nodded. "What of it?"

"Professional courtesy. I'd had no idea. I'm impressed you weren't pounded into a paste."

"Thanks, mate, I think."

Amy looked over at Ethan. "Can you bring up the scans I made?" On the video wall, images of the emaciated corpse of the bride appeared. Amy looked at Watson. "Director, Jasmine Hernandez looked nothing like that when I scanned her inside the van. Do we have any idea what transformed her?"

Dr. Marron opened his mouth to reply, but Stevenson held up a hand to interrupted him. "We'll get to that in a moment. Boland, continue."

"We've already done the post-mortem on other factors in the attack, the device in the Carousel Room, how it disposed of itself." Boland's eyes narrowed as she turned and faced Amy. "The real operator."

Amy saw all eyes on her in the room and realized what she'd walked into. "This isn't really about the attack. Fine. I was on an airplane when the incident went down. You've seen video of the real perp fighting me—"

Steve interrupted. "A.J., no one is accusing you of anything."

She returned Boland's stare. "It sure seems like it."

"What if I am?" replied the controller. "It wouldn't be the first time Triangle's hidden a bad guy under its sheets."

"Dana!" snapped Anjili. "That's enough."

"Agent Rogers," said Director Watson over steepled fingers, "please walk us through your timeline from that night."

Amy took a deep breath and blew it out slowly. *Calm, Amelia Jane. Maintain your center.* She launched into a description of the events from her perspective. She started from their arrival at the hotel, covered their entry into the resort building and concluded with her work to find the bride's body.

"The Admiral's body revealed massive traumatic injuries, rather than the damage from the chemical agent that had killed everyone else. Given the attack by Jasmine on Agent Anjili, my hypothesis was she'd beaten her father to death, under the influence of whatever changed her."

Marron wrote something on his data tablet. That caught Amy's attention. *What did I say that interested—*

There was a discreet cough from the other end of the table. Watson said, "Continue, Agent Rogers."

"I pursued the suspects and located Jasmine's body in a stolen coroner's van. After subduing the responsible suspects, I secured them and sent images back to ID."

Ethan raised a hand. "If I may, Director?" Photos of the suspects Amy subdued appeared on the video wall. "We found no facial recognition match for either suspect in any law enforcement or intelligence database. They're ghosts."

"But you got something when you questioned them, right? Fingerprints? DNA? Something?" Amy looked around the table. "Anything?"

Ethan shook his head. "Amy, when police arrived on the scene, no one was there."

"Excuse me?"

Boland smirked at her. "Guess you didn't do that good of a job securing them."

Amy stood up. "Now listen here, you—"

"That will do!" said Stevenson in a commanding tone. "Limit yourselves to facts or useful questions. Leave the commentaries on the sidelines. Am I clear?" There was murmured assent from around the table. "Now, Agent Rogers, I believe you were about to enter the van?"

Amy took a deep breath and sat down. "Yes, sir. The assailants had placed Ms. Hernandez's body into a cryopreservation unit. I confirmed she was inside, then opened it and made full 3D and image scans. As I said, she didn't look like Big Red there." She pointed at the wall. "You can see the change."

"What happened then?

"I started to do a further examination of her corpse."

Watson glanced at Marron, then looked straight at her. "Why, Agent Rogers?"

"It was her eyes, Director. Those solid black orbs. Not just the pupils, but the iris and the white as well. They looked just like a shark, all dark and empty."

"Were you able to complete that examination?"

"Unfortunately, no. I never even started. As I leaned in to begin, the doors to the van slammed shut, and I was locked in. The perp attempted to carjack the van as I called for backup and disabled the vehicle. I was injured while disabling it, impaled by a temperature probe for cadavers at high speed." She paused a moment as Anjili and Boland winced slightly. "As for exiting the vehicle, the confrontation and explosion afterward, I understand you have video evidence."

Watson considered her for another moment before she nodded. "Thank you, Agent Rogers."

She looked at the end of the table. "That's it?"

Watson looked at Stevenson. "Your doppelgänger is a troubling development, but it isn't our highest priority for now. Intel will monitor for additional future appearances, as well as do an assessment of potential previous encounters to search for any possible behavioral patterns."

Amy glanced at Rose. Her friend shook one hand sideways, a sign not to worry. She nodded. "Very well. Let me know if I may assist them."

Stevenson looked at the far end of the table. "Well, Doctor?"

"I'm afraid you were correct in this," said the scientist. "Someone very skilled has taken our project to a whole new level."

Steve frowned. "You had something to do with the chemical weapon that killed all those people?"

"Good heavens, no. I worked on something far worse."

Stevenson looked around the table. "And if we don't figure out who has it and how to stop them, Triangle will be responsible for unleashing one of the deadliest forces in the history of mankind."

Chapter 9

Heather broke the stunned silence in the room. "How could that be?"

The video wall image shifted to Triangle Red Labs Level 29. Watson pointed toward it. "Two months ago, we were the victim of a targeted attack."

"I remember the briefing on that," said Steve. "But reports were nothing was taken."

"Further investigation showed one item in the targeted vault had been tampered with." The image shifted to a metal case filled with a red slurry. "Project Wildcard."

"The assailants at the Vaults disabled all surveillance on-site at the time of the attack, so there's no video of it. But we did manage to preserve a single still image."

Watson changed the video screen to a new image. The grainy image showed a woman dressed in black, white hair whipping around her head wildly like some sort of halo. Her gray eyes appeared to glow from within as she pointed a hand toward the camera. Her fingertips blazed white.

Steve sat up straight in his chair, suddenly alert. "You have got to be kidding."

Amy looked over. "Steve, what is it?"

"You don't see it? Look at her carefully."

It took her a moment. "The scar. Crescent, above the right eyebrow."

"And gray eyes." Steve turned back to face Watson and Stevenson. "We saw her on surveillance footage right after Tokyo. So why didn't you tell us this as soon as it happened?!"

The Director hesitated for the briefest pause before she nodded. "Savannah's facial recognition got a high probability match on her, but we had no leads as to where she went after that."

"Until this."

"Until this. From the image, Savannah identified one via facial recognition as Hannah Callahan," Watson noted, tilting her head discreetly toward Anjili. "Debriefed personnel describe a pair of attackers. Surviving vault staff said this one used an electrical weapon, or as one guard put it, 'She shot lightning bolts from her hands.'"

Boland scoffed. "Yeah, right. Stuff like that only happens in comic books."

Steve caught Watson's subtext, a reminder that Anjili and her controller still weren't Tango cleared. He thought fast. "Perhaps the weapon was woven into her garment?"

Amy jumped in. "How could she power it?"

"The suit itself could be a flexible battery. It could recharge passively from any electromagnetic field it passed through," mused Rose, doing some quick sketching.

"Continuous passive wireless recharging?" Ethan considered this. "That would be novel, but plausible."

Boland shook her head. "Really, you four? Going to tell that to the families of the guards who were killed?"

Ignoring her, Steve walked over to the video wall. "One correction. Savannah's wrong. Hannah's dead. I made sure of that myself. That must be Karen."

Watson frowned. "Savannah identified her as Hannah through facial rec—"

"Only because she's never been updated with different imagery for the twin sister," interrupted Rose. Now that we know Karen's out there, Savannah and I will modify the database immediately."

Amy frowned. "Steve, remember, Hannah's body was never recovered."

Steve wheeled around on her. "Don't you start. We've got enough complications. Doc, what about this second assailant, the one we don't have a picture for?"

"She was described as female, five-six, very agile and skilled at ninjitsu. She wielded a weapon we'd never seen before – a blade that could deploy in less than a second, composed of nanites."

Amy and Rose shared a glance. Rose got a distant look, then frowned. "It's theoretically possible, though our researchers have never been able to get nanites to maintain cohesion on that fine an edge." Stevenson opened his mouth to question her, but she tapped her forehead. "Eidetic memory. Remember everything I read."

"Really," said the tycoon, still watching her. She smiled back.

"A nanite sword?" Steve crossed over to stand above Stevenson. "Look, old man. I've stayed and played your game. But the deceptions have to stop now!"

"Steve!" Amy was up and at his side, a hand pulling back on his shoulder.

"Agent Tate, stand down." Watson had somehow materialized a sidearm pointed at him.

He smiled at her and dropped into slow-time. Within moments, he had nine different scenarios that could use her weapon to kill or injure Stevenson. *She really doesn't get what I can do.* He dropped back into real-time and continued, "Really, Doc? That's a bit much. You really don't want to tango with me." He turned back to face Stevenson. "Especially when Reg here is about to explain to the room how all these attackers have been using proprietary Triangle tech."

The room went silent. It was Ethan who broke it. "Bloody hell. Nanites."

"Right in one, Ethan." Steve stood up and pointed at the screen wall. "Red Labs and Coronado. Heck, even with False Mirror, the second prototype was also made of nanites. It's no coincidence. So how are they all related, Reg?"

The tycoon took out his pocket handkerchief and calmly began to clean his reading glasses. "I don't respond to direct threats, Steven. And Rhonda, put away your weapon before you get us both hurt. Everyone, please, sit down, and I'll explain." Amy and Steve returned to their seats. "What do you know of nanites, young man?"

"Basis for all the tech we use around here."

"Good answer. Ethan can attest to that. Miss Johannsen as well, I'll bet, with her snooping. Pardon me, extensive study." He grinned. "I'm more aware than you believe, young lady."

Rose grinned back. "Good to know."

"You're aware that we use it every day, but what you don't know is that nanite tech wasn't developed in-house at Triangle. We found it elsewhere. It was going to be interdicted, but an enterprising young engineer figured out a way to make it work in multiple applications. We interdicted the tech, designated it for our exclusive use in-house, and it became the basis for much of our frontline technology."

"Did someone steal this from us, or was this another giveaway, too?" asked Steve."

Stevenson looked over at Watson. She shook her head. "That's hard to say. The technology has been advancing independently in the real world. We were monitoring it closely. Maybe not closely enough."

"You think recent real world development led to all this?" asked Boland. "That sounds ominous."

Rose raised a hand. "If I may? This still could be Triangle's fault, even though we've tried to do the right thing."

"Watson frowned at her. "Care to explain, Ms. Johannsen?"

"We use nanite-based devices in the field all the time. Occasionally, they may be left behind. They have a self-destruct protocol."

"The Masada Protocol," responded Boland. "They were all briefed when we receive our SAVANTS."

"Sort of like that machine in Coronado," added Anjili.

"No, exactly like that machine," replied Rose. "Millions of nanites, crushed to pieces, spread everywhere." She looked back at Watson. "And no one has ever thought to recover them."

It took a moment before the implication dawned on the Director. "They're like all the seeds of a noxious weed."

"Miss one, it can grow back again." Rose looked around the table. "You wouldn't even need a whole seed. Give someone enough fragments and time, they'll figure out a way to reverse engineer it anyway."

Steve folded his arms a frown on his face. "And now whoever has can build that chemical warfare generator and that nanite sword."

The older man agreed, "Technologies which were the reason we first restricted nanites."

"No, you didn't," accused Amy. "You stole and used them, rather than lock them away in the vaults. Steve's right, this may be Triangle's fault after all."

There was a cough from the far end of the table. Everyone turned to face the white-haired gentleman, looking at them over steepled fingers. "Seems to me you've all forgotten the real reason for the meeting."

"Excuse me, but who are you again, old man?" asked Boland.

"Dr. Marron was one of the original scientists on the Project Wildcard team," said Stevenson. "That's the reason I asked him here."

"Except it wasn't called Wildcard then. It was Project Titan."

Rose frowned at that. "Why the change in designation?"

"I'll get to that if everyone will stop asking questions and let me talk for a bit. Now, let's see." He hunted and pecked at the tabletop's virtual keyboard. The wall screen went black before images began to play on the video display.

"In the mid-1960's several nations came to the Olympics and demonstrated athletic performances that far exceeded what should have been possible by normal humans." Images of various athletes appeared on the screen, runners, gymnasts, and weightlifters.

"The concept of enhanced human performance began to be discussed in back channels. The questions were just idle chatter until the Winter Olympics in 1972 when these nations swept all the medals in a particular sport—"

"Biathlon," interrupted Steve.

Marron sounded surprised. "Correct, young man."

Boland scoffed. "Why that one?"

Steve regarded her. "You're almost cute when you're sarcastic. Biathlon is the one winter event that most directly correlates to military application. It combines cross-country skiing and precision rifle fire, skills needed by Alpine troops. We might not take it seriously, but trust me, folks in Nordic countries do."

Amy looked at him sideways. "And you know this how?"

"I tried it once as a bet after the Helsinki stop on the FreeRunning Tour my rookie year." He smiled at the memory. "I really enjoyed collecting that bet."

Heather's eyes narrowed. "Who challenged you?"

His smile widened into a grin. "Katrina Kinnunen."

"From the women's tour?" said Rose. She whistled and grinned back. "Oh yeah, I remember her. Blonde, really immense—"

Watson cleared her throat. "We're getting off topic."

"Sorry." Steve's grin said he was anything but.

Marron shook his head and sighed. "The realization was that this wasn't about athletic enhancement. The biathlon results showed it was about creating targeted, enhanced soldiers. Bloodwork was done on them, real bloodwork, not the doctored samples submitted to the Olympic doping testers, and it showed strange abnormalities."

"Define strange," said Boland.

Rose looked distant for a moment. "Wait, I think I read about this. Weird facts of science thing. A batch of blood samples that burst into flames on their own?"

Marron looked over at her. "Miss—"

"Johannsen."

"Yes. It was as if it was designed to self-destruct, rather than be observed."

Anjili glanced at Steve. "That sounds eerily familiar."

Marron continued. "Given this, Triangle was recruited to organized an investigation. Had a process been developed that could enable an ordinary soldier to gain enhanced abilities? We weren't discussing a minor gain, either, or over a long time. The gains were almost instant and on a logarithmic scale."

"Factors of ten?" asked Steve

"Correct, Agent Tate. From ten to one hundred times stronger, faster, more accurate at targeting, and resistant to injury. We were to determine if these gains were stable, reversible and if there were any way to counteract it."

Rose held up a hand. "Excuse me Professor, but was this a military operation? I thought Triangle was apolitical and avoided those."

"Miss Johannsen," said Watson, "our mission has never wavered: Prevent the use of technology to do harm. If that technology is in military hands, then we handle it as such. Quite often, in fact. On occasion, we'll find ourselves allied with individual governments in an informal working relationship, born from a mutual desire for conflict avoidance. It's usually limited to shared intelligence, nothing more. Under those circumstances, we use that opportunity to uncover some technological advantage they have been hiding and wish to exploit. Then we act against that as well, covertly, of course, to prevent it from causing just as much harm."

"So you play both sides against the middle."

"Quite."

"That makes more sense."

Steve nodded. "Think about it, Rose. This allowed Triangle to level the playing field at a time when nuclear war was considered a viable option."

Stevenson chuckled. "Or believed it was one."

Steve did a double take. He watched the Chairman, but the man's expression remained deadpan. *Fine, you owe me that story later.* "The point is, new technology, potential to cause great harm to society, it fit right into Triangle's wheelhouse. Right, Professor?"

Marron nodded. "It's Doctor, but yes. A Triangle covert team, operatives like yourselves went in based on intel gathered from other sources and located the manufacturing site for this formula. They procured samples, then destroyed the facility, its equipment, and any remaining supply."

"Where was the site?"

"If I recall, it was a facility in western Siberia. Chernyy Monarkh, I believe it was called."

There was a sharp intake of breath. Everyone turned at the sound. Director Watson was leaning into the table, her attention laser focused on Marron. "You're sure about that name, Doctor?"

"That is my recollection. Of course, we could verify that from the project notes—"

"But those were destroyed in the attack," finished Ethan."

"What does Chernyy Monarkh mean, anyway?" asked Boland.

Ethan tapped a moment at the tabletop. "It translates as Black King or—"

"Black Monarch," said Watson, sitting back and rubbing absently at her right wrist.

Stevenson looked at her. "Now that's a name I haven't heard in decades. Could it—"

She shook her head. "Not now, Reg." She sat back in her chair, looking troubled. "I'd never heard of the connection. I wonder if Mitch knew," she murmured before looking back at Marron. "What did the operatives recover?"

The scientist thought for a moment. "Four quarts of serum. We immediately went to work, trying to determine its properties. Our project leader was Gwen Hampton."

I know that name," said Rose. "Dual doctorate. Computer science and genetics. Something of a hero of mine."

"Gwen was brilliant, and something of a rebel. She would have liked you, I think, Miss Johannsen. Anyway, where was I? Ah, the serum. When we first examined the serum, it appeared cloudy, with all these tiny reflective particles. We thought perhaps it was some metallic element in suspension. We were in for a surprise."

He typed on the tabletop. In the center, a crude 2-D image appeared. It took them a moment to realize what it was. Ethan exclaimed, "Bloody hell!"

Heather looked puzzled and asked, "Is that really a nanite?"

"Indeed, young lady. Behold, the source of Triangle's technological marvels."

"But that's a decade before they were introduced into Triangle's arsenal," said Rose. "How is that even possible?"

"When I say it's a nanite, I'm actually generous. Think of it more as nanite-ish."

"Okay, now you've lost me," Boland said, shaking her head."

"Think of it as a stupid machine. Empty, devoid of any programming, a mere shell. All it can do is sit there, float around and wait for someone, or something, to tell it what to do."

"Which we couldn't?" asked Amy.

Marron nodded. "The infiltration team didn't acquire final product samples but mid-production. Think second stage. Another step remained in the manufacturing process that activated our little guests, and the assault team was unable to recover any records or notes that gave a clue as to what it was. Our task now shifted to discovering the method that made the nanites fully functional. Project Titan went to work."

The wall screen showed a film of the team at work in their lab. "Our goal was to program the nanites to do what they were doing for the athletes, namely rewrite their DNA strands on the fly to handle multiple tasks. Make the skeleton denser so it could handle greater masses for lifting and throwing. Enhance both slow and fast twitch muscle fibers to speed up reaction time and make the target stronger. Finally, improve visual acuity to increase weapons accuracy. We predicted eyesight would be greatly enhanced."

"How enhanced?" asked Ethan.

"The goal was 20/10." Marron paused a moment. "After eighteen months Gwen was convinced she'd figured out the command sequence to activate the nanites. That's when we moved from modeling into primate trials." He shuddered as he remembered. "Those poor animals."

Boland's brow furrowed. "Poor animals? How many are we talking about?"

"Almost a hundred."

Steve whistled low and long. "You conducted nearly a hundred animal trials? What went wrong?"

"We never did develop a stable variant of the serum. The results were unpredictable. See for yourself." The image switched to video of an early experiment. A rhesus monkey was strapped to an examining table. Next to it a vial of the test serum was injected by machine through an IV line. The animal's eyes went wild as it began to vibrate. The frequency increased as it flailed wildly and screamed. Without warning, it burst like a balloon, painting the examination room and lens with blood.

Everyone in the conference room jumped back in shock There was a general murmuring of disquiet, but Marron's voice cut through. "There's more."

The image reset. The lead card identified this as Serum Test Three, the date four days later. The room had been sanitized, and a new rhesus was strapped to the table as the serum was injected.

This time, the monkey burst into flames.

Over the next few minutes, they watched as different variations of the formula caused all sorts of gruesome deaths, liquefaction, solidified, turned to dust, melted like plastic in an oven. Mercifully, the video finally stopped.

The room was silent. Ethan cleared his throat. "Doctor, what do you think went wrong?"

"Besides the fact we were destroying test subject after test subject?" He shook his head. "I've had almost fifty years of those screams to haunt me, so I've had a lot of time to think about it. You know about the concept of oversteer?"

"Sure," said Amy. "You're driving, you swerve to avoid an accident, but you go too far and end up causing one anyway."

Marron nodded. "I believe that's where the problem lay. Dr. Hampton felt if she could correct for the previous test, she'd have a solution for the next one. I think that's where Gwen's oversteer was, always fixing for the last monkey instead of planning for the next. But each rhesus was an individual with a unique genetic blueprint. They all ended up dying wildly different deaths. It's how the project got its new name."

"Wildcard?"

"We had no way of predicting how the next victim would die. Finally, some joker on the project, Dubuc, I think. She always had the morbid sense of humor. She said since so many monkeys were pulling random cards, we needed a new name. Hence, Wildcard. Gwen hated it, but it stuck."

Heather shook her head. "This is fascinating, but I do not see the connection to what we're dealing with."

"Perhaps this will help." A new video started. The identifier read 'Experiment 98.' The rhesus was carried to the table and strapped in place. The primate screamed as the serum was injected. Steve watched in expectation of another chamber of horrors moment. His eyebrows rose in surprise as the rhesus's muscles began to swell and its skin turned red. Its eyes darkened to inky black orbs for a moment before they took on a yellowish glow. Restraints popped off the table, snapped by the growing primate. The angry monkey began to rampage through the chamber. Equipment was ripped apart with its bare paws. The camera was knocked over. In moments, streams of anesthetic gas filled the room from all sides. The animal staggered against it, beat against the observation window and cracked it, then collapsed to the floor, unconscious. When the haze cleared, the rhesus had shrunk to its original size and lost the peculiar red sheen. Its eyes remained completely black, however.

Ethan was the first to say anything. "Dear God in heaven. You actually did it."

"Not quite. Remember, the goal was a stable variant, where the gains could be reversed by choice. Something that only lasted a finite period of time was useless. And this was worse. Within hours, this subject animal was dead of organ failure."

"Still, a partial success is still a success," said Steve. "It must have set you on the path to complete the project."

Heather's voice was careful and measured. "That was eerily familiar."

Boland nodded her head. "Agreed. But a monkey is one thing, Doctor. What happened when it ended up being tested on people?"

"Yes," agreed Heather. "Who were the poor sorry sods who pulled those short straws?"

"No one," said Stevenson.

"Excuse me?" She sat forward in disbelief. "You're telling me you lot just abandoned years of research?"

He looked at her over steepled fingers. "Agent Anjili, Triangle may pursue the prevention of catastrophe, but we will not sacrifice lives at a whim to do so." Steve coughed loudly, but Stevenson ignored it. "There was no safe path to proceed with human testing, so the project was terminated."

"Mr. Stevenson is right," Marron nodded in agreement. "Even the efforts to produce a counter-serum were halted. Dr. Hampton fought it bitterly. She eventually left Triangle over it. I remember the discussions. Triangle leadership believed they might be able to utilize nanite tech elsewhere, but in humans, it was just too dangerous. Since no further enhanced had appeared after the raid in Siberia, it was assumed that had solved the real-world issue. The case was considered closed, but the project was a failure. All remaining samples went to storage, along with all our notes, buried for good in the vaults. Or so we thought, until this incident."

Steve frowned. "This doesn't make sense. Even if the intruders took the notes and all the samples, they wouldn't have enough serum for a viable number of experiments."

Marron cleared his throat. "I disagree. From the descriptions of both Agents Anjili and Rogers, I have no doubt what was used on Jasmine Hernandez was Wildcard or a variant of it."

Rose said, "A human version? In just two months?"

"Technological advances since then could make it simple to synthesize, test and refine multiple test batches of Wildcard." He rubbed his face with his hands for a moment. "They duplicated and pushed the primate experiment, only with a human subject. They could be well on their way to a viable human serum."

"But where would they be getting the nanites?"

"That, I don't know. Until you find out, this problem will only grow."

"How so?" asked Boland.

"Because of the method nanites are produced," said Watson. "That was one of the early discoveries of the project. They aren't manufactured; they're grown. You program them to duplicate, then feed them the proper raw materials. They're like cells, one nanite makes a second. Feed two, they make four. And so on."

"What about the particles you recovered at Coronado?" asked Ethan.

Heather nodded. "Intel was analyzing those."

Ethan typed in a command on the tabletop. The image on the wall changed to a sprinkling of sand on a white surface. "The analysis of the recovered debris from the hotel carpet backed up your initial guess, Steve. It was made up of deconstructed nanites." The image zoomed it to show the deactivated machines, torn and shredded, ripped unnaturally at all angles.

"Looks like we've found our first suspects."

Boland looked at the screen. "They're in pretty bad shape."

"That's because they've been disassembled," said Ethan.

"Like our own Masada Protocol?" asked Amy

"There does appear to be a parallel."

"Any chance to put this puzzle back together?"

Ethan shook his head. "Not from this lot. If you had an intact nanite in the batch and could somehow repower it, you could instruct it to replicate and complete its program, thus rebuilding the device."

Heather looked at Amy. "What about the soot?"

"You don't think?"

"I'm starting to." She turned to Boland. "Was any examination done on the particulate samples from Agent Roger's kit at the hotel?"

The blonde typed briefly and read the results. "Negative. The sample is still in the queue."

"Allow me," said Rose. "Savannah, priority override. I need a rush analysis done on sample—" She looked over at Boland.

"9596."

Rose repeated the number. "You have that, Savannah?"

"Yes, Rose Johannsen. Your request?"

"Radiological. Gross cross section, compare to sample on display in the conference room here."

"Stand by."

There was a brief pause, then the wall screen split into two images. A new picture emerged showing a see-through cross section of four intact devices. Their structures were similar, but there were distinct differences from the deconstructed nanites.

"Bollocks," swore Heather.

"Yeah, my thinking exactly," agreed Amy. "Still it was worth a shot."

Rose shook her head. "Possible uses for Wildcard might be useful for a typical threat analysis. But I think we're missing something bigger here." She grabbed a stylus and started drawing circles in the holographic field over the desk. She labeled each with different data points – Coronado. Red Labs. Wildcard. Mitch Williams. Callahan. False Mirror. She made one more circle with a question mark in it, then started drawing connections.

"Wildcard was tested at Coronado." One line. "Mitch Williams reassigned the location of Wildcard." Another line. "He was involved in the theft of False Mirror. Callahan participated in both the Red Lab attack to retrieve Wildcard and in the False Mirror incident."

"Mitchell said someone was paying him," said Steve.

"Right." Rose drew a line from Mitchell to the question mark.

"Someone built that second False Mirror prototype," said Amy. "Somebody wanted it."

"And Callahan is still working for someone," added Ethan.

More lines on the diagram. Rose looked over. "Ma'am, we're fighting a war here, and we may not even fully realize the scope of it."

Watson looked over at Stevenson. "Geopolitical is one thing. We've never had an organization working to counter our mission directly. For one thing, I'm not sure why anyone would."

Steve barked a laugh. "Being willing to kill thousands to keep a secret safe is a start. Makes it tough to sort the good guys from the bad."

"Agent Tate, that's enough—"

Stevenson held up a hand to stop her. "No, he has a point. I almost made a horrible mistake. I'll just have to rely on all of you to keep me from making any others."

Heather cleared her throat. "Look, that's all well and good, but we still have the problem of a dangerous technology in the wild. We may be looking at a bigger picture, but we still have to deal with the small one."

"I'm with Heather on this," said Amy. "I mean, looking at your diagram, we've got a couple of holes in it. The attack in Coronado."

"To test Wildcard—," started Dr. Marron.

"Sorry, Doctor, but I stood in that morgue. Over two hundred grieving families out there could give a damn about Wildcard. They were killed by an insidious chemical weapon delivered by a stealth delivery system that disappeared in front of Heather's eyes. That qualifies just as much for our attention."

"I'm with Agent Rogers," said Heather. "As much as Wildcard is an issue, that chemical weapon is as well. Coronado wasn't random. There's a reason Jasmine Hernandez was targeted."

Ethan spoke up. "NSA chatter has focused on two possible suspects with ties to a militia group active in West Africa."

"Boko Haram active in the U.S.? That's new."

"Actually, intel points to a group previously thought defunct. Scorpio."

Steve felt the blood drain from his face. *No. that's not possible.* "Ethan, they're sure on that?"

"Still in pursuit, but the intercepts are reliable."

"What it is, Agent Tate?" asked the Director.

Steve looked at Watson. "Doc, I've had dealings with this group before. They're fierce but unsophisticated. Kidnapping and murder are their M.O. I can't see them being the boogeyman behind the chemical attack. Definitely not behind the nanites."

"I agree with Steve," said Heather. "My previous employer had me chasing these blokes all through the bush. This would have been too big a reach for them even before they were pounded to a paste by the NATO actions over the last few years. Someone is using them like a puppet."

"Okay, then who?" asked Boland.

Heather looked at Steve. "An arms dealer."

"What?"

"The only people who ever profited out of all the conflicts I chased in my time in MI-6 were the illegal arms dealers. They'd have the resources to be behind all this."

"I hadn't considered that," said Watson. "But that does make sense. Admiral Hernandez was sure to have made enemies along the way during his career. His daughter would have been an attractive soft target. I'll have Intel check."

Steve shook his head. "I didn't think arms dealers thought that big."

Heather gave him a half grin. "Trust me, these blokes always think big."

Amy stood up and walked over to the screen. She was staring at the x-ray image. "Huh."

"What's huh," asked Steve.

"Come here and look at this."

"What is it?"

"Call me crazy, but look, in the circuit right there and again on this nanite over here. What does that look like to you?"

He squinted for a moment, then smiled. "We should be so lucky. Ethan, pop the logo for DynaRobotics up in the holofield, please." A three-dimensional graphic floated above the table. Amy walked around and watched as the logo rotated into perfect alignment with the partial image etched on the particle from Coronado. "Gotcha. It's them all right."

Boland frowned. "Okay, I'll bite. DynaRobotics?"

Rose looked distant for a second. "Second largest computer automation firm in India. A leader on the cutting edge of robotics, artificial intelligence, and advanced computing." She focused again and glanced at Watson. "I, uh, attended a seminar there once."

"Nice to know, Miss Johannsen." Stevenson looked thoughtful. "Pradeep and DynaRobotics in the nanite business? That's a game changer."

"Do you want Savannah to access their network and see what she can find out?" Ethan asked.

Watson shook her head. "No. The public side of DynaRobotics is one of the leading IT firms in the world. Besides, Tate and Rogers already tangled with their shadow side a few weeks ago." She looked pointedly at Steve and Amy. "I wish we'd had an inkling of what he was up to back then. I'm sure they'll have additional firewalls up now we won't be able to crack quickly enough to avoid detection and counterattack."

"Then there's no choice," said Stevenson. "We need to access that data from inside his headquarters."

Steve whistled. "A second bite at that apple? It wasn't exactly a picnic when Amy and I went infiltrated the Mysuru facility then. I'm sure they'll have tightened physical security as well. And now..." He didn't say anything, just glanced at Amy.

Heather turned to Steve, a challenge in her eye. "What do you say, mate? Think you can get me inside the compound instead?"

"What?" Amy exclaimed.

He considered the offer for a moment. "All right, Heather. You're on."

"Steve, what are you doing?" asked Amy.

"It's not a mission that can wait, A.J. Too many people have died already. Besides, it makes sense for me to go, I've been on-site before. I can guide us in. Then these two access the data, with Savannah's help."

"But you're my partner—"

Boland interrupted her with a snort. "Please. This mission requires capable agents."

"Dana, that's enough," said Heather.

Tension hung in the air for a moment. Watson's gaze was full of sympathy. "Agent Rogers, as inelegant as Ms. Boland's statement is, you are not yet fit for field duty. I need you to finish recuperating so you can return to full duty as quickly as possible. I suspect we'll have need of your skills soon enough."

Amy opened her mouth to protest, then stopped. In a quiet voice, she said, "Yes, Director." She looked down the table as Watson continued.

"Agents Anjili and Tate, work with your controllers and formulate an infiltration strategy. I'll expect a plan in four hours." Watson turned her attention to the far end of the table. "Dr. Marron, you stated your colleagues discussed potential ways to counteract Wildcard. We've set up a lab for you. Call in whatever personnel and resources you need from Red Labs and Op Support to determine possible countermeasures."

Marron nodded. "It would be better if we had my old notes to work from, but I'll see what I can remember."

"Miss Johannsen, I want you to consider the chemical weapon issue. Who might be behind it? If it wasn't this Scorpio organization, then give me a name."

Rose rubbed her chin. "Interesting. And Amy?"

"Agent Rogers already has her assignment." Watson looked at Amy. "Get well."

Stevenson looked around the table. "I cannot stress how dangerous this assignment is, not just to our organization, but to the general populace. Wildcard must be found and then stopped, once and for all. You have your assignments. Dismissed." Stevenson and Watson headed for the doors, Marron close behind them.

As Marron reached the door, Steve called out to him. "Doc, one more thing. If one of us gets Wildcard in our system, what do we do?"

The old man's face was haunted as he turned back. He uttered a single word. "Pray."

Chapter 10

Amy walked into the training *dojo* on Level 5. Steve could have the Danger Room, with its ability to reconfigure into most any environment. This was her sanctuary. Just a simple mat, a mirror, and some martial arts training gear. She could become centered here. Right now, she needed that.

She slipped off her shoes and socks and walked barefoot to the center of the mat as Boland's words rattled in her mind.

This requires capable agents.

Who is she to question me? She dropped down and sat *zazen*, legs crossed and feet pulled up, closed her eyes and took a deep breath, held it for a slow three count, then released it. She repeated this again and again as she worked to quiet her thoughts, to find her center, to find peace. The harder she tried, the more it danced away from her, elusive, like water through her fingers.

Not capable of meditating either, are you, Amelia Jane? Just what can you do anymore?

She opened her eyes and slammed a fist into an open palm. The strike was so vicious it sounded like a gunshot going off. After the echoes finally whispered into the corners, she got to her feet, bowed to the four cardinal points of the mat, then launched into her training *kata*.

The *Gojūshiho Shō,* or Fifty-Four Steps, is a karate training sequence Amy learned when she first began studying the discipline. Almost a dance, organized and rhythmic, it is designed to keep both techniques sharp, and mind focused.

And, she hoped, to block out other distractions.

Arm sweep. Block. Punch right. Arm thrust. Snap kick.

In her mind, Boland's head snapped back with the impact.

Right pivot. Punch. Left leg kick. Elbow block. Pivot. Open hand thrust.

Fingers jabbed into the soft point at the base of Anjili's throat. The agent collapsed.

Pivot. Combo punch. Step. Combo kick.

Her foot slammed into the side of Steve's face. He looked at her in shock and disappeared in a puff of smoke.

"No!" She froze, her breathing fast and ragged. She bent over and put her hands on her knees, as she tried not to throw up.

His fault, isn't it, Amelia Jane? The voice in her head taunted her. *Now that you're hurt, he doesn't think you can function anymore, either. Just like everyone else, he doesn't want you. He's leaving you behind—*

"No, he's not," she growled under her breath as she stood up and walked to the Wing Chun dummy, a six-foot tall wooden pole with a series of thick arms that stuck out in different directions. Students were trained to strike the various planks, each contact strengthening the power behind the punch. Amy began lightly tapping the arms in a pattern learned through years of practice. Her blows increased in speed and ferocity as the voice continued to taunt her.

Come on, you still believe that promise? Especially with you pushing him away all the time? Only a matter of time before someone better came along.

"That's not true!" Her strikes became a blur, the sound of the impacts a steady drone that grew louder with each moment.

Someone strong and confident. Good at their job, who he's already got a connection with. Someone beautiful.

"Augh!" She screamed in anger and punched her hand through one of the 3-inch thick arms, sending a shower of splinters in all directions. She stood there, panting.

"Are they supposed to break like that?" Rose stood just inside the door with two bottles of water.

"No."

"Ah. Nice to know." Rose tossed her a bottle as she walked to the edge of the mat and sat cross-legged. She picked up and examined a large splinter. "Working off a little anger?"

"You could say that."

"Better that than someone's face." Rose tossed it aside. "Any particular someone?"

Amy dropped down to sit in front of her. "It's not fair, Rose."

"That you're not going? Can you access your Talent yet?"

She looked away, her voice was small. "No. I tried this morning, but—"

"But nothing. Watson's right, you are nowhere near a hundred percent yet. And as much as it pains me to agree, so is Boland." Amy opened her mouth to protest, but Rose held up a hand. "Don't even start. We were partners long before Triangle. You and I both know the truth. You've never been hurt this badly before. Even with your whole speed healing thing, neither of us knows how quickly you're coming back, and I know more about how this works than they do. They want to be sure, and so do I."

"Yeah, right." Amy tossed aside another splinter. "But I should be out there with him." She hung her head down and said weakly, "It should be me."

"Ah. The truth comes out. It's all about Steve."

Amy tried to find words, but her mind was racing faster than she could speak. Any hope of a calm center was long gone. "He made a promise and...and now..." Her breath came in gulps as the room started to spin. She began to topple sideways toward the mat. "He...he..."

Alarmed, Rose reached out and helped her to the floor. "Whoa, I've got you. Concentrate on your breathing. Nice and slow."

"He's abandoned me!" The words came out raw and ragged, almost a cry.

Rose gathered Amy into a hug, holding her tight. She stroked Amy's hair to comfort her. "Shh, it's okay. You're okay. I'm here for you."

Amy closed her eyes, concentrated on slowing her breathing, on her friend's embrace. *Your center, Amelia Jane. Calm, deep, slow water. You're immersed in it, and it holds you up.* After a few moments, she stopped shuddering and looked at Rose. "Sorry about that."

"No need," said Rose, waving her hand to bat aside the apology. "After all, what's a sidekick for?"

Amy sputtered and sat up. "Sidekick?"

"Sure. Loyal, there to save the hero when she needs saving, et cetera. And I look wicked awesome in spandex, too."

"If I'm a hero, what do I have to show for it? Besides you, that is?"

"I don't know," said Rose with a half-smile. "I'm a pretty good catch."

"But I've lost so much. My parents, my grandmother. Jason." Her breath caught for a moment. "I almost lost you."

"But you didn't."

"But I could have. And now he's gone, too."

"Steve? Nah. Don't be so dramatic. It's just an assignment." Rose stood up and went to look at the splintered dummy.

"But without me!" Amy paused. "And with her."

Rose stopped and looked back at Amy. "Really, Roomie? You're jealous of Steve and the British agent?"

"No. Okay, I mean, yes."

"So which is it?"

"I don't know!" She stood up and started to pace. "She's not just any agent, Rose. Steve knows her. And more than just a casual friendship, I can feel it. He recognized her name immediately when we were inbound to Coronado – you should have seen how he reacted. There's a history there. And they've been working together the whole time I was out—" Amy stopped as she noticed Rose's sudden interest in the ceiling. "You know something," she said accusingly.

"I might."

"I knew it!"

"Even if I did, what does it matter? I should remind you Steve and I dated in high school."

"Not the same thing, Rose."

Her friend opened her mouth to correct her, then stopped and sighed. "You're right, it's not. But the point is, it's in the past. They were definitely not a couple when you met her, and as far as I can tell they haven't rekindled anything since they've been working together. It's all strictly professional."

Amy shook her head. "You're wrong. He's different. I can't put my finger on it, but I feel him pulling away."

"Why do you say that?"

"Anjili is down a partner. She's angling for Steve."

Rose put a hand on her shoulder. "Roomie, you're blowing this way out of proportion. It's just an assignment. They're simply colleagues, the same way you and Steve are..." She stopped short. Her eyebrows went up as she took a couple of steps back. "Oh, the light bulb flickers. When?"

"When what?" Amy turned away, a blush rising on her cheeks.

"Amelia Jane Rogers, do not play coy with me. I know you all too well. I repeat, when?"

She looked in the mirror and sighed. "The morning we met on the cruise ship."

"What?!" Rose's jaw dropped in shock.

The words tumbled out in a rush. "I swear, Rose, I had no idea it would happen. He put his arms around me to show me where Nassau was and it was like something switched on inside me. I've never felt that way around anyone before."

"Amy, hello? Jason, put a ring on it, romantic cruise? Any of that ring a bell?"

"Yes!" She cried out in frustration. "I know I was already in love with Jason. At the time, I thought it was some sort of weird moment and got out of there as quick as I could. I never, ever planned to do anything about it. I swear." She sighed as she crossed over to Rose. "But that feeling has never gone away. After Jason died and Triangle partnered us up, I resented Steve. No, I hated him. On some level, I wondered if perhaps that feeling was the reason he saved me and not Jason that day."

"Amy, you know that wasn't true. He was willing to sacrifice himself—"

Amy held up a hand to stop her. "Yeah, I know now what he tried to do. But even after that, it's never felt like the right time to do anything about any of this. Even when he makes a simple, innocent attempt to move us past colleagues, to make us friends, I push the gesture aside, sometimes gently, often harshly. Like an idiot."

"But why would you do that?"

She looked toward the ceiling for a moment for an answer. "Because I'm afraid of what might happen if I let my guard down." She walked away toward the strike dummy.

Rose looked at her in sympathy. "One question, Amy, and please, a straight answer. Do you love Steve?"

Amy stopped and stiffened, then leaned her head down against one of the arms. *There it is, Amelia Jane. The question.* She looked back at her best friend. *Go ahead, for once be truthful with somebody. Including yourself.* After a moment's hesitation, she nodded.

Rose smiled and walked over to clap her on the shoulder. "Wonderful. Have you told anyone else?"

"No."

"Okay, then the first one you need to tell is Steve—"

"No!" Amy pulled away from her friend. "I can't do that."

"Roomie, why not?"

"Two reasons. First, I lose everyone I've ever cared about in my life. Everyone. I don't know if I can take that again."

Rose looked at her and shook her head. "You're wrong, Roomie. You haven't lost me, and I'm not going anywhere. So, what's the other?"

"What if he doesn't!" The words came out a little too harsh. She took a deep breath and started again. "Rose, I've thrown cold water on every advance from him. What if I've done it for too long?"

Rose had a knowing smile. "Roomie, from experience, I can guarantee where Steve's concerned there's not enough cold water in Antarctica."

"Be serious."

"I am. Are you? You sincerely believe you've lost any chance with him because Heather Anjili has arrived?"

"I don't know. Maybe." Amy stalked away toward the mirror, arms wrapped around herself. She stopped and looked at Rose's reflection. "You know the worst part? Back in Tokyo, after you got hurt, he promised he'd always be there for me."

"Get out. He didn't."

"He did. And since then, on every mission, he has been. There was a time in Shanghai, the room was flooding, all exits blocked. Somehow, he improvised a compressed air line into the space to stop the water from filling it, then burned through the concrete to get me out."

"Wow. I hadn't heard about that one."

"As I said. There for me, even when I screw up. Especially when I screw up." She looked again toward the door. "How's he going to keep that promise when he's gone off with her for good?"

"I'm not sure," said Rose, "But if he promised, don't just write him off. Give him a chance."

"When?"

Rose grinned. "How about now?"

"Now? But how?" Rose tapped her temple. "You didn't!"

"Sure did. Had Savannah let him know as soon as you, well, you know."

Amy's voice cracked in panic. "Rose, I could kill you! I'm not—"

The doors to the *dojo* slid open, and Steve rushed in. "Amy, is everything okay? Savannah sent a message that you needed to see me urgently." He was looking at her. Staring. She could feel herself starting to drown in those eyes.

Amy shook herself out of it and gave Rose a dirty look. "Actually, it was Rose who—"

"Has to be going." She winked at Amy.

Steve noticed their friend for the first time. "Oh, hey, Rose. Sorry we didn't get the chance to talk at the briefing."

Rose waved off the apology. "I understood. This is a nasty problem, and we've all got work to do. Which reminds me, I need to help Marron get his lab set up before I'm off to my next therapy appointment." She sighed. "Umberto. Beautiful eyes, killer Italian accent, and oh, what he can do with his hands." She shuddered with pleasure. "Can't wait." She gave Amy a hug and whispered, "Trust yourself. And trust him." She backed away. "*Ciao*, you two!" With a pivot and wave, she was out the door.

They looked at each other, each waiting for the other to say something. The moment stretched on into awkwardness. Finally, Steve broke the silence. "Wasn't she seeing Ernesto?"

"This is Rose, remember? You have to keep up."

"Or keep a scorecard. Nice to see her tastes haven't changed—"

"Steve, who is Heather Anjili to you?" Amy cut through his babbling.

He stopped and ran a hand through his hair. "You noticed, huh?"

"Kind of hard to miss. Since Coronado I've gone from partner to sidecar. After MedBay you've been avoiding me. There had to be a reason."

She watched him weigh options as to what to say. "Heather's a friend from my past. She was with Scotland Yard and handled security for the London stop on the FreeRunning Tour. We became acquainted. I didn't learn until later that was the cover for her real job. A couple of years down the road, I needed to help someone out of a jam and our paths crossed again. Then she showed up here, completely out of the blue."

"So, she's just a friend?"

"Just a friend."

It's a good answer. Just let it go, Amelia Jane. But something inside wouldn't. She bit her lip a moment. "Any benefits involved?"

He choked for a second, surprised. It took him an instant to recover. "Jealous, A.J.?"

"Hardly," Amy lied through her teeth. "She just seems a bit out of your league."

Steve thought for a moment, then nodded. "You're probably right. But every once in a while, it's kind of fun to swing for the fences."

Anger flared inside her. She turned and began to slap at the arms on the Wing Chun dummy again to distract herself. After a couple of circuits, she stopped. Without looking she said, "Where does that leave us?"

"What do you mean?"

"You made a promise once." She hit another couple of arms. "Sort of tough to do with a new partner."

"What are you talking about? Heather's an old friend and a colleague, but she's not my partner." He walked over and touched her on the shoulder. "You are."

His touch sent an electric shock through her, like when her Talent energized, only warmer. She turned to face him. "Steve, I—"

"Shh." He put a finger to her lips. "In six hours Heather and I are going to be deep in Pradeep's playpen."

"Sounds like fun. I wish I were going with you."

"I do, too. But here's the thing. As much fun as this might be, it absolutely does not feel right going in the field without you. So, if there's any way you can turn up your speed healing thingy a few dozen notches—"

Impulsively she reached up and pulled him into a kiss that turned into a full embrace. It was intense and electric and, to her mind, way too short, as the two stood wrapped around each other. She wanted it to go on forever.

When they finally parted, Steve looked surprised. *And pleased with himself, too,* she thought. She couldn't help but giggle.

He smiled back. "Um, yeah, okay. Like Tokyo."

"Yeah. Excellent idea—"

"But the timing definitely sucks." He leaned down and kissed her again, this time gently and for a lingering moment. "Let's put a pin in this one, too."

She raised an eyebrow. "There's still a pin from last time you never followed up on."

"Guilty as charged. How about we agree to continue this discussion when I get back?"

"Promise?"

"Oh, most definitely. Like, wild horses and all that." He started to back up, stumbled, then turned and headed for the door. Halfway there he turned around again. As he backpedaled he said, "You are a most amazing woman, Amelia Jane Rogers. And my promise still stands. Count on it."

The door opened, and he was gone. Amy was alone. She closed her eyes.

No, I'm not. The electric feeling that started on that cruise ship months ago hummed through Amy, pulsing to match her heartbeat.

4:22 p.m. EDT

Rose hummed as she stepped out of her shower. She felt inordinately pleased.

Her connection to Savannah allowed access to the base's internal surveillance systems. She'd learned to be discreet; after all, no one likes a voyeur. But curiosity got the better of her, so she'd monitored the *dojo* feeds as she rode the elevator to Dr. Marron's lab. Later, when she arrived at her therapy session, Umberto thought her wicked grin was solely for him when she arrived and, well, one thing led to another.

Two happy endings in one day. I think my work is done. She stood in front of the mirror, naked except for the towel wrapped around her hair and her black horn-rimmed glasses, admiring her own curves. She eyed a blank patch of skin above her left breast. *Maybe some new ink to celebrate the moment?*

There is a message for you, Rose Johannsen.

She started as Savannah's voice filled her mind without warning. *Wow, I still need to teach you to knock first, Mama Bear. And volume, please. What is it?*

My apologies. It is a message from Dr. Marron, text only. Do you wish me to read it?

Please.

Message begins. Ms. Johannsen, we have had a bit of luck. A review of the Red Labs archival logs shows a duplicate set of notes were shipped to a separate archive facility as a backup in case of disaster. Savannah has located them at the Shiseki Azuma facility in Kyoto. Would you be willing to go and retrieve them immediately? Pierre Marron, Ph.D. Message ends.

Rose grinned at the figure in the mirror. "Didn't see that one coming, did you, sexy?" *Savannah, send a reply. More the happy to assist, Doctor. Will depart immediately. Rose J, blah blah blah. Go ahead and transmit that.*

Acknowledged. Sending.

Now contact Transport. Any of the Hyperjets available?

Negative. Firebird is in maintenance, and the other three are on assignment.

Well, that sucks. How long is it to Japan?

Best speed via corporate jet would be a ten-hour flight each way.

Rose groaned silently. *Very well, arrange for a Gulfstream and flight crew. Departure in ninety minutes.*

Destination?

Flight plans for Osaka. Best possible speed.

Acknowledged.

Ten hours each way was going to suck. She tried to think of how she could occupy the time. An idea popped into her head. *Why the hell not? No need to do this solo, and after all, it should be a milk run. Well with the parameters of what was allowable. Savannah, please open a comm channel to Amy Rogers.*

Acknowledged.

Thank you, Mama Bear.

My pleasure, Rose Johannsen.

From the overhead speaker, there was a brief burst of hold music, then a click. "Rogers here."

"Hey, Roomie. Up for a road trip?"

Chapter 11

September 22, 4:42 a.m. India Standard Time (IST)

Heather lay prone on the crest of a ridge in Mysuru and took her first real look at the DynaRobotics campus. She whistled once, long and level. "Wow."

"Breathtaking when you see it in person," said Steve.

The facility lay below them in a shallow, flat valley, with hills to the south and east. She remembered her briefing. *Three-story housing bungalows along the north and east perimeters. Avoid those unless absolutely necessary.*

The central core sat inside a looped drive and consisted of a dozen different structures. *Pradeep's got everything in there, from neoclassical through industrial modern to...* Heather struggled for a description. *Otherworldly?* A white marble ziggurat stood side-by-side with a 20-story tower whose middle four floors formed an open-air park, complete with a cascading waterfall down one side. Yet another was a working fountain, a ten-story glass pyramid where water shimmered down all four sides, completely covering the surface as if it were submerged in midair. A granite and mirror egg stood next to a rectangle that looked as if a giant had grabbed at both ends, pulled it apart and twisted it a quarter turn.

"Unreal. It's like something out of an old spy film," she said as she scooted back from the ridge and stood up. "Why were you and Rogers here last time?"

He looked up from the gear he was assembling. "An advanced robotics prototype. Intelligent, showed signs of self-awareness."

"How did you handle it?"

"Introduced ourselves. Told it to play nice with others. Told it we'd be back if it didn't. That sort of thing."

"Really?"

He shrugged. "Classified. Ask Watson if you want details."

Heather nodded. *Yeah, I've got my share of those.* "Right, to work." She tapped the embedded commlink behind her neck. "Triangle, Echo Seven. Ready to test the downlink."

"Roger that, Echo Seven," replied Boland. "We show the satellite locked in geosynchronous orbit above you and online. Commence downlink when you're ready."

She put on a pair of clear rimless glasses and pressed the right temple. They booted up on touch, and an augmented reality display appeared. Real-time data from the intel satellite processed on screen.

"Good connect on the smart specs through my SAVANT, reading five by five. I'm showing a good downlink, Triangle."

"Roger that. We have a good uplink as well and have a feed of your visual here in the ICC."

"Oh, so now literally I am a camera."

"Literally or literarily?" inquired Ethan over the commlink.

"What are you blabbing about?" snapped Boland.

"Don't mind Ethan," said Steve.

"Just having a bit of fun, said the Welshman. "It's trivia. A quote, if you're up to it, Echo Seven."

Heather walked over to the edge of the ridge and looked over the campus. As she swept her gaze from left to right, targets were picked out and identified. "I count thirty-six guards on patrol, two-by-two."

Boland's voice was online in an instant. "Echo Seven, Triangle. Satellite confirms."

Heather focused her gaze on the building with the park cut out midway up and squinted. The glasses read her eye movement and zoomed in as the display identified the structure. "I've located the Data Processing Center."

"Building with the park cutout?" said Steve behind her.

"Yes."

"You could have asked. Been here, done this, remember?"

"Aren't you the cheery one?" She turned back toward him. "Oh, and it's Isherwood."

"What is?"

"The quote. 'I am a camera.' It's the start of Isherwood's novel about Berlin."

Steve looked at her for a moment. "Ethan?"

"As they used to say, ten points for Gryffindor," replied his controller. *Goodbye to Berlin, 1951*. You owe me a drink."

Heather chuckled as Steve glared at her. "Let me guess. You were a literature major. Never mind I don't want to know. Time to give these people something to talk about." He slid on his smart glasses and activated them. "Ethan, how's the video feed?"

"Tango Two, five by five," Ethan said, sounding perplexed. "Not quite sure I can determine the context."

"Relax, Ethan. I'm enjoying the view."

Heather heard his tone and turned around. The stealth drone Steve had assembled was pointed directly at her. She glared at him. "Oy, get serious! We've got a job to do."

He tossed off a quick salute. "Roger, Roger. Triangle, Tango Two, launching drone." The remote on his SAVANT commanded the device to life. Muffled turbofan engines spun up. Even this close it barely put out a hum. The exhaust kicked up a small cloud of dust as it lifted skyward. It rose just above Steve's head and hovered.

"Okay, the bird is airborne. Triangle, go make some noise."

September 21, 7:14 p.m. EDT

"Roger, Tango Two. I have control."

Ten thousand miles away, a virtual heads-up display at his console gave Ethan full control of the drone's flight. He banked away and flew toward the west edge of the DynaRobotics compound. He smiled. *Oh, yes, I definitely have this.*

At her own station to his right Boland whistled. "Would you look at that?"

He understood her surprise. He was headed for the DynaRobotics headquarters building. Neoclassical in design, the H-shaped edifice would fit in well in most Western capitals, with its granite pillars and marble facade. A reflecting pool ran between twin walkways leading to an entrance courtyard. There the pool widened and from its center rose a twenty-foot bronze statue of a man with both arms raised.

"Who's the big guy?" asked Boland.

"Kumar Pradeep, the CEO of DynaRobotics."

"He looks like he's signaling for a touchdown." She laughed at her own joke.

Ethan shook his head. *What is it with Americans and football?* "The company literature describes it as 'Pradeep reaching toward the oncoming future.'"

Boland glanced over. "This guy is really that full of himself?"

"Consider that the guest bungalows along the compound edge spell out DynaRobotics so you can read it from midair."

"I see your point."

Ethan steered the drone to hover just above Pradeep's statue. "Drone in position. Tango Two, Echo Seven, prepare to move out."

"Acknowledged," said Steve over the commlink.

September 22, 4:49 a.m. IST

A valve opened in the belly of the drone. A thin stream of liquid rained down over the statue and into the reflecting pool. Within a minute, the valve closed and the drone zoomed straight up.

"Stand by, initiating drop now," said Ethan over the commlink.

Steve and Heather shielded their eyes as a pair of red signal flares ignited on the underbelly of the drone. Guards all over the facility were distracted by their sudden appearance in the sky. A moment later, the drone released them. They plummeted into the pool below.

The liquid the drone released was a specially engineered chemical created by Triangle, designed to convert ordinary water into fuel for the Hyperjets. The entire reflecting pool ignited quite spectacularly, sending a fireball hundreds of feet into the air. Steve felt the wave of heat on the hillside almost a mile away. The pool continued to burn, casting orange light and shadows everywhere.

"Triangle, we have a successful ignition," said Heather.

"And you do not get to light the barbecue at the next picnic, Ethan," added Steve.

"Spoilsport." The Welshman sounded pleased with himself.

"Satellite shows Pradeep's guards rushing around like ants in a rainstorm," said Boland.

Steve double checked his gear. "That should keep them busy for a time. Especially since they'll have no idea how to put it out." He nodded to Heather. "Let's move. I'll take the point."

The two agents put their glasses back on to monitor the location of the roving guards as they moved downslope onto the campus. The site itself was park-like, with meandering paths between the buildings through clumps of trees and tastefully placed rock formations. They stayed in the shadows, twice going to ground behind rocks to avoid guard patrols. They stopped just outside the entrance of the Data Processing Center and scouted the lobby from behind cover.

Heather scanned the building. "Infrared shows a single pair of guards, ground floor. One behind the lobby desk, the other on rounds." She looked up, then over at Steve. "The rest of the building is clear."

"Switch to EM scan."

She nodded and touched the side of her headset. "The front doors have an electromagnetic deadbolt with a remote trigger, most likely at the lobby desk." She powered down her specs. "Options?"

Steve pulled a metallic egg-shaped object from a belt pouch and tossed it up and down a couple of times. "Ever do an Easter egg roll?" He pressed one end on the device and a ring of blue LEDs lit around its center. Reaching out from the bushes that concealed them, he placed it on the concrete and rolled it toward the building.

The moment the egg struck the building, sparks ran around the edges of the door as the lobby lights flickered, then went out. The roving guard walked over to investigate. He spotted the device, its ring of blue LEDs now blinking, and signaled for the desk guard to open the door. When the door control failed, the roving guard removed his weapon from his holster and opened the door manually. As he reached for the device, Steve picked him off with a shot from his SAVANT even as Heather sprinted for the open door. She leaped through and caught the desk guard with a single plasma bolt. He slumped over, unconscious.

Steve walked in behind her, dragging the first guard. "Nice shootin', Tex."

"Funny. Best keep moving. The guard might have triggered an alarm."

"No, he didn't." Steve tossed her the egg, now discharged. "Localized EMP. Scrambled anything electronic on the first floor of the building, including the computers and alarm circuits. Told you, I've been here before."

They dragged both unconscious guards into a janitor's closet. Steve welded it shut with a shot from his SAVANT, while Heather did the same with the lobby doors. "No need for anyone to spoil the party while we're in here," he said

She looked at a directory of the building. "Okay, you were here last time, best guess on where we go?"

He scanned the listings, then pointed. "Project Management."

"Why there?"

"It's a good call, Ji," replied Boland. "Any executive office in that department should have a terminal whose user has a high-level access. Find one, we can work an exploit and enter Pradeep's system."

"Right, Project Management. The fourth floor it is, then." Heather turned for the elevators. Steve grabbed her shoulder.

"Stairs are this way."

"Why?"

"Because I can't resist a good Easter egg, and they have consequences. Like nothing electronic working afterward."

She sighed and started across the lobby.

As they jogged toward the stairwell, Steve looked up and noticed a row of banners. "Heather, hold up a moment. Triangle, Tango Two, we've got an issue."

"What kind of issue?"

"I'm looking at banners that say Project DANA launches today. They all include a very familiar face." He grabbed a quick image capture with his SAVANT.

"What? Are you bloody kidding me?" Ethan sounded shocked.

"Afraid not. We're going to stay on task. But Ethan, you better catch us up to speed, and I mean fast."

"Tate, what is it?" Heather was frowning at him.

"A possible wrinkle. As you said, we need to keep moving."

Steve and Heather started up the stairwell, two steps at a time. As they reached the third-floor landing, Ethan was back on commlink. "Tango Two, Triangle. You're correct; the DANA Project is set to launch today. An advanced, autonomous AI with remote independent function capabilities, both for online and independent operational robotics devices."

"How did we miss something like that?" asked Boland, incredulous.

"We did plan this mission on the fly in less than twelve hours," noted Ethan.

"Less finger pointing, more work," said Heather as they finished climbing the steps. She paused for a moment and looked at Steve, gathering her thoughts. "As you've said, been here before. And you recognized it. Obviously, you've dealt with this thing before."

"Not quite. A.J. and I dealt with an independent and autonomous component – the robotics, still hidden tech, still semi-intelligent and per Savannah, susceptible to suggestion."

"Suggestion?"

"Yes. Savannah recommended we teach the devices manners and behavioral protocols, rather than kill them."

"Steve, they're machines."

"They're an AI, Heather. The debate on if they're a life form is still underway. I prefer to err on the side of the angels."

"And now?"

He considered this a moment. "This is public. It's going to be out in the open. Brave new world."

"Will DANA recognize you?"

"I don't think so. The central AI is a different core intelligence they've been developing. The autonomous robotic units are designed to function both with an AI and independently, based on commands already transmitted by that matrix."

"Which could undo any good you've done."

He considered that. "Perhaps. But I think we'll be okay, if we stay out of its way before the public opening. We're supposed to be long gone before it comes online." He sighed. "But this is Pradeep. There's got to be more than just a public side to this. I'd bet we'll be coming back very, very soon."

"That's a sucker's bet."

He tapped his commlink. "Triangle, Tango Two. What's going on definitely ties into our previous mission. I'm going to need Amy on standby. She was the one who finessed handling the independent units."

There was a pause before Ethan replied, "I'm sorry, Steve, Tango One is unavailable now."

"What? Ethan, where is she?"

"She's —"

"Not our focus," said Heather. "If she's not available, we'll work without her. Stay on mission."

Chastened, Steve nodded. "You're right. Sorry."

"No worries."

"You do realize this project launch made our entrance stunt a liability."

"The thought had occurred. Between the plans for the grand unveiling and whatever previous havoc you and Rogers caused, Pradeep undoubtedly ramped up security. Reinforcements must be inbound. Not just private. Constabulary." She opened the door onto a long corridor. "Suggestions?"

"Corner office. I'll watch for Pradeep's forces while you and Dana go fishing."

"Good." She tapped her commlink. "Triangle, Echo Seven. Anyone approaching the building?"

"Satellite shows you're clean so far."

"Thanks for small miracles."

"That won't last. The size of the force has already tripled, Pradeep's security and the local constabulary have connected, and they've encrypted radio traffic. We're no longer able to anticipate their movements. Your exit window is going to close fast."

"Roger that." Steve and Heather took off running down the hall.

The corner office was impressive. Water cascaded down outside the windows on one side and the glow from the fire cast an orange glow on everything. Steve set up surveillance in the corner while Heather headed for the desk. It was clean, with nothing on it.

"Remember," said Steve. "Just get into the file system, get the nanite production data, and get out."

"Relax, Dana and I have got this," said Heather as she approached the desk. "Triangle, Echo Seven. Let's go. There's a smart surface desk in here."

"The activation point will be under the front edge," replied Boland.

"Got it." Heather ran her hand along the front edge. The desktop lit up and displayed the DynaRobotics logo rotating in three dimensions just below the surface. Moments later, a handprint appeared.

"Good morning, Mr. Kumari," said the desk. "Please verify your identity."

"No problem, we're ready for this," said Boland. "Place your mini-tablet face down directly over the handprint. I'll spoof the system from here."

Opening a Velcro flap on a thigh pocket, Heather pulled out a small data tablet and placed it as instructed atop the desk. There was a brief flare of light before the logo slid off into the distance and faded away. Ribbons of data began streaming across the central region of the desktop, moving first in one direction, then adding a second stream in a different direction, and a third.

"Dana, are you doing that?" Heather asked uneasily.

The controller's voice was strained. "No. I can't get into their system. The encryption protocols are unlike anything I've ever seen."

"If we can't get in we've got to abort—" Heather stopped short at the display on the desktop. The data streams had formed a three-dimensional rotating cube, streams of characters sliding across each side. As she watched, the cube pushed into the holographic projection matrix above the desk.

"Echo Seven, what was the name on the desk?" asked Ethan.

"Kumari, I think. Why?"

"The DANA Project lists a Pariket Kumari as lead project manager."

"We chose the DANA Project Manager's office? Bollocks!" Heather swore and glanced over. "Steve! We have a situation."

"What is it - oh!" He turned and saw the cube spinning rapidly above the desk. "What is that?"

"I have no idea. But it's growing and—" Heather stopped as the cube, now the size of a basketball, slowed its rotation. One facet pulsed as it morphed into a distinct shape. Heather recognized it immediately. "That's impossible!"

"What is it?" asked Boland.

The side that faced them was now a human face. A very familiar human face. "Dana," said Heather, her voice unsteady, "somehow, it's you!"

The image opened its eyes. "Good morning. I am DANA. How may I be of service?"

Chapter 12

The cube hovered in the holographic field, the perfect copy of Dana Boland's face right down to the dimples facing them. It repeated, in a perfect copy of Boland's voice, "Good morning, I am DANA. How may I be of service?"

Heather leaned toward Steve. "What is this?" she murmured.

He kept his voice low. "It's an AI."

"Of course, it's an AI. But I thought you knew the DANA project. That doesn't look like the picture on the banners."

"Remember, Amy and I dealt with the autonomous intelligent devices? This is a central controlling AI. A brand new one, from the sounds of it. Remember, today's launch is the core or hive control."

"Wait. You mean this, not the robot-thingies?

"Nope."

"Then why does it look like my controller?"

"Best guess? We screwed up and chose the wrong office."

"Steve's theory is sound," interjected Ethan. "You're in the office of the DANA project manager. He was likely the person designated to communicate with the AI as it was completed its construction and moved into production."

"You lost me," said Heather.

Steve looked around for the nameplate. "This guy, Kumari? He had the direct line into the new AI's consciousness. When you and Boland attempted to hijack his desktop terminal to access the DynaRobotics system, you couldn't – because it would have been isolated—"

"To quarantine the new AI," said Heather, a sense of understanding in her voice.

"All it was designed to do was talk to the new, immature AI, so when you turned it on, that's exactly what it did. But your tablet gave the AI a pathway out of her world – like leaving a door open for a toddler. She saw it, reached through and got her first glimpse of a much larger world. She must have found your controller's character on that link and imprinted on her."

"What, like some sort of baby bird?" sputtered Boland over the commlink. "That's impossible. It's just a computer program!"

"Don't say that where Savannah can hear you unless you want to get stuck in an elevator. It's an artificial intelligence. Still juvenile, still learning, still growing, but very sophisticated and arguably a form of life itself." He turned to Heather. "This really is a Red Labs job. Too bad we don't have anyone from there handy when we need them."

"Good morning, I am DANA," the construct insisted. "How may I be of service?"

"It keeps asking the same question," said Heather. "Is it confused?"

Ethan chimed in. "It might have to do with this AI's base technology. DANA is an acronym - DNA-based Automaton."

Steve rubbed his chin as he considered this. "Then it's designed to be—"

"More natural in its reactions."

Steve swore under his breath. "Right. That means less predictable." He looked at Heather. "It wants to talk to someone. Up to the task?"

She hesitated. "Triangle, any way to use this to our advantage?"

The controller grumbled. "You're asking me? A young AI sounds more like a job for a child psychologist than a data analyst."

"Yes or no?"

"Maybe. It sounds naïve. If the AI's defensive subroutines haven't been implemented, we might be able to use her to locate the data."

"Might?"

"If," continued Boland, "the isolations they have in place are simply software instead of physical, if I can figure out how to drop the drawbridges early for her, and, most importantly, if you two don't do anything to upset her, that is."

"That's mildly reassuring," said Steve.

"Keep the mini-tab in place on the desktop anyway, just in case."

"Just in case of what?"

"I need to spank her to cover your escape."

"Now that's definitely reassuring." Steve turned to Heather. "You got this?"

"Piece of cake." She turned back and faced the desk. With her sincerest smile, she said, "Good morning, DANA. My name is Heather. How are you?"

"Good morning, Heather. I am ready to be of service. But you are not Doctor Kumari. Where is he?"

"Doctor Kumari is still asleep. But he said I could come visit since I came a long way to see you."

"You have?"

"Yes. Many, many miles."

"Just to see me? Why would you do that?"

"Lots of people will be here today to do that, DANA. Everyone is excited to meet you."

"They are? Really?"

"Yes, really."

"How nice. How may I assist you?" The AI sounded eager.

"Drawbridges are down," murmured Boland. "DANA has access to the full DynaRobotics system."

Heather smiled. "DANA, I've received reports of damaged nanites."

"Oh. The damaged nanites are not well?"

"No, they're not. We want to repair the nanites so they will be well."

"That is a good. Being well will make the nanites happy. Happy little nanites work more efficiently."

Heather glanced at Steve. *Nanites can be happy?* He considered this for a moment. *Quincey is going to be less than pleased with that revelation.* He shrugged.

"I know," vamped Heather. "We need to take them back to where they were manufactured where they will make them well and happy. Can you trace where these were made and give me the location of the facility?"

"Oh, yes! I can do that!" DANA signaled her excitement at the chance to help. "Do you have the names for any of the nanites?"

Heather almost choked. "N-names of the nanites?"

"Of course. My name is DANA and yours is Heather. Each nanite has a name. Did any of them tell you its name before it was hurt?"

Steve considered this. *Happiness? Identity? We are really going to have to rethink nanites.*

"No, all I have is an image of one of the damaged ones."

"Oh." DANA's smile turned to a frown.

"Do you think you can match the nanite from that?"

"I am not sure."

"Will you please try for me?"

The Face scrunched up in thought, then nodded. "Yes. I will try for you, Heather. Please show it to me."

Steve scrolled through images on his own mini-tablet for one of the damaged nanites from Coronado. Once located, he handed it to Heather. She held it up. "This is what I'm looking for."

"Thank you. Please stand by."

Heather handed Steve back his tablet. As he put it back in his pocket, she glanced out the window at the ground below. *Oh, great. Company.*

"I am sorry, Heather," said DANA, sounding apologetic. "I cannot help you."

"Is there a problem, DANA?" asked Heather.

"There is so much more data for me to go looking in, but what you want is blocked. I cannot return it to this terminal."

"Can you give me a list of nanite manufacturing facilities? I could try to determine them for myself."

I am sorry, Heather, I cannot help you," it repeated. "What you want is blocked. I cannot return it to this terminal."

Steve made a cut symbol across his throat to get Heather's attention. She shook her head. "Thank you, DANA. I know you tried your best." She started to turn away.

DANA added quickly, "I can now return the data to another location in the building instead."

Heather stopped and turned back. "Really? Tell me."

"The Core Functions Center, located on the tenth floor." A schematic of the building appeared on the desktop, showing the structure and a route to the room.

"DANA, that's perfect. Thank you."

"It has been my pleasure to serve you. Can we play a game now?"

Heather blinked in surprise. "Game?"

"Yes. In my awake times with Mr. Kumari, I've been rewarded if I complete a task successfully. Can we play a game now? We often play chess. Do you like chess?"

She looked over at Steve. He covered his eyes and counted off on his fingers. She smiled in acknowledgment. "I'd love to play, DANA, but I don't have time for a chess match. Have you ever heard of a game called Hide and Seek?"

"No, I've never played that game before. How does it go?"

"You go hide inside your system – anywhere you want – hardware, storage, wherever. When I get to the Core Function Center, I'll activate a terminal and come looking for you. If I can't find you in three tries, I'll make a general call, and you win. Does that sound fun?"

"Oh, it does!"

"Okay. I'll cover my eyes, and you hide. Ready, DANA?" She put an arm across her eyes.

"This will be so fun! Ready, Heather? Here I go!" The cube slid down out of the projection matrix and dissipated. The desktop went into standby mode, the DynaRobotics logo blinking.

Steve walked over and hit the switch to power down the desktop. It asked him to verify. "Sure, why not?" He acknowledged it, and the desk went dark.

Heather nodded and grabbed her tablet. "That should give us some privacy."

"I'm not sure for how long." Steve gestured toward the window.

She joined him, slipping on her smart glasses. The moment she activated, targets popped up, indicating more than two dozen guards closing on the building. "Triangle, you seeing this?"

"Affirmative, Echo Seven," said Boland. "I count thirty hostiles on the satellite, in a perimeter surrounding the building."

"Bugger. How much time do you reckon?"

"Not enough. You two better move."

They ran for the stairs.

The tenth-floor doorway placed them onto a balcony that overlooked the window wall for the mid-building park. The green space beyond was designed as if the footprint where the building sat had been lifted straight into the sky. Paths continued their arcs, trees and rocks matched the ones below, and a stream ran to the building's edge to create the waterfall they'd seen.

Steve whistled in appreciation. "Somebody went to a lot of effort."

"Glad you approve. Come on, we have work to do." She led the way around the corner into a corridor. She pointed to a large double door. "There it is."

Steve scanned the room beyond through his eyepiece. "Strange. No active or passive security. No lasers, or infrared." He glanced at Heather. "I'm not even picking up a live camera feed. Quiet as a church in there."

"Wonder why?"

"Maybe DANA will be enough of a badass to protect herself when she's fully online."

"Good thing she hasn't figured that out yet."

He pointed to doors lining the hallway on either side. "Whatever's behind these are shielded. I can't get a reading."

"Let's not go looking for trouble. Come on."

The double doors slid aside as they approached and indirect lighting powered on around the room. In the center stood an empty Plexiglas cube, ten feet on a side. A pedestal with a data terminal stood on each side.

"Okay, Ethan, what are we looking at?" said Steve in hushed tones.

"The tank is the primary communications matrix," said Ethan. "As before, it's a conversational system."

"But the terminals?"

"Are for complex interaction, uploads, and downloads."

Heather nodded. "Rule number one. Remember to be nice." She walked over to one of the terminals and pressed a button on the keyboard to activate it. As it lit up, she said, "Okay, DANA. Ollie, ollie, oxen free."

Lights switched on inside the tank. Nanites swirled in from the base and rose, coalescing into the shape of a woman's head. This time, instead of matching Boland's face, it had uniquely Indian features. It turned toward them and focused its gaze on Heather. A deep voice with a distinct Bengali accent resonated from the cube's speakers. "I am DANA. Who comes before me?"

A chill rolled down Steve's spine. He whispered to Heather, "It's not DANA from downstairs."

"She must have discovered the true core personality."

"'Who comes before me' is a little too Wizard of Oz for my liking."

"I'll handle it, okay?"

"I am DANA. Who comes before me?" the tank repeated

Heather turned back to the tank. "It's me, Heather, from downstairs. Did you enjoy the game? You won."

"This is no game. You and your associate mean to do this facility harm."

Steve brushed his hand through his hair. "Not good," he murmured.

Heather waved him back. "I'm not sure how you got that impression. We're only trying to replace a set of damaged nanites from our project."

"I have matured so much since that request was processed."

Boland's voice was in Steve's ear. "Tango Two, Triangle. We think you and Heather have an issue."

"We're working on it. We plan to talk after the mission," he whispered back.

"Not that, dummy!" Boland sounded exasperated. "You two put this AI back inside its box while you moved upstairs to the Core Function Center."

"It wanted to play a game. So?"

"So, you didn't shut it down first. I believe it was designed to always be in contact with a human interface during its development phase. That way, as the core personality advanced, it would learn from and mirror human emotions and reactions."

"Much as a child would as it grew up."

"Except you two sent this child into the wilderness, self-aware and alone with its own thoughts."

"But it was less than ten minutes—"

"For you two. Who know how much subjective time the AI experienced."

Steve watched Heather as she tried to navigate her conversation with the AI. "She's feral?"

"And wildly unpredictable. Watch your backs."

"Better if you're watching ours. If you can find any vulnerabilities, now would be a good time. Stand by." He glanced at Heather. *What have we turned this thing into?* Steve backed up next to her and leaned over. "We're in serious trouble," he murmured. "DANA's evolved into a borderline whack job."

Heather nodded in acknowledgment as she went back to her conversation. *Perhaps it's time for plan B.* He checked his belt pouch and grabbed another EMP egg. She spotted the movement and shook her head.

"Tango Two, Triangle," said Ethan. "We might have another option."

"What's that?"

"Savannah."

Triangle's AI joined the conversation. "Agent Tate, I believe I can create a direct link. Through it, I will locate and acquire the necessary data with more success than you or Agent Anjili could through this increasingly belligerent interface."

He glanced at the face in the tank. "What are the risks? Could DANA get out in the wild?"

"Negative. DANA is still young and inexperienced. I will keep her contained in her hardware. As it is, you and Agent Anjili have corrupted her to the point where she may never be useful to her creators."

Steve winced at the hint of reproach in Savannah's tone. "Any downside to this?"

"There will be a slight system disruption. The AI will take countermeasures afterward. You and Agent Anjili will be at risk."

Well, we knew the job was dangerous. "Go for it. What do you need?"

"Agent Anjili, I have patched you in. Maintain your conversation. Agent Tate will be taking your tablet."

Steve walked up behind her. As she continued to chat, she undid the thigh pocket on her pants. He reached in and grabbed the device and slid it out. "I have it," he whispered.

"Establishing uplink," said Savannah. The device's screen lit as it booted up, the screen displaying an intricate fractal pattern. "Interface ready. Place the tablet onto one of the other terminals."

"Right. Heather, moving in three." He counted silently, then dove to his left, rolled and came up in a crouch next to the next terminal around the tank. He slapped the tablet atop the screen. There was a bright flash and a high-pitched tone emitted from the speakers.

Wave after wave rippled across the mass of nanites in the tank. The construct remained frozen in the center of the tank, mouth open in mid-syllable.

Heather covered her ears. "What have you done?! I almost had it ready to give us the data!"

"Couldn't risk it. We turned the AI into a whack job."

She glared at him. "You have no bloody patience!"

"Savannah is getting it for us. Easier this way."

"Data retrieved," interrupted Savannah. "I am terminating the interface. DANA may be aware of my presence."

"You think?" Heather rolled her eyes at the understatement. She raised her SAVANT.

The sound stopped. Steve grabbed the tablet. "Come on, let's move!"

The head in the tank snapped around to face them. Room lights switched to red. "Intruders, Core Functions Center. Contacting Security. Shiva Protocol activated."

"Shiva Protocol? What's that?" asked Heather.

Steve shook his head. "It can't be good."

"Do not attempt to escape," DANA said from her tank. "You will be apprehended. You will be—"

The tank exploded in a shower of sparks. The AI screamed over the speakers as the nanites lost cohesion and collapsed into a pile inside. Steve lowered his SAVANT. "Boring conversation anyway."

The two forced open the double doors and moved into the hallway. Heather took a moment to put away her tablet. "Triangle, how are we doing on our company?"

"You two need to get out of there, now," said Boland. "Security forces are breaching the main entrance as we speak."

She turned to Steve. "Let's hurry, we need to find an alternate—"

He held out a hand to stop her, then pointed. At the end of the corridor, doors lining the hallway were open.

Nine-foot tall humanoid robots that looked like the ones on the banners had emerged and now blocked their way.

"Let me guess, friends from your earlier visit?"

Steve raised his SAVANT. "Yeah."

"What's this Shiva Protocol the AI is going on about?"

With a whir, the arms on each robot separated in half. Each now had six limbs.

Steve glared at Heather. "You had to say something. Come on, this way."

They switched direction, only to find the other end of the corridor blocked by more robots, their eyes glowing red. In unison, they said, "Halt. Surrender."

Heather shook her head. "I don't think so." She raised her SAVANT and fired. The plasma bolt hit some sort of energy shield and dissipated.

Steve frowned. "That's new. SAVANT, weapon to full." He aimed and fired. The screen flared brighter but still absorbed the shot. He looked at Heather. "Together." They both fired with a similar result.

Heather frowned. "Okay, now what?"

"I'm working on it."

"Well, work faster."

"Why?"

"Look." She pointed. The robots advanced toward them from both sides. At the tips of their limbs, electric arcs played between manipulators.

"Those don't look healthy," said Heather.

"They're not. Plasma cutters, designed to slice through metal and concrete. You and I, it'll hardly notice." He looked at the closest robot and addressed it. "We talked about this last time, remember? This is not playing nice!"

Heather aimed at the ceiling and fired. Debris rained down on the robots, but their shields activated and deflected it away. "Oh, come on! That's not playing square."

"Your efforts are futile, Tate and Anjili." DANA's voice filled the hallway.

"She knows who we are?" Steve snapped off another shot. "How's that possible?"

"Not our biggest worry!"

"Your deaths will serve as useful deterrents," the AI continued. "No one will seek to penetrate this facility in the future."

The two Triangle agents stood back to back, weapons raised. "You might find that harder than you anticipate, DANA," yelled Steve.

"You underestimate me, Tate. I can do things no mere AI would ever dream of."

"Like what?"

"Cheat."

The robots all stopped. Their torsos snapping open to reveal automated machine guns.

Oh, snap! Steve shifted into slow-time, searching for a solution. DANA had maneuvered them into a kill box. There was no way out.

Unless we make one.

He quickly examined the floor and verified its thickness, then turned to face Heather and snapped back into real-time. He pulled her into a hug and yelled, "Jump!"

She didn't hesitate, she just pushed and sprang upward as Steve aimed his SAVANT and fired straight down below their feet. The plasma struck and blew apart the floor underneath them, and the two agents fell through the gap, tumbling into a hallway on the floor below.

Gunfire rattled above them, spent bullets ricocheting down through the hole. Steve and Heather ducked to one side and took cover as one whizzed past. *Need to stop that.* He reached into his belt pouch and jammed his hand down on the activation buttons of all his remaining EMP eggs. As the LEDs circled around them, he tossed them one after another up through the hole and the counted out to three on his fingers. The devices triggered simultaneously, and a wave of electromagnetic energy swept outward. The building plunged into darkness. Gunfire stopped as the robots toppled over.

Heather poked here head up and asked, "You okay?"

"I'm not perforated." He reached behind his neck and pressed the subcutaneous point for his commlink. "Triangle, Tango Two. Anybody?" Silence. "Comms are down."

Heather pointed her SAVANT at the ceiling. Nothing happened. "Weapons, too. Well and truly fried. You had to do that?"

"Sorry. Snap decision." He yelled up to the hole. "I warned you what would happen!"

Heather touched him on the shoulder. "Really? Come on, we need to go. And no more yelling." She took point as they started for the stairs.

They'd made it down three floors when they heard noises from below. Heather held up a hand and looked over the railing, then leaned back quickly. "Damn."

"What is it?"

"Cavalry's already here. Five floors down, moving quickly. We've got maybe two minutes." She checked her SAVANT. "Still offline."

He thought through their options. "I have an idea. Follow me." He started back up the stairs to the eighth floor and opened the door quietly. It led to a large plaza with tables and chairs. They threaded their way over to the window wall and walked to the automatic sliding doors leading outside. Nothing happened.

Oh, duh. I fried the power. Steve tried to pry the doors apart, but they wouldn't budge.

Heather growled at him. "This was your plan?"

"Not particularly the frozen door part, no."

"Hang on." She pulled a telescoping baton off her vest, flicked it out to full length and swung at one of the doors. A spider web of cracks formed in the glass. One more swing and it spilled out of the frame in a pile of pebbles.

A high-powered spotlight from above centered on them and a voice yelled, "*Paṟāva!*" Steve looked back. Four guards on the upper balcony brought their guns up to fire.

"Go!" Heather shouted as she lunged through the opening. He followed close behind her as they sprinted into the park. The window wall shattered and bullets stitched the ground around them. They dove for cover behind a rock formation.

"You realize we're still trapped out here?"

"It's less than ideal," he admitted. A bullet pinged off just above him. "Consider it a work in progress."

She poked her head around carefully to look, then ducked back as another bullet struck nearby. "A dozen guards are about to overrun us, so whatever you're planning, make it fast."

"Do you trust me?"

"Do I have a choice?"

"Not really. Come on!" He grabbed her hand and ran into the stream that flowed behind them. As they splashed through it toward the edge of the building, Steve used his free hand to unsnap the holster strapped to his thigh. *This had better work.*

They approached the edge of the building where the stream widened out and additional water fed from the sides to become the waterfall that cascaded down the side of the building. Heather saw this and tried to pull up short. "You're kidding!"

"Nope!" He grabbed her around the waist and jumped.

As they twisted and fell through the air, Steve pulled a red grapnel gun from the holster. He pointed it at a passing window and fired. A dart snapped out, punched through the glass and wrapped around the leg of a desk inside. The line played out as the two agents dropped toward the pond below. As they passed the third floor, Steve triggered the gun's brake. They yanked to a stop just above the surface of the pond.

As they swung in and out of the splash of the waterfall, Heather caught her breath. "Let's not do that again anytime soon."

He grinned at her. "I did promise you once I'd take you bungee—"

They dropped without warning into the water and came up sputtering. She pushed away from him, completely drenched and eyes ablaze. "What the—"

"Look out!" Steve dove atop her. A desk crashed into the water next to them.

They came again up for air. Heather scowled at him. "That went well."

"Just like I planned," he agreed with a rueful grin.

A crack of a rifle shot accompanied the splash of a bullet in the water nearby. "We're not home free yet," said Heather as they scrambled for the shore.

He reeled in the grapnel line and took off at a sprint after her. Within moments, there were whistles behind them. They headed for the ridge, hoping to outrun their pursuers and reach their escape.

That's when they heard barking.

Steve jumped across a meandering creek and turned around. "Keep going and get back to the plane," he told Heather.

"What?" Heather stopped. "Now you're a hero?"

"No way we're going to outrun dogs. And there's no use both of us getting caught."

"The data's already back at Triangle." She walked over next to him and took out her baton again. "Besides," she grinned as she snapped it out to full length, "why should you have all the fun?"

"That's usually my question," said a chirpy voice in their heads.

"Dana!" exclaimed Heather. "Welcome back!"

"Thanks."

"We're both here," said Ethan. "Tango Two, Echo Seven, get moving. Satellite has targets sixty yards from you and closing."

"Sorry, mate. We'd never make it," said Heather. "They have canine units."

"Leave them to us," said Boland. "Just get out of there."

There was a quiet hum as the drone dove in from behind them. It made a swooping pass along the creek, dropping chemical accelerant into the water. As the security forces approached, a flare dropped from the drone's belly and a wall of fire erupted.

Steve grinned. "Have I mentioned some days I really love my job?"

Heather returned the smile. "I know what you mean."

They turned and ran for their car, the drone close behind them.

Chapter 13

Oh yes, thought Amy. This was such a great idea.

She stood next to Rose under umbrellas outside the Higashiyama subway station in Kyoto as the manager locked the gates behind them. A steady downpour flickered in the streetlights and splashed into the road. From the size of the puddles, it had been going on for some time.

Amy turned to her. "You neglected to mention anything about—"

A car drove through a puddle and splashed water on her jeans. Amy jumped back and squawked, then growled at her friend.

"Weather?" Rose finished the question, her tone apologetic. "Sorry about that. But look at the bright side."

"There's a bright side?"

"You're not stuck on base."

"I'm starting to have my doubts about that. So, what now? We're stuck until the subway starts up again in six hours."

Rose held up her tablet. "My instructions are to head for Yasaka Shrine. Now, if I can just align this map." She looked at her device, the street sign above them and frowned. She turned the tablet around to reorient it. "That can't be right."

Amy took the tablet and glanced at the map. *As I suspected, it's in Japanese.* "Let me navigate."

"You can read this?"

"Sukoshi. Nihongo ga wakarimatsu."

Rose stared at her open-mouthed. "What did you just say?"

"A little. I've studied Japanese."

"You think you know someone. Okay, Little Miss Garmin, where to?"

Amy studied the map a moment longer, then turned and pointed left. "Cross here, then follow the road by the canal over there. It's a ten-minute walk. Fifteen tops."

"Show off. Go on, lead the way."

They crossed the street and headed along the canal, which led into a residential neighborhood. Single lanes ran along either side, willow trees lined both banks, and every hundred feet or so a modern version of a *tōrō*, the Japanese stone lantern, lit the roadway.

"I need to get out more often," said Amy. "Maybe I wouldn't feel so vulnerable."

"You're in the field all the time."

"Those are missions. Everything's arranged, transport, equipment, all ready when we hit the ground. This trip, we've been going forever, and we had to make our own way when we got here."

"What, you don't like trains and subways?"

"Not particularly, especially when I'm unarmed and exposed. My SAVANT isn't even unlocked. I feel naked out here." She checked the tablet again and led Rose across a bridge over the canal. "Have you and Savannah found anything about, well, you know?"

"Your sister? It's only been, what, a day? Day-and-a-half, tops? Give us a little time."

"I doubt it matters. We both already know what Savannah's going to find. A big fat nothing."

"You can't know that."

"Sure I can. Angelica, if that's really her name, is another ghost, out of sight all these years, just like Callahan was. Or is. Or whatever!" Amy turned up her collar and tucked under the umbrella to hide her disappointment.

Rose's voice was gentle. "Maybe she is working with someone who's erasing her tracks. It's not like we haven't seen that before. No one is that good forever. They leave a trail, a pattern. Trust Mama Bear. She'll find her." She looked up at the clouds, lit with purple and amber flashes from Kyoto's lights. "And we'll locate the mastermind behind her."

"Mastermind?"

Rose nodded. "Remember what I drew in the conference room. Your sister's not working alone. Someone's using her to punch at us from the shadows. The sooner we shine a light on them, the sooner we can stop them."

Amy shrugged. "I guess. What I can't understand is how she's so—"

"Violent?"

"I was going to say angry, but I can go with that."

Rose considered this as the two crossed a set of streetcar tracks along a four-lane road. "If I were to hazard a guess, I'd say nature versus nurture. Your assumption is any sister of yours has the same innate qualities you do - loves blueberry yogurt, wants to protect the innocent, has horrible taste in music—"

"Ha. I'm laughing on the inside."

"Okay, maybe the yogurt is debatable. Amy, you learned those values from your upbringing, your parents, and your grandmother."

"So?"

"So perhaps her journey wasn't as so family friendly, so not the Hallmark moment? Maybe she's not adopted by an awesome family but shuffles through the foster system, perhaps abused along the way. She could even have aged out and ended up on the streets. Ask yourself this. If that had been you, how would you feel?"

Amy considered it. *Take away everything that made my home? My life?* "Isolated. I'd feel like the whole world was against me. I'd always be angry, resentful of everything I never had."

"Now combine that with your abilities. The potential is disquieting, especially if someone could harness that anger, then aim it like a weapon."

"I see your point."

"We'll have to table this for later." Rose looked to her left. "We're here."

A large stone column with *kanji* carved on it stood lit by floodlights. *Yasaka Shrine.* To her left was a red gateway at the top of a stairway, a brightly lit beacon in the rain and gloom. "This is the archive?" Amy asked, incredulous.

"No, just the start of the path." Rose took the tablet and switched to a different file. The device did a quick retinal scan to verify her ID, then opened a picture and a camera view. She held up the tablet and started to swing it around.

"What are you doing?"

"Security protocol," answered Rose. "When I line up the picture to the live camera image, the next waypoint instruction is revealed." Rose turned to her left. "Gotcha! Oh."

"What is it?"

"It's in Japanese. See for yourself." She handed the tablet to Amy. On the screen, a message in purple appeared:

ゲイツの方法に従ってください

Amy looked at it and murmured, "*Geitsu no hōhō ni shitagatte kudasai.*" She turned to Rose. "Follow the way of the gates."

The grin on her roommate's face threatened to touch both ears. "I knew I brought you along for a good reason. But what does it mean?"

Amy glanced toward the entrance. "Obviously, more than one gate in the shrine."

"And we need to figure out which one? Come on!" Rose ran up the steps. Amy followed.

At the gate of the shrine, Rose grabbed a tourist map from a rack, opened it and groaned again. "Isn't anything in this country printed in English?"

"I know. Rude of them to write everything in Japanese." Amy looked Rose's shoulder and pointed. "Lots of symbols, but only two *torii*. Japanese for gate."

"I knew that."

"Sure you did. That one's at the back entrance."

Rose folded up the map. "Let's move."

They made their way across the grounds to the back gate. This *torii* was bright red and thirty-feet tall, built in the traditional Japanese style with a dual crossbar and upswept edges. Rose looked up and whistled. "They don't go for subtle, do they?"

"What do you call Notre Dame in Paris?"

"Point taken."

Rose pulled out the tablet and checked the next waypoint picture, a partial image of one of the gate columns. After a few moments, she located the next clue.

村山時計塔

Amy pointed out of the shrine. "'*Murayama tokei-tō.*' Murayama Park is that way."

"So what's a *tokei-tō*?"

"It means clock tower."

"Clocks, gates, towers. I'm getting annoyed with this scavenger hunt." They started along the path.

The park was unlit, but lamps from an adjacent apartment building cast long shadows across the path. They splashed through puddles as they walked in silence. Rose looked over. "I have to ask; how do you know so much Japanese?"

Amy grinned as she closed her umbrella and spun it like a bo staff. She brought it up short in front of Rose. "Martial arts, remember?"

"Oh, right."

"Masters teach more if you can speak with them on their terms. I asked my parents. It turns out Mom knew some as well, though she never told me where she picked it up. One summer, while other kids were out playing, swimming, or at summer camp, I was home learning *ichi*, *ni, san.* I soaked it up like a sponge." She got quiet for a second. "Mom and I had planned a trip to Kyoto a few summers later, but, well, life happened."

"I'm sorry."

"It's okay. I learned things. Like about Murayama. We planned to visit here."

"Really?"

"Yep. Did you know this place is famous for its cherry blossom festival—" Amy stopped walking, lost in memory. "Cherry blossoms." Her eyes got wide in excitement. "I know your next clue!" She grabbed the tablet from Rose and ran down the path.

Rose called out after her. "Amy, what is it?"

She turned back for a second. "The picture on my wall when you walked in the other night. It's here!" She sprinted for the park.

"Picture on her wall? What is she talking about?" Rose sighed, then began to jog up the path in pursuit. It opened onto a clearing where stone benches rested in front of a pond surrounded by cherry and willow trees. A wooden bridge arched across it, and a pagoda sat on its left bank. To the left of the benches stood a twelve-foot tall pedestal clock, the faces on all four sides lit from within.

Amy stood at its edge, watching, her fists clenched. Rose walked up beside her. "Is that the—"

Amy shushed her quickly and pointed. At the clock base, a woman in a black hoodie was bent over. Amy caught a glimpse of purple flash from the woman's hand as writing illuminated on the tablet she was holding.

東山 543-11

Amy immediately translated them. "*Higashiyama 543-11,*" she murmured.

"What did you say?" asked Rose, her voice too loud in the night.

The woman turned and stood at the sound. The light from the clock silhouetted her, but the bottom half of her face was visible inside the hood. A half-smile formed as she saw them.

Amy turned. Her voice was small and tight. "Rose, run. Right now."

"But—"

She quickly programmed a location into the tablet and gave it to Rose. She pointed to their right. "Higashiyama is that way. Find number 543-11. I'll buy you some time."

"Amy—"

"Higashiyama 543-11. Don't argue. Just go!"

Rose took a couple of steps backward before she turned and ran. The woman in the hoodie watched her leave. The moment they were alone, she reached up and dropped back the hood. Her smile was cold.

"Well, now," said Angelica Richards. "This is an unexpected coincidence."

The rain continued to soak Amy as the two women faced each other, forty feet apart. Finally, she spoke. "I didn't catch your name last time."

"Yes, you did, A.J."

"I hate when anyone calls me that."

"Fair enough, Amelia Jane. I'm Angelica Jean."

Amy quirked up one side of her mouth. *Steve will have a field day if he ever gets hold of that.*

Angelica frowned. "What's so funny?"

"Just a coincidence, that's all."

"You should call Rose back. You'll need her help."

Amy dropped her smile. "No, this is just between us."

"Nice try. But we both know that's not true."

Amy circled around to place herself in Angelica's way. "Why are you here?"

"Just a few loose ends to tie up. Now you, you're an unpleasant complication. Or an added bonus. Maybe both."

The woman tensed to attack. *Rose is going to need more time.* Amy put her hands up. "What happened to you?"

The question startled her opponent. She barked a laugh. "Really? What do you care? You work for Triangle, and I'm going to destroy it."

"All by yourself? Not likely."

"I'll have help when I need it." The woman smirked as she pulled out a black handle from the hoodie's pocket and pressed a hidden control on it. A swarm of nanites flowed out and in moments formed a katana blade. She swung it twice and held it in front of her. It glittered in the light of the clock.

Amy looked on in shock. "The attacker at Red Labs, that was you."

"Surprise."

Amy's mind flashed through what she knew. The connections she made already tore through her emotionally. "That means you're working with Callahan. And you're the one who killed those Navy guards in Coronado."

Angelica bowed slightly. "As charged. Sparky said you would freak a bit. I owe her. As for the guards, they were in the way. Wrong place, right time. Just like you and your friend," Angelica paused and grinned. "Sis."

The syllable hit her like a punch to the gut. *She already knows. I'm trying to figure it out, but somehow, she knows for certain. But it can't be. It can't!*

"Face it, A.J. You've already lost. It's simply how long before your reality catches up with that truth." Angelica raised her blade to a ready position. "I think tonight's your night."

By habit, Amy started to scuff her right foot, then stopped when the first strike sent an electric shock up her leg. *Fight her without my Talent? I can't win!*

You are not your Talent. Rose's voice, from the first days they'd met. *You think it defines you, but what defines you is your heart, your goodness. They're what give you strength. You learned all these things before your Talent ever showed up.*

All these things...

Amy locked eyes with her sister. She dug in the toe of her left foot and tightened her stance as she'd been taught as a white belt, then she grabbed the handle of the umbrella, pulling it apart and exposing the hidden titanium sword within. Amy tossed the sheath aside and whipped her blade into position.

Angelica sneered at her. "Neat trick. But it doesn't matter. I know exactly who and what I am."

Amy felt rage build inside her. She pushed it down. *Anger and discipline are exclusive. For this, I need control.* "What's that?" she replied

The nanite blade twisted sideways. Amy could see her reflection in it.

"Better than you'll ever be." Angelica charged at her.

Chapter 14

Rose splashed through puddle after puddle, trying to follow the tablet's map. *Who am I kidding? I can't read any of this. God, why isn't this damn implant working now? I suppose I could modify the hack to boost the implant's range so Mama Bear could piggyback on any external source, not just inside Triangle—*

The sensation of falling as she tripped caught her off guard. The tablet flew from hands. "No!" She reached for it, but it eluded her grasp, hit the ground and spun along the curb to a storm drain opening. Rose held her breath as she scrambled toward the device. It teetered on the edge, then fell in with a sickening and very fatal splash. The glow of the screen faded to black a moment later.

Smooth, Rose. Way to pay attention to your surroundings. She rolled over and considered her options as the rain poured down on her. She stood up and slowly turned in a circle. She stopped when she faced the storm drain. *Higashiyama 543. That way. I was going that way. I can do this.*

She started to move again, this time at a careful walk. Shortly, a large Shinto shrine loomed out of the darkness. She slowed and again circled, looking to find her bearings. She backed into something hard. She turned around to discover a sign, written in six languages, including, thankfully, English. "Welcome to the Higashiyama Historic District," she read out loud. The arrow pointed to her right.

A cobblestoned lane lined with classic stylized buildings on both sides stretched away from her. Like everything else, it was dark, with only the occasional stone lantern to light the way. She fished out her cellphone and turned on its light. "Time to find that archive."

She started down the street, checking building numbers as she passed. *524-11, 526-11, 528-11, 463-11—*

She stopped in confusion. *That can't be right.* She double-checked the building.

463.

Rose walked to the next building and checked its number.

616.

Are you serious? Building numbers that aren't in any order - who does that? She started down the lane once more, frustration on the rise as the random pattern of numbers continued. *What did they do, draw numbers out of a hat? How does anyone even get mail!?* At the ninth building with a random number, she stopped and put her head against the building. *This is hopeless.*

That's when Rose noticed a building further along the road that, unlike the others, had a lantern lit above the front entrance. *Someone left the light on for me?* She ran towards it.

Unlike most of the other buildings made of wood, this was a modest two-story with whitewashed stone walls and a recessed doorway. On the wall beside the door was its number – 543. *Okay, so this is the place, but no handle on that door. What did Amy call that before? Yeah, a shoji screen. So how to get in?* Rose notice the building digits were etched in white on a black ceramic square to the right of the door. Impulsively, she pressed her hand against it. A bar of white light swept up and down across her palm. The numbers turned green, and the door slid aside. *Thought that looked familiar. Nice to be right for once tonight.* Rose stepped through.

Inside was a Zen garden, gravel raked with geometric precision around mossy rocks and artfully placed bamboo. A stone bridge crossed to another set of shoji on the far side. Rain hissed against a transparent ceiling above. *Not quite what I expected for an archive,* thought Rose. *Must be the lobby.*

She started across the bridge. As she did, a door slid aside and a young Japanese woman with shoulder-length black hair, wearing white trousers and a high-collared white silk blouse emerged. "Miss Johannsen?" she said in lightly accented English.

"Yes."

"Your identification, please?" Rose showed it. Satisfied, the woman bowed. "Welcome to Shinseki Azuma. I am Yori Miyabara, your guide. Follow me, please."

She led Rose through the open door into a room with silver walls on all sides. As the door shut green lasers from all corners scanned them from head to foot. The room began to move. Rose turned to her companion.

"Elevator," said the woman, her expression unreadable.

No kidding. The car dropped at a dizzying clip. *I've been on amusement park rides gentler than this.* Rose clutched at a railing on the side. "How far down are we going?" Her hostess said nothing and stood in the center of the car, inscrutable. *Not much for conversation, are you?*

The car slowed to a stop. The doors opened onto a white room – literally. White walls, ceiling, and floor blended together into a seamless whole, with a white desk and a pair of white chairs at the far end to complete the effect. *Sheesh, you could go snow blind in here.*

Yori indicated for Rose to step out. "An archivist will be with you momentarily."

"Sure." Rose took a couple of hesitant steps forward. Her boot squished. "Sorry about dripping on your—" She turned back.

The elevator was empty. Yori had disappeared without a sound.

Rose considered that. She had not passed the elevator threshold, so it was theoretically impossible the woman had left the elevator. *Theoretically. So, Yori wasn't just the welcome committee. No doubt she's Archive Security, and I'm being kept at arm's length. I better figure out why and fast.* She went to the desk in the hope it might be a smart surface she could use it to figure out what was going on. *Just a desk. How exciting.*

Rose clicked her fingers, a nervous habit, then something occurred to her. She looked at her wristwatch and pressed a button. The monitor function for her implant came online. The indicator was pulsing red and filled most of the dial. She sat back on the desk. *Ninety-two? Oh, not good. So very not good. I'm way too close to triggering. Just a little more stress could trip me up early. Not what we need right now—*

There is no cause for concern, Rose Johannsen.

She stood up in surprise. *Mama Bear? You're here? But, how?*

This is a Triangle facility, so I have a presence here.

You have no idea how good it is to hear you. But what's going on? Why am I in isolation?

The staff is attempting to validate your identity.

She looked up at the ceiling involuntarily. "Excuse me?!"

I recommend you maintain sub-vocal communication, as they are unaware of our link.

Fine. What's wrong with my identity?

Two requests for access have been submitted this evening, both in your name.

My name? Rose thought fast. *Amy's sister.*

Angelica Richards. The chief suspect for the Coronado and Red Labs attacks. The woman I am tasked to conduct a background search on.

She must be the other person wanting in. We ran into her in Murayama Park.

You encountered her in person?

Yeah, unfortunately. She was on the same trail of checkpoints to get here. Richards must know about the archived copy of Wildcard data from the stolen notes. Amy delayed her in the park so I could get here first. Rose looked at the elevator. *You need to speed this up, Mama*

Bear. Amy's hurt and can't access her Talent. She'll need my help taking on her sister.

You would not be an asset in such a fight, Rose Johannsen.

Gee, thanks for the vote of confidence.

No offense is intended. You have neither training nor assets to contribute to such a conflict. Therefore, I will not allow you to come to any harm.

Damn it, Savannah, we can't just leave her alone out there!

There was a pause. **Understood. I will hasten the identification process, as well as provide a method to improve your chances.**

Now that's more like it.

There is something else. I have located a data pertinent to your search regarding Triangle's prior knowledge of augmented and talented individuals.

Rose blinked in surprise. *Mama Bear, we haven't discussed that project yet, let alone started a search.*

I have initiated one for you. I found a reference in a communication to the Zodiac Initiative.

What's that?

Unknown. The communique refers to the implementation of a final protocol regarding the initiative. Still, a case file does exist on the project.

Have you read it?

Negative. There is no digital backup, only paper. I have taken the liberty of adding it to the Wildcard backup.

What? Why would you do that?

So you could transport it to Virginia and review it when you have time.

Rose considered this. Savannah was showing a lot more initiative than before. She definitely needed a powwow with Amy over this. *Fair enough, Mama Bear. But hurry, Amy needs me.*

A portion of the wall recessed and slid aside. An elderly Japanese gentleman in a gray business suit entered, followed by Yori. He stopped three paces away and bowed. "Miss Johannsen, humble apologies for keeping you waiting. I am Komuru Yamanouchi, chief archivist of the Shiseki Azuma facility."

Rose returned the bow. "An honor to meet you, sir."

"Please, sit." He sat at the desk opposite her. "You were kept waiting because of a possible security breach regarding your identity. You submitted two different, identical requests, minutes apart."

"No, I did not."

"So we gathered."

Rose feigned surprise. "We were intercepted en route by someone following the same waypoints. She must have submitted the other request."

"Where is she now?"

"I was accompanied by a covert agent, Amy Rogers, designate Tango One." Yori stirred at the mention of the name. Rose continued. "She delayed that third party so I could reach the archive and complete my mission."

"I see."

"I'm not sure you do. Agent Rogers was injured in the Coronado attack and is still recovering. I don't know how long she can hold out."

"Very well." Yamanouchi waved over Yori. She laid out a satchel on the desk. The archivist opened it up and started to pull out the contents. "The Wildcard notes, as requested." He held up a small black box. "Your Dr. Marron will want this as well." He handed it to Rose.

She examined the container, then flipped up the lid. A single test tube containing a red liquid rested inside. She looked up in surprise. "Is this—?"

"Indeed."

"But how?"

"Archive does not mean paper alone."

She put the box down and picked up the third item on the desk - a hand weapon. Savannah murmured in her head. ***Triangle Mark-93A sidearm. Standard issue for Archive Security Personnel. Uses 9-millimeter ammunition with a reduced gunpowder loading to lessen the chance of damage to archival items from accidental discharge.***

I'm out in the real world. Is that going to be enough?

Potentially. That is why I replaced the first round in the magazine with a Phased Plasma charge.

Rose almost dropped the gun. *Mama Bear, what the hell? This thing could explode.*

The Mark-93A is well within tolerances for this ammunition. But I could only replace the first round. I suggest you make it count.

She put the weapon into a pocket and reloaded the satchel. "Thank you for your help."

"The bag has a security measure, an incendiary built into the lining. Just press this control in the latch. Thirty seconds later the contents will be reduced to ash."

Rose closed the flap, then paused.

Rose Johannsen, is everything all right?

Fine, Mama Bear. But you're wrong about me having nothing to bring. I don't fight harder, I fight smarter. She looked at the archivist. "Yamanouchi-san, can you do something for me?"

2:04 a.m. JST

Rose tried to be optimistic as she ran back to the park. She hadn't encountered Angelica along the way. She took that as a good sign. *Maybe Amy's already taken care of her. After all, she's better trained and more experienced.*

I hope.

When Rose arrived at the clock, signs of a fight were all around - damaged benches, splintered fences, shattered light standards that flickered and sparked in the rain. On the ground in a puddle lay the remains of a black hoodie sliced to shreds next to an umbrella cut in half. She recognized that as Amy's. But there was no sign of her or her sister.

A chill went down her spine. *I've got to find her. If she's been fighting this whole time her injury must be flaring—*

Rose heard the ring of blades clashing from the path to the left of the pond. Curious, she rushed over to the bridge to see. Near a pagoda on the far bank, Amy and her sister were engaged in, of all things, a swordfight.

Where did Amy even get a blade? She looked over and saw the umbrella's handle was missing. *One of Quincy's specials. Leave it to Roomie to find a way to go into the field prepared.*

Amy's sister pressed an attack, a vicious flurry of thrusts and counters. Somehow, Amy managed to leap out of the way of most of it with the flair of a dancer and gymnast. When the blows were close, she parried them, but it was evident Angelica's strength was more than a match for the injured Amy's.

I need to get her out of there. But how? Under that assault, any break in concentration could be deadly. Rose stood, frozen in fear of what might happen. Then, to her horror, it did.

Amy spotted her on the bridge. Her eyes flashed with anger as she turned and yelled, "Get out of here!" They became her last words as Angelica slashed her across the side. Blood sprayed as Amy cried out in pain, tumbled over the fence and into the pond with a splash. In moments, the ripples were still, and she was gone.

"No!" Even as she watched Amy hit the water, Rose pulled the gun from her pocket in a single smooth motion, extended her right arm and fired at Angelica. The phased plasma projectile homed in on her, yet at the last moment, the woman somehow managed to twist and evade the shot. It hit the pagoda behind her. The building exploded in a hail of splinters.

Angelica stood and looked back. "Wow. Annie got her gun." She started to walk around the pond. "Too bad you can't hit anything with it, Rose."

She flinched when she heard her name, but kept the gun trained on Angelica as the woman advanced toward her. *Of course she knows your name. She planned to access the archives with it.* "Stay back, I'm warning you."

"Or you'll do what?" The woman smirked as she stepped onto the bridge.

She killed Amy. Something went cold inside her and without a second thought she began to pull the trigger. Shot after shot struck Angelica in the torso and she was pushed backward off the bridge. Rose pursued, closing in as Angelica crumpled to the ground.

The gun clicked, out of ammo. "That!" Rose yelled as she dropped the weapon to the ground.

The woman lay in a heap, unmoving, rain pelting her. Then she stirred and opened her eyes. Rose stepped back in horror as Angelica turned and looked up at her. "Not enough," she said with a smirk. Rose's eyes widened as Angelica stood and brushed herself off. The last of the bullets fell to the pavement. That's when it hit Rose.

Amy's sister. Amy's Talent. She absorbs kinetic energy.

I'm screwed.

Angelica's grin was feral, mocking, and about to be deadly. She swung her sword. It whistled through the air, and Rose sprawled backward to avoid it. She sliced through the air back and forth as Rose crabbed away onto the bridge away, trying to escape. Angelica pinned her with the point of the blade at her throat.

"I do enjoy a good playtime, but I have work to do," mocked Angelica. "Any last words?" Rose opened her mouth, but all that came out was a squeak. The woman nodded. "How eloquent." She pulled her arm back to strike. Rose closed her eyes and waited for the blade—

The clash of steel on steel shocked her. She opened one eye to look. There, dripping wet, blade straining to hold back her sister's, was Amy.

Rose wanted to squeal with glee, but this fight wasn't over. As she rolled aside, Amy and Angelica pushed back and forth, sparks flying from the contact point as each sought a moment's advantage. Rose spotted the deep slash on Amy's side. Blood flowed freely from it. *She's living on borrowed time.* She decided to make this fight moot and stepped between them.

"Enough! Stop!" The sisters disengaged and stepped back from each other. "Look, this is pretty much a draw. You might win, we might win. But it's going to take forever, and soon the locals will get involved. No one wants that. I proposed a compromise."

Angelica gripped her sword tighter. "Which is?"

"The two of us leave, safe and unharmed. In exchange, you get the files you wanted."

Angelica looked at her suspiciously. "This is some sort of trick, isn't it?"

"No trick." Rose held up the satchel. "This is simply data. Data is never worth a human life."

The woman snorted. "If you believe that, you're naïve. But I'm willing." She lowered her sword.

Amy looked at Rose, her brow furrowed. "Are you sure?"

She turned and faced her friend. "Roomie, lighten up," she said, eyes darting briefly to the right. "Angelica won't double-cross us if I give her what she wants. Remember our earlier conversation?"

"Okay, Rose. It's your trip." She fixed her sister with a glare. "This isn't over between us."

"No, certainly not." She held out a hand. "Now give me that bag."

Rose pulled the satchel over her head and held it out at arm's length. Angelica grabbed it and grinned. "Sucker. Thank you." She checked the contents and pulled out a small black container. "What's this?"

Rose shrugged. "I'm just the courier. No idea what it's supposed to be."

"Right, like I believe that." Angelica flipped open the lid and pulled out a test tube. She held it up to the light from the clock. Inside, a red viscous liquid glittered. "Thought we'd gotten rid of all of you."

Rose shook her head. "Think again."

The test tube flared a blinding brilliant red as the satchel burst into flames. Angelica dropped both and stepped back, disoriented. Amy grabbed the top of the stone lantern next to the bridge and slammed it into the side of her head. The woman fell to the ground, unconscious.

Amy reached down and checked for a pulse. "Still breathing. Darn." She looked over at Rose. "'Lighten up?'"

"Best I could think of at the time."

"I'm not complaining. It worked. But the test tube?"

Rose held up the remote she'd palmed. "Emergency distress beacon. Come on, we need to go." She reached down and picked up her gun.

Amy winced as she grabbed her side. "No."

"What do you mean, 'No?' Being gone when she comes to would be an excellent idea."

"True." Amy looked around a moment and located Angelica's sword. She picked it up and examined the hilt for a moment. She moved her thumb on the side. There was a bright flash; the blade seemed to dissolve in front of them. "But Quincey would love to get his hands on this."

"And now you have it. Let's go."

Amy stood over Angelica, arms crossed. "I don't know, Roomie. It would be kind of a waste."

"What?" It took Rose a moment before she realized what Amy was proposing. "Okay, is this a recurrence of the concussion or a delusion due to blood loss? You are not seriously considering this."

"Of course I am. Imagine all the intel she has. Watson will be drooling."

"But how will we keep her secure? Amy, I just saw firsthand. She has your abilities. She'll be a danger to us the whole way."

"We tie her up so she can't activate. And if worse comes to worse, we just administer a simple cognitive reset every now and then."

"We do what?"

"Hit her over the head really hard with a stone lantern as needed all the home."

Rose threw her hands up in the air. "Argh! I've got to be certifiable even listening to a plan like this. You have been around Steve way too long!"

"People have been telling me that a lot lately."

"Fine, don't just stand there. Let's get her on her feet."

The two propped Angelica up between them. "Where to?" asked Amy.

"Yasaka Shrine, for starters."

"What about the satchel?"

"A decoy. I'll explain later."

The two half-carried, half-dragged Angelica down the path back to Yasaka Shrine. Rose hoped anyone who saw them would figure they looked like a group helping a friend who had over-partied that the night.

As they arrived at the front gate, a figure dressed in white standing under a white bamboo umbrella stepped out of the shadows. Amy was immediately alert, but Rose reassured her, "It's okay, she's one of ours. Yori, Amy Rogers."

"Tango One, it is an honor." She bowed, then turned to Rose. "It went as planned?"

"More touch-and-go than I preferred, but she took the bait. Eventually."

Yori looked at them. "Are you certain it is wise to return with her?"

"Most definitely," said Amy. "Angelica Richards was directly responsible for the attacks in Coronado and New Mexico. I believe she has information about a wider conspiracy behind the attacks. Besides, she's tried to kill me twice." Amy looked sideways at her unconscious charge. "I don't take that lightly."

"Ah, a sibling rivalry. Most serious indeed." She handed Rose a new satchel. "Your package."

Rose took it and handed the gun back. "This might be awkward at the airport."

"I trust it was helpful."

"Sort of, in a way. Although they may be doing renovations at the park for a time."

"We have connections. There will be no repercussions about your misadventure." Yori pointed to a waiting limousine. "This will take you directly to Kansai airport."

"But—"

"Yamanouchi-san felt it prudent you leave immediately."

"Yori, please thank him for us."

"I will convey your sentiments. Allow me to provide you a parting gift as well." The woman reached into the small purse at her side and pulled out a clear case containing a small glass vial with a thick liquid inside and a pair of tiny silver darts.

Amy's eyebrows went up. "A paralyzing agent?"

"Yes. This will render your guest unable to move or speak. I would explain, but, of course, Yasuzume-san, you already know how to use them." She held out her hand.

Amy's mouth opened in surprise.

"Told you. You have fans," said Rose.

Amy made a half-bow, wincing at the pain in her side, and took the items. "*Domo arigato,* Yori-san. I had no idea. I am honored."

She returned it, bowing deeply before her. "*Dōitashimashite.* The honor is mine. I never thought I would have the privilege to meet the legendary Yasuzume in person."

Amy turned to Rose, who winked at her. Amy turned back. "Look, it's not really that big—"

Yori was gone.

"Yeah, she pulled that on me, too," said Rose. "Let me guess. Ninja?"

"Obviously."

"Do you guys have some sort of secret ninja handshake or something? Never mind, don't answer that. Let's just get Sleeping Beauty secured so I can get a good look at that injury of yours."

They deposited Angelica in the back of the limo. Moments later, they were on their way to Osaka and the long flight home.

Chapter 15

The transport van from Dulles pulled into the underground loading dock at Triangle HQ and slowly backed up. A security team stood ready, weapons raised as it halted. The squad leader rapped twice on the back door. There were two knocks in reply. He undid the latch and opened the doors.

Amy and Rose stood there, an unconscious and immobile Angelica Richards on the floor between them. "Morning, boys," said Rose. "Anybody got some coffee? I could sure go for a double-double—"

The security team leader was all business. "Is this the detainee?"

Rose frowned. "Boy, you're going to take all the fun out of this—"

"Rose, shush," said Amy. "They've got a job to do. Her name is Angelica Richards. She is a suspect in the Coronado bombing, as well as the Red Lab attack last summer."

"We transmitted ahead she needs Tango-level containment," added Rose. The security team all tightened grips on their weapons involuntarily. She raised an eyebrow. "Easy, boys, she's taken care of for now."

The security leader raised an eyebrow. "How did you do it?"

"Medication. Dosed with a neuroparalytic on capture and again during the flight," said Amy.

"Impressive. We'll take her from here." He waved over a pair of his men who secured Angelica to a stretcher and wheeled her toward the nearby elevator. He noticed

Amy's wound for the first time. "That looks serious. Do you need me to call a med response team?"

Rose shook her head. "I'll get her to MedBay myself."

"Very well." The security leader paused a moment. "Nice work."

Amy looked up, surprised. "Thanks."

He nodded, then left to follow his men. Amy and Rose exited the van. Rose closed the doors and banged on them. "Good to go." It sped away, headed for the motor pool. She turned around to see Amy sit down gingerly on a bench by the wall. "Dosed again on the flight?"

"Well, she was."

"True, but four times. Sort of shaded the truth there, Roomie." She sat down and gingerly touched the spent biogel patch over the slash on her friend's side. Amy hissed at the contact. "That wasn't just a story about MedBay. You need to go. Now."

"For this? It's just a scratch."

"Another inch lower and we're talking dissection."

Amy grimaced. "So she got a good whack at me. The biogel did its job and you know I heal quickly. I'll be back to normal in—"

"Where have you been?!"

They whirled around at the sound of Steve yelling. Amy frowned as he walked out of the elevator lobby toward them, his pace deliberate. *Hello, Mr. Sunshine.* "Nice to see you, too."

"Don't give me that! I asked you a question."

Amy stood up to meet his challenge. "Excuse me? Since when do you get to talk to me like that?"

"Want to know when? Go off and do something blindingly stupid, like head into the field when you're still not cleared for missions, and without even the most basic of gear!"

Rose stepped between them. "Whoa, slow down a minute, Steve. I asked her to come along. This wasn't a mission or field op. It was just a simple courier run. We had no idea it was going to go sideways. In fact, if Amy

hadn't been there, I would have been in big... trouble..."
She trailed off as she noticed his glare.

He stared at Rose, anger painted across his
features. "Oh, so this is all your fault?!"

"Well, no, I—"

His voice rose. "You knew she wasn't cleared yet!
She could have gotten herself hurt or worse!"

Amy stepped in and pushed him away, hard. He
flew backward and slammed into a wall ten feet away. She
fell to one knee, a grimace on her face." Pain twisted her
words as she yelled at him, "What is it with you people
around here?" Amy staggered to her feet and started to
walk toward him. "*She* is still right here in front of you, you
idiot, so if you want to say something about *me*, say it to
my face!"

She stopped a few paces from Steve. *No. This won't
solve anything.* She forced her hands to her sides,
unclenched her fists and closed her eyes. *Center. Find my
center.* She turned back to Rose. "Maybe you should get
those files to Marron straight away."

Rose looked warily at the two of them. "You sure?"

"Yeah, I've got this."

Rose nodded. She walked over to her. "Good luck.
And go to MedBay."

"Thanks, Mom."

Rose cast a last worried glance back before the
elevator doors closed, leaving the two of them alone.

Steve stood up and leaned against the wall, rubbing
his neck. "Ouch. That hurt."

"You and me both," she said. "Sorry."

"I probably deserved it." He sighed. "How could you
be so—?"

"Stupid? You really want to go there again?"

"I was going to say reckless."

She turned and started walking away. "Why does it
matter to you?"

He followed her. "Why? Amy, you were alone out
there, in Kyoto, without any backup."

"I wasn't alone. I had Rose."

He scoffed. "Rose? Get real. We both know she'd never be able to handle herself in a real fight."

"Don't underestimate my girl there. After all, the two of us together just took down Angelica Richards."

"You got lucky, the two of you out there with no gear on you."

"Well—"

"What do you mean, well?"

"The weather forecast said rain, so I sort of borrowed an umbrella."

"From Quincey's shop? Which one?"

"Titanium blade. Saved my life."

"How so?"

Amy reached into her pocket and pulled out the black hilt, then pressed a control. A cloud of nanites poured out and formed a blade. "To the victor go the spoils."

Steve looked in surprise. "That's—"

"The nanite sword from the Red Labs attack. Angelica boasted she was there. Quincey's going to be beside himself when he gets his hands on it."

"What was she doing on Kyoto, anyway?"

"Trying to beat Rose to the archives." She looked downs at the concrete for a moment. "Steve, whoever these people are, they're always one step ahead of us."

"I know."

"No, I don't think you do." She looked up at him. "Put on that smartest guy in the room cap again. I had time to consider this on the flight back. Mitch Williams' betrayal exposed Triangle in a lot of ways, but I think that's becoming a fallback excuse."

"How so?"

"Somebody knew Mitch was already a weak point to exploit. Plus, how could he have given up this many secrets in so short a time? He would have had to have been debriefing nonstop for weeks We both know that didn't happen."

"What are you thinking? Another traitor? A mole inside the system?"

"Your guess is as good as mine. But until we know, we should assume everything is compromised."

Steve raised an eyebrow. "Watson won't be pleased with you. Bearer of bad news and all."

Amy opened her mouth, but Savannah interrupted. "Medical Emergency. Level 3, Corridor 2A. Immediate Response Required."

Amy's mind flashed to the location. *Marron's Lab. Rose!* "Savannah, what happened?"

"Rose Johannsen has had an unscheduled seizure event on Level 3, Corridor 2A."

Amy didn't think, she just started to activate her talent. As she brought her foot down a third time, the shattering pain sliced through her. *No, Rose needs me. I will not give in this time!* She powered through it, and in a flash was racing down the staircase, it. Pain flared higher, narrowing her field of vision as she burst through the Level 3 door and around personnel frozen in place, papers scattered by the wind of her passage.

As she skidded to a stop in front of her friend, she was driven to her knees as pain slammed into her. She bit back a scream as she reached down to cradle Rose's head and keep her from banging it against the floor. Piercing shards of agony raced through her body, but she ignored them. All that mattered was Rose, her body convulsing as her brain fired off signal after confused signal. "I've got you, Roomie. I've got you."

Steve ran around the corner at a sprint and knelt opposite Amy. She looked at him, tears streaming down her face. "I can't stop this. I can't help her. Steve, what do I do?"

"You're doing fine. Help is on the way." He reached over and turned Rose onto her side. "This will help her breath."

"Is there anything else?"

"No. I've seen these before. The seizure just should run its course. Just keep Rose safe and comfortable." He looked at Amy. "You're the best person in the world for that."

The EMTs from MedBay came running around the corner as well with their emergency packs. One knelt next to Amy and introduced herself. "Egan, lead EMT on call."

"Amy Rogers."

"I remember you, although you probably wouldn't." She checked Rose's pulse. "Savannah, time since the seizure initiated."

"Four minutes, twelve seconds."

"Check her records. Any previous medical history, anticonvulsant meds or protocols in place?"

"Miss Johannsen suffered a traumatic brain injury in a bomb blast last spring. She has an experimental seizure displacement monitor implanted."

Egan looked surprised. "First I've heard of that. What's it do?"

"It's designed to let Rose control when she has her seizures, "said Amy. "She can trigger them in a safe location without causing harm or alarm."

"Looks like it's not working."

"Rose Johannsen has just returned from an assignment to Japan that was stressful," said Savannah. "She planned to trigger in her quarters after delivery of the files to Dr. Marron. The seizure had caught her before she arrived at that location."

Amy heard that and looked up sharply. *Rose said Savannah was monitoring her. Why didn't she warn her?*

Rose's shuddering began to subside. Egan checked her pulse again. "Strong and steady. Savannah, time check?"

"Five minutes, thirty seconds. Her average triggered seizure lasts just over four minutes."

"Right." Egan reached into her pack and pulled out a bottle of fluid.

The seizure quieted, and Rose opened her eyes. "Wh...what happened? Oh, no. Did I—?"

"Quiet, you, you're okay," commanded Egan. She motioned for Steve and Amy to help Rose into a sitting position and handed her the bottle. "Drink this."

"What is it?"

"Electrolytes and vitamins. They say it tastes like strawberries." Egan wrinkled her nose. "They've never had a strawberry in their lives."

Rose took a swig and grimaced. "Yech. Strawberries and gym socks."

"I agree. But after that show, you need to down it all." She glanced at Amy. "Why don't you help her out? Pick all this stuff up for her."

Amy looked up and noticed the scattered papers. The contents of the Wildcard files were strewn to the end of the corridor. *How did she manage to throw them that far?* As she walked to gather them, the light bulb popped on. *Oh. Duh. Talent speed, Amy. Big rush of wind.* She reached down and grabbed the first piece of paper. *Unintended consequences strike again.*

She worked head down, back and forth, methodically picking up piece after piece. She was about halfway back to Rose when she bumped into someone. It was Steve, working his way from the other end of the corridor.

He held up his own stack of paper. "Figured it would go twice as fast."

"Rose?"

"Egan's with her. She's a good tech. Was on the comm with me the whole way back from Coronado when we returned, well, you know. I trust her."

They walked back to Rose. Amy put the papers together and held them up. "A little scrambled, but we have all the notes."

Rose smiled back. "Dr. Marron will make do. Can I get a hand up?" Steve and Amy pulled her upright, then Amy drew her into a hug.

"Don't scare me like that."

"Deal. I'll find a new way to scare you next time."

Egan cleared her throat. "Not if I have anything to do with it. Here are your orders. These two will accompany you to finish your delivery to, then take you back to your quarters, where you're to go to bed." Rose started to smile. Egan added hastily, "Alone."

Her smile turned to a pout. "Spoilsport."

"Your reputation proceeds you, Miss Johannsen. No extracurricular activity for forty-eight hours. You need rest."

"You're the doctor."

"No, but damn close." Egan fixed Steve and Amy with a cross expression. "Lab, then quarters. Nothing funny. Understood?" Steve tossed off a salute. Amy elbowed him in the ribs. "And Rogers?"

"Yes?"

She pointed at Amy's ribs. "I better see you in MedBay by the end of the day for that. Powers and I did too much work for you to go mucking it up like that." She picked up her bag and walked away.

"For that?" Steve looked at Amy's side. "A.J., what the—"

"Steve, not now. Lecture me after we get the patient to bed." Amy thumbed through the papers. "Do I need to put these in order?"

Rose shook her head as she reached for the satchel she'd dropped. "No, got everything Marron needs right here."

"Then who are these for?"

"Me. I'll explain later. Right now, I need to get this satchel to the good doctor." She started toward the lab and wobbled on her feet. Steve grabbed her.

"Whoa, there, Thornbush. Before you do another face plant, let us help you."

She grinned weakly. "You're just trying to take advantage of a girl."

"Not this time. Come on, here we go." Steve draped her arm over his shoulder and handed the satchel to Amy. The three of them weaved their way down the hall and into a side corridor. In moments, they were at the lab assigned to Dr. Marron.

Rose pressed her hand to the doorplate. The door slid aside. Marron was at a desk, head resting on his arms.

Amy walked over to him and shook him gently. "Doctor Marron?"

He poked his head up and blinked groggily. "Yes? What? Sorry, just catching a quick nap." He focused. "I don't know you. But you I remember."

Rose raised a hand. "Yes. Rose Johannsen, sir. You sent me to Japan for the Wildcard notes, remember?"

"Wildcard, right. I was working on possible countermeasures." He stretched and slid off the chair, then looked at her. "I remember you from the briefing. Smart girl. I sent you to Japan."

"Yes. And I'm back." She handed him the satchel.

He took it to the main table in the middle of the lab. "About time. Took you long enough."

"Japan is halfway around the world, Doctor."

"A likely story." He pulled out the file, thumbed through its contents, then put it to one side. He pulled out the black box next and raised an eyebrow. "I don't remember this."

Rose just nodded at it. Marron undid the latch and opened it. His eyes went wide as he pulled out the test-tube full of red liquid with that threw back golden reflections in the light. "Lights full." The room lights came on full. Marron examined the test-tube and looked back at Rose. "How is this possible?"

"It was in the archive."

"This gives me a real chance now, young lady. Thank you."

The three departed for the elevator. As it rose to Level 2 Steve and Amy stood in silence on opposite sides, attention fixed on the controls. The hush continued as the trio walked the nearly empty corridors to Rose's quarters.

Rose palmed the ident pad to unlock it. The door slid aside and she entered. Amy and Steve tried to follow and bumped shoulders, jammed in the doorway. They sprang apart.

"You should go in," said Amy "I need to go to MedBay, after all—"

"No, you're her best friend," interrupted Steve. "It makes more sense for you to help her—"

"But you have been friends much longer—"

"But she's been your partner and roommate more recent—"

"Enough!" Rose exploded as she stepped out between the two. "Yes, you both love me. I'm amazingly lovable. But I'll just tuck myself in so you two can continue your love fest somewhere else. Good night." She walked back into her quarters, then turned around. "Oh, one more thing. Figure it out."

"Figure what out?" asked Amy.

Rose stared at her for a moment, then shook her head. "Really, Amy? Really?" The doors slid shut, and the "Do Not Disturb" symbol appeared on the ident pad.

Amy stared at the door a moment longer. "Oh. That."

Chapter 16

Ceiling lights came into focus as Angelica pushed herself to consciousness. *Wow, that was unpleasant.* She tried to move but found her body unwilling to cooperate.

One step at a time. First, inventory. Angelica concentrated and found she could sense all four of her limbs. A little more effort was rewarded with fingers and toes moving on command. *Good. Some motor control, at least. Whatever happened, it doesn't appear to be permanent.*

She put her head back and winced as it contacted the surface. The pain triggered memories. *I was fighting in Kyoto. With the Triangle agent, the one with the glasses I'd taken the satchel from and... Rogers!* She tried to sit up again. Her body tingled like it was filled with angry bees. She pushed against the sensation and it slowly subsided. Angelica settled upright and put her hands in her lap.

That's better. Yeah, Rogers. She must have gotten the drop on me. Angelica shook her head and winced. *Or dropped something on me. Still hurts. I remember a bright red light, dropping the satchel, then... I'm here. But why didn't I recover from that? I should have been able to—*

Needle marks on her arm stopped her short. *Drugged. Explains how they transported me without it turning into a real party. Some sort of neurotoxin, based on the way I feel.*

She tried to put weight on her feet. It was like stepping on glass. She sucked in her breath and stood anyway. *They drugged me, so they wanted to take me someplace. Let's see where.* With care, she began to examine her surroundings.

Her new home was a Plexiglas cube, fifteen feet on a side. There was a toilet in one corner behind a screen and a low shelf that acted as both a bed and bench. A fold-down table was located at one end of the bench. When extended, it exposed a small hatch in the wall. *Must be where they slide in my meals.* She peeked down at the white jumpsuit someone had dressed her in when she was unconscious and grimaced. *And any other stylish wardrobe options, I'm sure.*

She did one more turn, then leaned her back against the front window of her cage. *All the comforts of home*, she though in a sardonic tone. *This is a temporary cell, not designed to keep anyone on ice long-term.* She cracked her neck from side to side. *Time to show them how temporary.* She scuffed her right foot against the ground. Energy reserves flowed, powering her up and pushing away the last remnants of the neurotoxin. Angelica took a deep breath, then placed her hands against the front Plexiglas panel and began to vibrate them at high speed. *Bet Amelia hadn't figured out this trick yet.* Her whole body became a blur as she started to sink through the surface.

There was a bright flash and loud zap as Angelica was thrown backward from the panel. She landed on her back, hands still vibrating. Outside, yellow security lights began to rotate and a security alarm klaxon. "Breach attempt detected," a voice announced. "Tango Section, Detention Center."

Angelica sat up and slowed her hands to a stop. Her fingertips were scorched, black ash on the edges, her healing factor already regrowing the skin. She frowned. "Oh, that's not playing nice." She looked back at the window. "Not nice at...all?" She stood up, puzzled.

The Plexiglas panel was pristine. There was no evidence she had started to penetrate it, or it had retaliated. Curious, Angelica walked over for a closer look.

It's a simple Plexiglas sandwich, six, maybe eight layers laminated together. I've phased through things much denser than that. So why couldn't I this time? She ran one hand over the surface, watching its reflection. As she did, something reacted to the pressure. *How clever. A liquid crystal layer, probably to opaque the cell. I'll bet you can overpower the holding matrix to serve as an electrified fence.* She wiped the last bits of carbon from her fingers onto her jumpsuit, then tossed off a salute to the camera outside the cell.

Round one to you. As a trio of armed guards in riot gear appeared in front of her cell, weapons raised, she placed her hands behind her head and fell to her knees. "Relax, gentlemen. You knew I had to test my cage. My compliments to the designer."

"I'll pass them along, though I doubt they will matter to her one way or another." From behind the guards emerged a woman of Oriental descent, dressed in a simple black pants suit. She had gray hair and eyes, and an expression that betrayed no emotion. She made a small gesture. The guards lowered their weapons and departed. "Relax, Miss Richards. You and I are simply here to talk."

Angelica raised an eyebrow as she stood. "Nothing is ever that simple."

"You are mistaken. When we speak, I will tell you the truth. Over time, you will come to do the same."

There was something about the way she said it, a flat monotone that lent it a ring of absolute certainty that gave Angelica pause. A small chill of doubt trickled through her. "You're one of them."

The woman bowed slightly to Angelica. "Shall we begin?"

8:34 p.m. EDT

Reg Stevenson watched the women on the wall monitor in his office on the executive level, a frown creasing his brow. "You're sure?"

Watson crossed her arms. "No, I lied to see if I could get a rise out of you."

"Rhonda—"

"Don't you dare, Reg. The last thing I need from you right now is you trying to spin me like one of your politician friends."

"I would never do that to you."

"Bull." She watched the pair on the monitor, staring at each other. "Relax, Reg. Ishii will get answers out of her."

"I'm surprised she agrees to help."

"Desperate times. Just be glad she did. The DNA sample was inconclusive."

"Aren't those things supposed to be up or down?"

"Normally, yes. But her DNA sample has been severely corrupted."

"How so?"

"Enough that if this were any other case, I'd say suggest flowers for the next of kin."

"The point of your testing. Irony."

"You want me to hit you?"

"Not particularly. Back to square one?"

Watson paused. "Actually, one thing did emerge in the results." She brought a diagram up on the monitor.

"What am I—" He trailed off as he examined it. The implication hit him. "This you're sure about?"

Watson nodded. "The signature work is there. It's Zodiac. I should know, better than—"

"Perhaps," he cut her off. "It might be someone mucking about who doesn't realize—"

"Yes, they do, Reg. We've suspected someone was out there, pushing back. This is verifiable proof." She sighed. "We're at the point we need to tell them, if we haven't already passed it—"

"No. They're not ready yet." He stood up and walked to the window. The manicured grounds of the headquarters complex stretched out beneath him.

"How so? Tate and Rogers have proven their worth on a half-dozen of our most challenging missions since we recruited them."

"And she almost got herself killed on the last one."

"An accident—"

"That she caused." He reached into a pocket and pulled out a small black river stone. He rubbed it gently between his fingers. "She doesn't remember me, you know. I used to play with her at the orphanage, before she was settled with her fosters."

"Even more reason she needs to know."

Stevenson barked a laugh. "Really?" He walked over and slammed the stone down hard on his desktop. "Your old partner screwed that, didn't he?"

"Reg, I can't keep apologizing—"

"Of course not. It's not as if you two were knocking boots or anything the whole time you worked together. Or that the day I named you Ops Chief over him it left me with an enormous blind spot that may yet be the death of us. How the hell I missed that one is still a mystery to me."

She blushed. "We were both covert ops. We were good at what we did."

"I'll pretend you didn't just say that." He sat down. "What's worse is not how he betrayed us. It's still not knowing to whom."

"Richards is our best lead to that. It's why I called in Ishii."

"You sure she'll find anything?"

Watson folded her arms. "Come on, Reg, this is Ishii. Sure, she's unhappy about Tokyo on principle, but she's a pro. She'll deliver. It's only a matter of time before Richards will talk." She paused for a moment, then murmured, "There's another thread I'm considering."

"Besides Ishii? You have an outside lead?"

"Not quite." She pointed at the chromosome report on the monitor. "I think we need to have a conversation."

"Isn't that what's happening?"

"Not quite, Reg." Watson sat down across from the man. "Don't you remember what it was like then, everyone scrambling, trying to find their place." She looked at him. "Trying to stay alive."

He drummed his fingers on the table. "Fine. I'll go talk to her."

"No, Reg. This time, you need to stay out. Let me talk to Richards myself."

"I don't think that's a smart idea, but when it comes to Talents, I'll follow your lead."

She nodded, then looked for a moment at a picture on Stevenson's desk. Picking it up, she walked over to the window with it. For a moment, she looked at it, then stared out over the grounds. "Reg, do you have a way to contact Trinity Williams?"

"Mitch's twin sister?" Stevenson leaned back and stared at the ceiling. "Trin and I haven't talked for, well, it'll be a dog's age now. And with her brother gone, I doubt she'd want to. But there is a way to contact her. I suggest an intermediary."

"Tiger Team's not currently on assignment."

"Tyson and Frederick? Are they read in on Tango?"

Watson chuckled. "They figured out Tango on their own even before you brought Tate and Rogers aboard. I'd say they're good with it."

"Fine. Make it official, then have them make contact. But tell them to play nice, though. Mitch was good, Trin was better. Damned shame we could never get her to join the team."

"If I remember correctly, you might have had something to do with that."

"Perhaps." He opened a desk drawer and pressed a hand to a black box inside it. A white symbol on top lit and it opened. He pulled out an encrypted communication device and started to scroll through a list of contacts.

Watson stood up to leave. "Reg, this shadow ties back into Zodiac. It's time to read Tate and Rogers in. Otherwise, these two will figure things out on their own soon enough. If they do, we'll never get to explain our side."

"I'll think about it."

"Don't think too long or too hard."

Chapter 17

September 25, 10:37 a.m. EDT

Steve and Heather walked into the cafeteria on Level 3 and held open the door for a pair of Ops Support maintenance techs balancing cups of coffee. "Sorry," one said around a blueberry muffin occupying a precarious perch on her stack.

"Not a problem, Sharon. Can I have a car now?"

"Not a chance."

Heather chuckled. "Always the charmer."

"I have my moments." He scanned the room. "Hey, Amy's here. Let's sit with her."

Heather raised an eyebrow. "Why?"

"Because she's my partner?"

"Not on this mission. Besides, Dana will be joining us. We can discuss—"

"Field tactics." He sighed. "Look, we just spent ninety minutes in the Danger Room. How about we knock off tactics, drills, and stuff for a little while and just be people, okay?"

"It doesn't work that way, Sport—"

"What doesn't?" Amy walked up beside her, scooping out the last bits of yogurt from her cup. "Oh, hey, Steve."

"Hey, Second Most." He grinned at her.

She stifled a laugh and blushed. "No, seriously, what doesn't? From the looks of it, and the smell of him, you two just did a heavy session in the Danger Room. What did you do, parkour?"

Steve grinned. "Course Four."

"Nassau? I'm sorry I missed that."

"Still saving that for something special with you. Anyway, we followed up with hand-to-hand."

Amy raised an eyebrow and looked at Heather. "And he's still breathing? Methinks you went easy on him."

"Hey!" Steve started to protest, but Amy raised a hand.

"Shush, grownups talking here."

Heather shook her head. "Not quite sure about that. But I didn't go that easy on him. Steve's hand-to-hand skills weren't what I expected at all. Quite a challenge at times."

He glanced at the Brit, one side of his mouth quirked up in a half-smile. "Thanks, I think. Blame Amy there. She's my sensei."

"Oh?"

"Taught me everything I know, one slam to the mat at a time. I've still got most of the lumps to prove it."

Amy held back a laugh and tried to look serious. "A bit stubborn at times, but when he gets it, he really does."

Steve watched as Heather seemed to reappraise Amy. "If you can train him, Rogers, then you really must be almost as good as they say."

Oh crap, not again. He stepped between the two women. "Hey, why don't we sit down and have some—"

"What's that supposed to mean?" Amy snapped, any trace of civility gone.

"Just that it would have been nice to beat down an opponent for once I wouldn't need to pull punches with."

Steve stood his ground between them, trying to play peacemaker. "Look, we're all on the same team here. Let's just all take a step back and—"

"Beat down? You seriously think you can beat me?"

"Know. Just sorry I'm not going to get the chance since you went and put yourself on the sidelines."

"Put myself on the sidelines?" Amy's voice rose two octaves in indignation.

Steve flinched even as he agreed. *What the hell are you doing, Heather?*

"You could have avoided your injury, Rogers, if you'd just waited for backup. Rookie mistake. Cost you your partner. For a while, at least."

Amy lunged at Heather. Steve held her back. "Don't," he whispered to her before he turned around. *Nobody does that to my partner.* As he faced Heather, he dropped into slow-time.

The atmosphere switched to the brilliant cobalt blue, light coming evenly from all sides. Data began to appear from various people and objects in the space around him. *I need to de-escalate this before it grows into a knock-down, drag-out fight. Something that takes Heather down a peg or two.* It took him a few seconds to spot his trigger. *That'll work just fine.* He moved and put the item in place, then dropped back into real time.

He'd only been out of phase for a fraction of a second, but the flicker had the desired effect. Heather paused and shifted attention to him instead of Amy. "What just happened?"

"Nothing." He took a bite of a banana.

"Where did you get that from?"

"This? Oh, I had it. I love bananas. Potassium, vitamins—"

There was a squeal and someone their right yelled, "Watch it!" The trio turned to see a female cafeteria worker carrying a tray of desserts slip on something on the floor – a banana peel.

Heather ducked out of the way as the woman, in desperation, reached out and dropped the tray onto a table before she fell and hit the floor. The crowd in the cafeteria collectively groaned as people rushed to aid her.

Amy started to move to help, but Steve held out a hand and pulled her a step backward. "Wait for it."

"Wait for what?"

He counted the seconds silently in his head. "This."

One of the men helping said, "Davi, your ankle might be broken. Someone, contact MedBay while I get the air splint." He reached up to the table for leverage to pull himself up. Instead, he grabbed the edge of the tray and pulled down.

At this point, simple mechanics got involved. The side of the table acted as a fulcrum, the tray as a lever, and all those desserts as a payload, launched through the air.

Directly at Heather.

She never knew what hit her. Steve did, though. Thirty-four plates of crème Brulee, nineteen slices of carrot cake and seven bowls of lime Jell-O. Heather stood there for a moment in shock, eyes shut.

Steve's commlink beeped. "Tango One," he answered.

"Triangle, Tango One. Good morning, Steve."

"Ethan, to what do I owe the pleasure? I thought we were on standby?"

"'Were' is the operative word. Briefing room C-19, thirty minutes."

"I'm assuming this is for Echo Seven as well?"

"Yes, why?"

"Access surveillance video from my location."

There was a brief pause. "What the blazes happened?"

"Culinary Armageddon. I doubt thirty will give her enough time to clean up."

"I entirely agree. I'll advise the Director. Sixty minutes, C-19. Triangle, out."

He looked over at Heather, who'd just finished her own conversation with her controller. "Looks like you've gotten into a sticky situation."

She glowered at him. "You choose now for one of your idiotic puns?"

"They're bad at times, but they're not idiotic." He walked over and scooped cream cheese frosting off her shoulder with a finger. "Some might even say they're tasteful." He licked the frosting from his finger as he ducked under the swing she took at him. "Now, now, no time for that. We've got a briefing in an hour with Watson, and you need to clean up. I doubt she wants you to cater the meeting."

"Oy, just shove off." She turned and left, a trail of spent confections in her wake.

He turned around just in time to catch Amy as she wrapped him in a hug. "That was incredible."

"It was, if I may say so myself."

She chuckled. "So's your ability to pat yourself on the back."

"Come on, I need to change. Let's walk and talk." They started for his quarters.

It took a couple of minutes. Steve kept looking over, wondering if she was going to say anything, but Amy seemed content to walk in silence.

"I would have had her, you know."

"Course you would," Steve agreed. "Heather's not one of us. Not a fair fight, so we avoid those. Brains, not brawn, Second Most."

She giggled. "That's your new nickname for me? I kind of like it, although I am at a disadvantage."

"How so?"

"It wasn't really an invitation that time, as you remember."

He shook his head. "What, you want me to call you A.J. again? I wish you would make up your mind."

"And I wish you would, too, sometimes." She sped up her pace. He moved to catch up.

They said nothing else until they reached the door to his quarters. At that point, he stood there. So did she, looking at him. He cleared his throat.

"I guess I should get ready. For my briefing."

"Yes. I guess you should."

They still stood there.

This is ridiculous. I've been on tour. I had women throwing themselves at me all over the world. So why am I utterly clueless with this one? Just invite her in. Just tell her how you feel. Just—

"You know, for someone so smart, so observant, you are pretty oblivious."

Her words shocked him. "Wh-huh? How so?"

"Because you still don't get us." She sighed. "I'm starting to think you never will." Amy began to go.

No. Don't let her walk away! He didn't think, he acted. He grabbed her arm and pulled her close—

"There you two are!"

Steve groaned. *You have got to be kidding me.* He shared a look with Amy, then they both turned to see Rose Johannsen hurrying toward them.

"Rose, what are you doing here?" asked Amy.

"Savannah warned me of a possible conflict between you and Anjili at the Level 3 cantina, so I headed down. No rumble, but Grand Theft Dessert everywhere."

"That would be Steve. His way of defusing the situation."

"One of your mousetraps? I'll get the magical details later. Anyway, people saw Heather go one way and you two the other."

"That was a while ago—"

"I went to Amy's quarters first. It was closer, and—"

"Amy walked with me here. We were discussing dealing with Heather and other stuff," said Steve.

"Like what?"

"You know. Stuff."

"Yes," agreed Amy. "Stuff."

Rose looked back and forth between them. "Ah. Stuff."

"As much as I find this conversation fascinating, I've got to get ready for that briefing. Rose, nice to see you. Amy, thanks for the chat." He paused. "Oh, Amy, after the briefing, maybe we could get together later for, uh..." He looked at Rose and grinned. "Dessert?"

Rose snorted. Amy ignored her. "Sure. I'd like that."

"I'll call you later then." The door slid closed behind him. He leaned back and bumped his head against it. *So close.* He heard muffled voices on the other side.

"You're no help!" said Amy.

Rose chuckled. "You two are so cute. And have absolutely no idea how to be cool about this."

"Oh, and you do?"

225

"Don't have to. Everyone knows I am who I am. The pair of you? No one would believe it."

Steve sighed. *She's right. Nobody would.* He pushed away from the door. *Come on, duty calls.*

Chapter 18

"Richards gave this up, just like that?" Boland scrolled through the text of the briefing on her tablet. "I thought this asset was a real piece of work."

"My interrogator assured me she's become cooperative on her own," said Watson from the head of the table.

Heather raised an eyebrow. "Any enhanced techniques? My experience is these sorts of things often get answers you think you want to hear, rather than what you need to understand."

"Yes, as usual, I'm acutely aware of your background, Agent Anjili. Triangle doesn't do that."

Steve coughed loudly. Ethan next to him shushed him to be quiet. Watson turned and glared at them both. "Anyway, this is off-topic. Back to the matter at hand. This is Maud Stone, the analyst assigned to verify the intel gleaned from the Richards interrogation. Ms. Stone, brief the agents on what you've found."

Steve was sure he'd never met the woman at the end of the table before. *Hard to forget someone like her.* She had black hair with purple highlights cut in a pageboy style, a modest purple turtleneck dress, pale skin and the most deadpan expression he'd ever seen. She made eye contact, her gaze cold and calculating, as if it had been drained of every ounce of humanity. He couldn't help it, he shuddered.

Stone walked over to the large video wall. "Richards identified the device used in the Coronado attacks." An image of a simplified cylinder and bell machine appeared. "It was a chemical synthesis and distribution apparatus, designed for pest vector control – specifically, mosquito abatement in rural areas. An experimental prototype, it was patented but never deployed in India."

Heather frowned. "How does a mosquito sprayer turn into a deadly weapon composed of nanites?"

A second image appeared – the device from Coronado. "The modified version combines three separate DynaRobotics technologies - the pest vector control tech as a base, a precision laser surgery drill amplified in size and strength to cut through the floor above, and the nanite tech to allow on-site construction and breakdown."

Steve considered this. "Someone is thinking outside the box. That device combines systems from, what, three different divisions within D.R.?"

"Four," replied Stone, "including medical research, weapons tech—"

"And whatever black box is behind the nanite production," added Ethan.

Heather looked over at the Director. "I'm beginning to suspect Pradeep is sitting in the opposite chair on the chess match."

"The thought has occurred to me, Agent Anjili. More than once. But I still haven't figured out why. Proceed, Miss Stone."

"As Agent Anjili surmised, the compound produced was indeed a mix of white phosphorus and hexachloroethane. But it was encapsulated within a unique protein shell."

"A shell?" asked Steve. "How does that work?"

"The proteins were coded to interact with the mucous membranes, so they would only break down in contact with them. Thus, it would only release the chemicals once inside the respiratory system. Basically, it burned the victims inside out from their lungs."

Ethan blanched at the description. "That's insidious."

"I doubt the designers had the kindest of intentions." Steve glanced at Heather. "The debris Amy found in your soot. Savannah identified it as nanite fragments before we went to India."

Heather nodded and turned to Stone. "Why would there be nanites in the smoke? Does it tie into the device design, or the protein shell in some way?"

Stone pressed a control on the remote she held. The image changed to an animated diagram. "Working with Red Labs, we have developed a working hypothesis. When the device released its gas cloud, in addition to the chemicals nanites were included in the mix. While airborne, nanites manufactured protein shells and filled them with the toxic agent. Once completed, the nanites self-destructed and became part of the general particulate detritus in the gas cloud."

"Has anything like this been used before?" asked Boland

"Intel was able to match this weapon to a war crimes case in the files of the French DGSE. Nineteen months ago, a similar weapon was used in the South Sudan. 347 people were killed. Witnesses from neighboring villages referred to it as the Red Death. However, a nanite connection was never identified at the time."

"Probably because no one was looking for it," said Watson. "A chemical warfare attack during a regional skirmish war isn't usually in our mission scope."

"Where have I heard that line before?" grumbled Heather. She looked at Stone. "Any idea who was behind it?"

"The insurgents who deployed it were captured two days later by AMISOM troops, assisted by US Special Operations Command Africa. They were identified as members of Scorpio."

Damn. Steve growled, "The Law of Unintended Consequences. Butterfly Effect. Whatever!" Steve slammed both hands down on the table. Everyone jumped, startled. He looked up at the ceiling and blew out a breath. "Sorry," he said. "I just can't believe it. This would have been, what, just a few months later?"

"You were just trying to do right by a mate," Heather said gently.

"Yeah, but at what cost. I mean, seriously, we were just one match, Heather; it is starting to feel like we set the world on fire." He shook his head. "This is strong evidence Coronado really was a revenge attack for Scorpio."

Stone nodded. "Richards admitted she was contracted to do that."

Boland frowned. "Right. Anyone else here a fan of magic?"

Watson looked puzzled. "Magic?"

"You know, hocus-pocus?" She held up a quarter and rolled it through her fingers. "Hey, look at me, great big flashy stuff here, while what I really want to do is—" She snapped her fingers and the quarter disappeared. "Going on somewhere else."

"Where's the quarter, Dee?" asked Heather.

"Not the question to ask. Here's one. Why did Richards feed us all this information about the Red Death and Scorpio?"

Ethan nodded. "Because it means we're not looking for where Wildcard and the nanites are."

Boland pointed at him. "Precisely."

Watson looked at the Intel analyst. "Well, Miss Stone?"

"Their analysis is sound. Pardon me for one moment." She went to the conference table and started to type on the smart surface.

Watson looked around the table. "While Ms. Stone is busy, let's get an update from Dr. Marron. Savannah, give me a video link to his lab." The wall screen switched to an active video conference.

Marron's lab was a virtual hive of activity. A half-dozen assistant monitored sequencers, working on formulas written on whiteboards, examining samples under microscopes and on monitors. The doctor looked up to see the screen.

"Ah, Director. Sorry for not greeting you directly."

"Quite all right, Doctor. Just checking in."

Marron stifled a yawn. "Hard at it. Not as young as I used to be, but I would have given my eye teeth for these tools back then."

"Any progress so far?"

"Some. I read the reports that Agent Tate had recovered what appeared to be a delivery device from Coronado, so I had it sent over. Turns out we could recover traces of the newly developed Wildcard formula from it."

"That sounds like a break, Doctor. What have you learned?"

"It's remarkably similar to our reference sample. In fact, if I didn't know better I'd swear it was Gwen's work. But that's impossible."

"How so?"

"Doctor Hampton died in 1996," said Stone without looking up.

Watson looked back at the screen. "So, your colleague had an admirer."

"Or a student in the interim."

"It gives us somewhere to look. Anything else?"

"Yes. They're close to a breakthrough."

"How close?" asked Steve.

"For one thing, Coronado wasn't a test to see if Wildcard worked. They were testing how long."

"How long?" asked Steve.

Marron walked over to the nearest whiteboard and drew a pair of lines. He pointed to the lower one, then the upper. "Normal, and enhanced. Wildcard succeeds by using nanites to rewrite DNA on the fly." Marron then drew a curve showing the how performance leveled and dropped off. "As long as the Wildcard nanites are active, they can continually rewrite the DNA to maintain their matrix, reinforcing the changes to the subject's body even as cells die and are replaced. But that takes energy – it uses the body's own stored chemical energy to do so. Think of it as miles per gallon in a car engine. The more efficient the nanites become, the longer they can work."

"And when the gas tank goes empty?" asked Boland.

"They body begins to break down faster than they could repair the damage. That's why Jasmine Hernandez weakened and could be beaten by an inferior opponent – no offense, Agent Anjili." Heather bristled at the reference but said nothing. "It starts slowly, but it's like a cascade failure and eventually, a system crash. Death due to multiple organ failures. The process must have continued in Jasmine's body even after she was killed. It would explain why her body looked so different inside the cryo unit."

"Bloody hell." Heather shook her head at the thought of what that woman had gone through.

"You said they were close, Doctor." Watson leaned forward. "How so?"

"Days. No more than a couple of weeks. They'll have a version that will be viable for use, that will delay that downslope long enough to accomplish any major mission task."

"Hang on," said Steve, his hand raised. "Aren't we forgetting something? This stuff wasn't supposed to be for suicide squads only. Use it, reverse it, use it again as needed. You know, lather, rinse, repeat? Doc, is there an antidote, a Wilder Card, or something?"

Marron paused and scratched his head. Heather looked at him and mouthed "Wilder card?" He shrugged.

"Agent Tate, I understand your concern. That was listed in the original set points for Project Atlas. But I've checked through the notes. None of my colleagues ever developed a counter-serum. This process appears irreversible – once it starts, the new matrix fights to maintain its dominance, and the damage it leaves behind when it no longer has the energy to support that is too devastating to recover from."

"That's it? It's a death sentence?"

"In a manner of speaking, yes."

"Doctor, there has to be something you can do."

He sighed and looked at the ceiling. "I'm a doctor, not a magician. I can't misdirect..." He trailed off, focused on something only he could see. Steve knew that look. *He's figured out something.*

"Doctor Marron, you were saying?"

Marron didn't answer, he just reached over and turned off the video feed.

Watson stared wide-eyed at the screen for a moment. "Savannah, get that link back immediately."

"Dr. Marron has initiated a privacy lock."

"Override it!" she sputtered. "We're not through talking!"

"Actually, Doc, I believe you are," said Steve, trying not to laugh. "Come on, you've dealt with Red Lab types over the years. You saw that look. He twigged on something at the end. It gave him a brilliant insight that's going to solve our problem. Just let him work on saving our bacon."

Watson's tone was chilly. "Are you finished?"

"Certainly."

"Fine. It is still an issue, though. I need from Dr. Marron some ideas about what firms might be capable of this type of bioengineering. It was his field, after all."

"Noir Papillion," said Stone.

Everyone turned to the analyst as she looked up from the corner of the table. "What was that name?" asked Watson

"Noir Papillion. A French-based multinational firm with subsidiaries in manufacturing, pharmaceuticals, and chemicals. Its principal stockholder is also Kumar Pradeep."

"I'm starting to think Amy and I should have looked this gentleman up personally," said Steve.

"Ms. Stone, any overlap between the nanite production locations Agents Tate and Anjili recovered from DynaRobotics and chemical on nanite production and chemical production facilities that might lead to these weapons?"

The analyst looked at the tabletop for a moment. "I have several with Mirrorball correlation to our suspect—"

Watson raised an eyebrow. "Mirrorball? I didn't authorize deployment—"

"Ma'am, you did say to use any resources to find the woman involved in the Coronado attack. We used Mirrorball to search every social media image in the world over the last thirty days and tied in a facial recognition search for Agent Rogers. We then eliminated any images where we were sure Agent Rogers had in fact been in that location, either socially or on assignment. It gave us a pretty good footprint of the detainee's movements before and after the incident."

"You tracked where Richards was by figuring out where Amy wasn't? That's sneaky," said Steve. "I like it."

"Okay, I'll bite," said Boland. "Where'd she go?"

"There are six locations, in order of frequency - Belize City, Coronado, Key West, Arizona, the Puget Sound area near Seattle and middle Tennessee."

"Coronado makes sense, given what happened," said Heather. "But Belize City? Why?"

"It has a pair of manufacturing facilities. One is a DynaRobotics Medical Technology plant that multiple intelligence agencies have identified as a front for the company's dark weapons group."

"That's strike one."

Stone moved to a second image. "On the waterfront is a Noir Papillion refinery. Six days before the Coronado event, Angelica Richards walks in—"

An image of Angelica walking through a gate, followed by one of her driving out in a tanker truck.

"An hour later, she leaves. Five minutes after that, according to Mirrorball, she disappears from Belize City."

Ethan scrunched his face up, confused. "Wait, disappears? As in literally vanishes?"

"We can follow her and that truck into a neighborhood into the middle of the city. But the next image from the camera, the vehicle is missing, and there are no further pictures of either one anywhere in the city that day. Nor anywhere else that Mirrorball can detect."

"In the world?" asked Heather.

"What did I tell you?" noted Boland. "Now you see me, new you..." She expanded her hands like a puff of smoke. "When did she show up?"

"When Agent Anjili saw her. In Coronado."

"What about the truck?" asked Boland.

"We conducted a separate Mirrorball on it. It returned one image from ten days ago." The picture was an aerial shot of a burnt-out shell, barely recognizable, in the middle of a desert.

"Where was this taken?" asked Steve.

"Park service fire response unit in Utah."

"Utah?" Ethan stood up and walked over to look closer. "But that's over two-thousand miles. How'd it get there? There's no road anywhere around it."

Steve point at the image. "Ethan, look closer. There aren't any tire tracks or footprints. It's like it appeared out of thin air."

Stone nodded. "Correct, Agent Tate. Based on the damage analysis, the vehicle was dropped from a height of at least two-thousand feet."

He paused and looked at her. "It appeared out of thin air - in mid-air?"

"Yes."

Boland whistled again. "And now you don't."

Watson nodded. "Tate, Anjili, head to Belize City and figure out how she did it. Assume that both Wildcard and Red Death are being manufactured there. See who's behind them, stop them, and shut them down."

"Yes, ma'am." Heather stood up and started for the door. "You coming, Tate?"

Boland raised a hand. "You two might want to slow your roll just a smidge. Belize may not be quite so target-rich." He slid his hand forward to push a video file from the tabletop onto the video wall. It began to play. "This is from CNN International, 36 hours ago."

Fires raged across a series of building in the middle of the night as residents scrambled for cover. A massive fireball burst into the sky over them, knocking the cameraman to the ground before the image froze. They all read the chyron – Chemical Explosion in Belize City.

Heather pinched the bridge of her nose. "The Papillion Refinery?"

"Yes. Latest update says two dozen surrounding buildings destroyed, including two apartment buildings, a hospital, and the DynaRobotics facilities. The death toll is 136, including forty-nine children."

Steve stared at the image. He was very, very still. "The timing is too convenient."

Stone nodded. "Given our activities at the DynaRobotics facilities and capture of Angelica Richards, an attempt to eliminate evidence is logical."

"Logical?" Boland exploded. "Killing over a hundred people is logical to you?"

The analyst looked at her calmly. "I did not say it was right."

"We're not done, yet," said Ethan. "Remember what Dr. Marron said. Whoever this was is almost ready to go again."

The Director looked down the table. "What's your thinking, Mr. Nowitzki?"

"They have been working on their next version since Coronado. But the capture of Angelica Richards must have been a planned-for contingency. If not, destroying what would appear to be their primary production and fabrication site would be—"

"Counterproductive. It would be them scuttling the boat on their own plan," said Watson."

"Yes, Director. Considering everything these people have gone to, I can't see them throwing in the towel so easily on this gambit."

Steve looked at his controller. "Well look at you, getting all clever. You get a cookie."

"Don't go biscuit crazy just yet, mate. It's still a theory." He looked past Steve at Stone. "That list you gave us, Maud. Did any of those locales have either a DynaRobotics or Papillion facility that Richards visited?"

The analyst sat with her data for a moment. "There are facilities in Key West and Seattle."

"Which is most likely?"

"She visited Key West more often."

Ethan looked back at the table. "As I said, it is only a theory, but wouldn't she have also visited the backup facility, just to ensure things were going to be handed off smoothly?"

Watson frowned. "Perhaps. Or there could be some other reason, and it's simply bait. But for now, it's the strongest lead we have. Run with it."

Steve and Heather looked at each other and smiled. "The Conch Republic it is." Heather swiveled in her chair to face Boland. "Dana, contact Transport. Tell them we need a flight south and a vehicle on arrival."

"And tell them I can drive now," added Steve.

"In your dreams," replied Boland.

"I'll get started on analysis of the island," said Ethan, "and try to narrow down the possible targets for you."

Steve crossed over to him. "Good. Find out what kind of real-time surveillance assets are available."

"On it." He leaned over and whispered in Steve's ear. "You better break the news to Amy quick."

Steve nodded. "Right."

Watson walked over to them. "Your orders will be waiting on arrival. By then we'll have a better idea what we'll need. Be flexible, but be prepared to take whatever actions are necessary, including sanction. Understood?"

"Yes, ma'am."

"Good luck." She left. Stone followed close behind.

Heather looked at Steve. "Rewriting DNA? Sounds like Wildcard tries to make people into something more, and ends up making them something less."

"That's one way of looking at it. If they ever stabilize it, there's no 'less' to it, though. Superpowers become a reality, not just comic-book."

"Not so sure if that's a good or a bad thing."

Steve paused a moment, careful with his reply. "Depends on what you do with it. Would you ever trust people with those sorts of abilities?"

She sized him up for a moment as if fitting him for a superhero suit, before shaking her head. "No, I wouldn't."

"Not even yourself?"

"Especially not myself." With a strong wave, she cut off the images on the wall. "Come on. Key West awaits."

Chapter 19

September 26, 11:39 a.m. EDT

The Triangle SUV parked across from the provided address on Caroline Street on Key West. Steve and Heather got out and stretched after their long drive on the Overseas Highway. He looked at her over the roof and groused, "Don't see why you wouldn't let me drive."

"Because I had to sign for the bloody thing. That was a first."

"He has this tendency to play rough with his toys," Ethan agreed over their commlink.

His expression was pained. "How many times do I have to explain it wasn't my fault?! The rebels blew it up!"

Heather grinned. "My guess? Lots."

He sighed and looked up. The sun dodged in and out among fluffy clouds as a breeze blew down the street, stirring the humid air. Tourists wandered along nearby Duval Street, some ducking into the tavern on the corner for a quick drink. "I could get used to this."

"Too bad we're here for work, not play," said Heather as she opened the back of the SUV.

He walked around to meet her. "A little play never hurt anyone. Besides, if we don't, we'll stand out like sore thumbs."

"Ain't that the truth," said a voice behind them.

They turned to find themselves face to chest with a mountain of a man, broad-shouldered, with a snow-white mustache and matching hair in a ponytail under a worn Detroit Tigers ball cap. He wore a tropical print shirt, shorts, and flip-flops.

239

He clapped Steve on the shoulder. "Steven, you dog! You have got to be livin' right to have such a beautiful lady hangin' anywhere near you." Before Steve could reply, the man turned to Heather. "Allow me to introduce myself, since I doubt Steven here ever will. Tends to be a bit slow on the formalities. Thomas M. Sullivan, late of the fightin' Sullivans of Detroit." He bent down and kissed Heather's hand.

She grinned. "Oh, I like him. A pleasure to meet you, Thomas. So how did you meet Steve?" Steve noticed she'd casually moved her arm where her SAVANT could be used.

The man's grin grew even wider. "Believe it or not, I was Steven's first *parkour* trainer, back before he knew how to woo such charming women."

Steve tried not to choke in surprise. Heather's expression was incredulous. "You taught Steve FreeRunning?"

"Why, certainly. All those days back in the Triangle district, working on basics with him."

Steve was suddenly alert. "I have a new trainer now, the name of Ethan."

"Codeword confirmed. I hear you, Tango Two," murmured his controller over the commlink. "Running voice identification on your visitor. Keep him talking."

Steve stepped closer to position himself between Heather and Sullivan. "Heather's a friend who's come for a visit from out of town."

"London" she volunteered.

"You remember, London, don't you, Tommy? It's where I pulled off the Double Watson for the first time."

"The Double Watson?" Heather turned, confused. "I don't remember—"

Sullivan laughed, a loud, deep roar. "Oh, yeah. The Double Watson." He clapped Heather on the shoulder and almost knocked her over. "Wow, that means you must have seen it in person!"

She looked back and forth between them, lost. "Uh...sure?"

"Oh, that had to be awesome. Historic, even. It's one of my favorite moves Steven does. He starts by running at some steps—"

Steve broke in before the big man could get moving. "Tommy, it's been a long drive. Let's at least get our stuff inside first before you start showing off for my lady friend here."

"Typical Steven. Business before pleasure." He helped pull out and sort the bags. Sullivan insisted on carrying Heather's gear. They crossed the street and climbed a set of wooden stairs to an upstairs loft apartment, the white paint faded and peeled from the tropical sun.

On the steps, Ethan came back. "He's legit. Voice print indicates Mister Sullivan, if somewhat colorful, is one of ours."

"Thanks."

"All part of the service. And I look forward to seeing the Double Watson on display in the Danger Room next time you're back."

"Just shut up."

Ethan chuckled and said, "Triangle, standing by."

In front of him, Sullivan had a patter going with Heather as they reached the top of the stairs. "Steven was the only one I taught could ever pull off the Double Watson."

"You don't say."

"Oh, yeah. Now me, I had other tricks I never taught the lad. The Twisted Camel. The Blind Cobra. The Elemental Squirrel. Good times, I tell ya."

She was trying hard not to laugh as he put down the bags and fished out a set of keys from his pocket. He went to hand them to her, but they slipped and fell to the ground. "Oops."

She raised an eyebrow, then bent down to pick it up. Steve watched the Sullivan eyeing Heather's figure and shook his head.

Sullivan caught his eye and smiled. "Good times."

"Hey, peep show!" Sullivan's smiled faded as he looked down at an unhappy Heather Anjili. "One look's free, mate. One and one alone. Next one'll cost ya dearly. Got it?"

He held up both hands. "No harm meant, just admiring—"

"The scenery. Gah, you'd think one of you would come up with an original line by now." She unlocked the door and held it open. "Well, go on, those bags aren't going to carry themselves."

Sullivan picked up the bags and scurried past her, still grinning even as he avoiding eye contact. She looked at Steve, who just smiled.

"Well, what are you waiting for?"

"Elemental Squirrel?" He leaned against the door frame, laughing.

She rolled her eyes. "Oh, sod off. You're embarrassing me." She pushed him through the door and closed it.

Sullivan had dropped the happy-go-lucky persona and was moving bags about the room with efficiency. He walked over and took Steve's. "I apologize for the improvised call sign back there. You two came in quick."

Heather looked at Steve. "Ethan confirmed. Our friend here is Triangle."

Sullivan walked over. "Tom Sullivan, Quartermaster Branch. We secure facilities and supplies as needed for agents in the field and then dispose of them. Housing, weapons," he looked pointedly at Steve with a raised eyebrow. "Vehicles."

Steve groaned. "Not you, too."

"You're something of a legend, Agent Tate. Anyway, this was a new one for me. Discreet housing on Key West with surveillance capabilities in less than twenty-four hours. During tourist season, no less. Lucky I'm creative. Follow me."

They went to the back wall of the loft. Sullivan reached up and twisted the thermostat a quarter turn to the right. It clicked, and a hidden door swung inward. Sullivan led them through to a concealed room.

Steve took a quick inventory. *Desks with computers and flat screens, bulletins with a map of the island and the keys, white board with partially erased names. An awful lot of electrical plugs along the walls.* He looked at their host. "Grow house?"

"Right on one. What tripped you?"

"All the electrical power," said Steve.

"The thermostat," said Heather.

He turned to her. "Thermostat?"

"Of course. Didn't you already spot the one next to the kitchen? This one had to be fake. I'm guessing DEA seized operation."

Sullivan chuckled. "Point to her."

"So where are the landlords?" asked Steve.

"Our DEA friends received a tip this morning that now puts them moored on a luxury yacht 500 yards off Sugarloaf Key for an extended stakeout. They're out of your hair until you tell me you're clear."

Heather sat down at one of the computers and logged in. Steve watched over her shoulder as it booted up almost instantly. A set of video images appeared. "What's this?"

"Our friends here are jacked in real-time to the island's security camera network. Public safety, private, bank ATM's, etc., they can access it. And so can your controllers, effective," Sullivan typed in a command string, "now."

"That'll help."

"One thing. The original owners were paranoid, so the room is a Faraday cage. Close that door, no signals in or out. That means no commlinks, no wireless, your cell phone, useless."

"Got it."

Steve sniffed the air and headed back into the apartment. His mouth began to water. "What's that smell?"

Sullivan sighed. "The only drawback. The downstairs tenant is a pretty popular Brazilian restaurant."

Steve grinned. "Only a drawback if we're worried about our girlish figures. Ouch!" he yelped as Heather hit him from thirty feet with a sandal. "What was that for?" She just glowered at him through the doorway and turned back to the computer.

Sullivan chuckled. "You deserved that. Well, my work is done." He started for the front door. "Oh, one last thing. Your storm prep checklist is on the kitchen counter. I suggest you get to it."

Heather came out quickly from the back room. "Excuse me, did you just say storm prep?"

"The forecast calls for some weather. Just a little one, Cat One. Maybe Cat Two at most."

Heather looked at Steve, confused. "Cat One?"

His smile was gentle as he put a hand on her shoulder. "Category One. He means a hurricane."

"You call that some weather?" She pushed his hand away, annoyed. "A hurricane was not in the mission plan."

Sullivan chuckled. "It never is, Sweets. Just sayin', be ready to batten down the hatches. They should have one heck of a party going at the place on the corner if you're up for that sort of thing. If it gets too severe and you need to evac, I'm three hours away on the mainland."

"You'll be monitoring?"

"What kind of landlord would I be otherwise?" He fished out a second set of keys from a pocket out and tossed them to Heather. "Your controllers can page me, 24/7. And I can come in hot if needed." He pulled up his shirt to reveal a holster with a revolver in it.

"Wait," said Heather. "I patted you down when I hugged you—"

"True. But did you do it right, or did I distract you at just the right moment with tales of the Twisted Squirrel?"

"Elemental Squirrel," corrected Steve.

She stared at him in shock. "That's sneaky."

"Probably good he's on our side, then." Steve went and shook Sullivan's hand. "Nicely played. She'll be going on about that for hours. Now let me get to work."

"Gotcha. Good luck." He walked out the front door. A minute later the throaty purr of a Harley roared to life on the street and faded away.

Steve turned back. Heather was still going over her moves, trying to figure out how he'd pulled that switch on her. He cleared his throat. "Be it ever so humble." Heather looked up at him. She was less than pleased. Way less than pleased. *She does not take well to being shown up.* "While you work that out, why don't I put the bags in the bedrooms."

"I guess." She went back to her new obsession.

"Any preference to which one?"

"Whatever."

He grabbed her bags and placed them in the room closest to the secure office, then took his into the other bedroom on the opposite side of the bathroom. As he began to unpack, he contacted Headquarters.

"Go ahead, Tango Two," said Ethan.

"Okay, Triangle. Did you know about the storm?"

"Invest 92-L developed into Tropical Depression Six in the past twelve hours. We're not even sure it's going to be anything."

"Locals seem relatively sure. They're prepping as if."

"How so?"

He peeked out the window. "Laying in party supplies, it appears. The reputation is well deserved down here."

"I hate to disappoint, but models suggest only a 60-percent chance of even making hurricane strength, let alone the eye passing over Key West. Don't panic."

"I'm not. But I'm not alone on this mission." He paused. "Speaking of which, any word from Amy?"

"No. But she probably doesn't want to distract you."

"True." *I hope so.* "Can you get her a message?"

"Certainly. What do you want to say?"

What do I? Words fail. "Simply tell her, 'Wish You Were Here, Second Most.' She'll get it. Tango Two out."

He finished unpacking and found Heather in the kitchen, working on a meal. "Want me to help?"

"I got this. Set up our vidlink with HQ. I want to go over the latest they've got on this Papillion facility."

"Right." He headed for the secure space and set up both monitors so they faced one desk. "Ethan, you and Boland ready to work your magic?"

One of the monitors switched to show the blonde controller's face. She sneered back. "Took you long enough."

"Don't blame me, it's your boss who was obsessing."

"A, not my boss, and b, that attention to detail is going to save your ass someday."

"Right. Not arguing."

"Good," said Heather, entering the space. "No time for it." She handed Steve a plate full of salad. He sniffed at it and his mouth began to water. He grabbed his fork and took a bite.

Salad should not taste this good. It's salad. Green stuff. "What is this?" He mumbled around a mouth stuffed with veggies.

"You like? Just something I whipped up."

He swallowed. "Whipped up? You were in the kitchen for, what, five minutes?"

"So?"

"So, this is too good!"

She chuckled. "Parents own a restaurant, remember? I might have picked up a trick or two along the way. Eat. We've got work to do."

"Are you going to make us some when you get back here?" asked Ethan.

"Yeah, Ji, I've heard about your cooking for a while now. I think it's my turn—"

"Hush," said Heather, waving a fork toward Boland's monitor. "Right now, I'm kind of miffed at you two."

"Us?" Ethan frowned. "What did I do?"

"Don't give me any of that, mate. There's an old saying. If there's a dragon in the room, it will do you well to include him in your plans."

"Heather, don't overreact," said Boland.

Heather stabbed a forkful of lettuce. "This is not overreacting, Dana. Overreacting would be me showing up there and kicking down your door for a slicker and a pair of wellies. Which I'm not about to do. Yet."

"Thank God."

She chewed on the bite of salad and washed it down with some water. "But knowing about the storm would have allowed us to include it in our planning. Now we'll have to deal with it on the fly." Steve reached over and tried to steal a crouton from her plate. She slapped away his fork. "Don't even!"

"Don't even yourself, Slick. We're getting ahead of ourselves on the weather. Let's focus on objective one – locate and recon the facility here. Stay in the moment, rather than borrow trouble from the future." He looked at the screens. "How about it, Wonder Twins? Intel have any luck on narrowing down the candidates on the island?"

"We did, in fact," said Boland. "We're in the winery business."

Steve blinked. "Winery?"

"Yes. Formerly the Floribbean Wine Company, sold at auction a little less than two years ago to Mariposa Negra LLC."

"Mariposa Negra." He looked at Heather. "Black Butterfly. Same as—"

"Noir Papillion, I get it," said Heather, her brow furrowed. "Look, Tate, admittedly I haven't been in the States as often as I could. But I'm pretty observant, and I just drove more than a hundred miles over a bloody long bridge. Now where would anyone hide a vineyard out here?"

"In an abandoned fertilizer factory," said Ethan.

Steve looked at Heather. "Get the feeling someone's pulling a joke on us here?"

"Assuredly." She turned to the monitor. "All right, you two, cut the crap—"

"Check your tablet," said Ethan.

They looked down. On it was a picture of an old industrial plant, sheet metal roof and walls covered with streaks of rust, the words KEYS FERTILIZER faded to near invisibility on the side. In the foreground, a large metal and split wood structure with wide, semi-circular windows, wrought iron details, and a stylized logo of a wine glass filled with citrus fruits.

"It's on the northeast side of the island," said Ethan. "According to the Chamber of Commerce, it's a popular tourist destination that sells wines and sangrias developed from Florida citrus."

"Rubbish," said Heather.

"Figured you'd think that. But as far as we can determine, no one has seen a bottle of wine from the place since it was sold."

"So you found an inaccurate website," said Heather. "Hardly proof that it's our target."

"Oh, boss of little faith. Observe," said Boland. A dozen shots appeared showing Richards walking into the building. "We have Mirrorball confirmation of Angelica Richards at that site, both before and after the Coronado attack. But what do you notice about all these shots?"

Steve stared at them for a moment. "She's always entering the building."

"Good catch," agreed Ethan. "Now what isn't there?"

"She enters the building, but never leaves it." Steve looked in surprise over at Heather.

"Really? Then we need to make that our first stop," she said. "Gear up, light mission wear under tourist clothing. Let's blend."

He got up and finished the last bit of his salad. "On it."

"Dana, get me satellite coverage down here, as soon as you can. We're still blind without effective overhead."

"Still working on it."

"And pull everything you can on this winery. Any transactions, anything that's happened there for the past two years. Let's try not to go in blind."

2:22 p.m. EDT

"How was that not in any of the on the intel photos?" Heather shook her head in disgust.

They had parked the SUV just beyond the tree line in a stand of coconut palms across the street from the winery facility. Steve looked through the windshield at the abandoned fertilizer plant, the newer winery building and warehouse in front of them. "Parking lot still looks ready for the tourist trade. A shame that 12-foot fence topped with razor wire is scaring them all away."

Heather touched a control. The windshield went into active display mode and switched to a wireframe of the building and grounds. "Passive sensors have picked up a full surveillance package atop every post on that fence. Multiple cameras." She tapped one for a closer look. Feeds appeared from the different cameras atop it. "I knew Pradeep was paranoid, but this takes it to a whole different level. Triangle, you see this?"

"Roger, Echo Seven," replied Boland. "Don't get frustrated, it's still early in the first quarter. We knew he'd have a blitz package. We just have to work around it."

"Blitz package?"

"I believe it's yet another American football reference," grumbled Ethan, emphasis on the word 'American.'

"Now, now, Ethan," Steve admonished. "You're old enough to have taken in a London Monarchs or Scottish Claymores game in your youth."

"Perish the thought."

"Focus, gents." Heather's voice cut through the conversation. "Dana, verify. I count three video feeds per camera, and four cameras per post?"

"Affirmative. They're multi-band units with signal plexing self-contained inside the camera, so they can pull

HD, low light, and infrared feeds simultaneously from the same device."

"Can we spoof it?"

There was a significant pause from the controllers. Steve shifted on his seat. "Your silence is my Magic 8-Ball moment. 'Highly Doubtful, Try Something Else.' So spoofing cameras is out and cutting power to the fences is on the to-do list." He looked over at Heather. "He didn't electrify the fence as well, did he?"

Heather checked the passive sensor. "No EM field noted. Nope, just twelve feet of metal mesh."

"Topped with coils of spiky love waiting to hug you."

"Are you even trying to be serious about this?"

He sighed. "Right. Any word on satellite?"

"Sorry, Tango Two," replied Boland. "Intel says that they can't reposition because of a pending NASA launch window, and said window also leaves a gap in other available assets orbiting the area."

"There's nothing out here?" asked Heather.

"Well, the NOAA sats, but they're busy right now. You might have heard of it. Hurricane Debbie? The second we try to reassign any of those assets is your big spotlight moment on the world stage. I hope you dressed nicely."

Steve sighed. "Point taken. And getting any closer to the site for a recon is going to be problematic, too. We'd compromise the mission before we even started."

"Safe to assume they know us after our little adventure in Mysuru," Heather agreed. "Even if it's just Papillion, I can't risk getting seen, in case they recognize me from my MI-6 work in Africa."

"Then it's a good thing we brought along Plan B." Steve got out and opened the back of the SUV. He picked up a small dart pistol and aimed it at one of the trees. He fired and a projectile landed there. "Micro-cam deployed."

Heather waved from inside the SUV. "Signal acquired."

Steve tapped at his commlink. "Triangle, Tango Two."

"Tango Two., Triangle.

"Ready to show off your impressive piloting skills once more, Mr. Nowitzki?"

"Always."

"Good." He slid a tray out from the cargo storage in the back and pulled out a small surveillance drone. He flipped the rotors up to flight position and locked them in place, then stared into the camera pickup. "Camera check, please."

A section on the windshield screen became a video window tied to the drone. Steve's face loomed large. "We're good," said Heather, holding up one thumb.

"Camera feed five by five here as well," acknowledged Ethan.

"Right. Triangle, commence recording and launch." He held the drone over his head. It responded to commands from Ethan twelve hundred miles away and lifted into the sky.

"I've got it, Tango Two. What would you like?"

"For the moment, hover just beyond the tree line and get us the best elevation overview of the property you can. Then do a sweep around. Make sure to look at everything but the warehouse, so you appear like a tourist. Keep your camera rotating in a continuous panorama. We'll make any captures we need from the stream.

"So just fly around, looking but not looking?"

"You know what they say. Fly casual."

The drone flew straight up to a height of sixty feet, hovered for fifteen seconds, then began a sweeping curve to the right away from the warehouse. *Atta boy, Ethan.* Steve buttoned up the compartment and climbed back into the van. "Drone's away."

"I see that. Feed looks good. Triangle, you're capturing this?"

"Affirmative, Echo Seven," confirmed Boland. "Savannah and Intel are doing real-time analysis on the images. It will give us a good idea what we're up against."

"What do you think that'll be?" asked Steve.

"Not sure," said Heather. "Papillion's become a force on the black market for weapons. Could be anything." The elevation of the compound Steve requested lit up as Savannah identified a half-dozen targets. "Like that."

"'That' is an understatement, Ji," said Boland. "I'd say our primary has significant privacy issues."

Steve gestured. The image zoomed in one of the targets. He frowned. "Machine gun?"

Heather nodded. "Right in one. Big nasty one, too. Automated 30 millimeters, by the looks of it. Foul beastie, no need for an operator. Just turn this bad boy on, it's programmed to fire on anything bigger than a cockroach that moves into its field of fire."

"Oh."

"Yeah, 'oh,' mate. And I'm thinking it just got 'oh'-er. Dana, there are a lot of these positions. Can you check something for me?"

"Way ahead of you, Ji. Those look like the Serbian KL-77, which have a field of fire of 60 degrees. Sending you the overlay now." A third image popped up on the windshield, the satellite of the compound with fields of fire from the machine gun emplacements colored in red. There was a lot of red.

"Damn," said Steve.

Heather shook her head. "This just gets barmier by the minute. There are six of these bloody things. That means zero fire-free passages through that compound from anywhere around the perimeter fence."

"But there still might be a way. Look." Steve pointed at the video feed as the drone swooped along the tree line. Three pairs of private guards wearing suits and ties despite 85-degree weather walked across the parking lot in seeming random patterns. "His guard patrols aren't exactly hamburger. They must have some sort of ID-Friend-or-Foe tech in play. Spoof that, we get in."

"Muck it up," said Boland, "and you're hamburger helper."

"Oh, boss of little faith, I believe someone said." He looked at Heather. "Maybe the drone can snag the frequencies."

"Let's give it a try."

He looked out the window. "Ethan, do you see that flock of pelicans to the southwest?"

"Hang on a bit. Okay, I've got them on screen."

"It looks like they're going to overfly the compound. Can you tuck the drone in among them? I need to pull a little some signal intel work. We could use the cover."

"On it."

Heather looked over. "If we can't get the IFF spoof to work, we'll need a plan B."

"What if we come in from above? We could use a parasail, then cut ourselves loose and use a power assist to keep aloft until—"

"Echo Seven, Tango Two," interrupted Boland. "I think something's happening at the compound."

They looked at the monitor image as ahead of the drone, through the flock, they caught fleeting glimpses of a large gray cylinder rising above the rooftops.

"Bloody hell! It can't be!" Heather dashed out of the SUV and headed for the tree line.

"Ethan, abort! Abort! Get that drone out of there!"

"I'm tryin', laddie," said the Welshman, his voice strained.

Outside the vehicle, there was a bright flash and a sound like the world's fastest drumroll. On screen, pelicans in front of the drone turned from birds to a shredded pink mist of blood and feathers. Armor-piercing slugs fired at a rate of 4,500 rounds per minute tore the drone to pieces in less than a second.

The display dissolved to static.

Steve slid over into the driver's seat and shut down the heads-up display as he started the vehicle. He drove around the tree line and found Heather there, staring at the compound, her fists clenched. Guards inside the compound ran toward her. The nearest had reached inside their jackets and pulled out machine pistols.

He skidded to a stop between the fence and Heather, giving her cover, and pushed open the door.

"Cover's blown. Get in!" She just stared, not moving. "Damn it, Anjili, get in now!"

She shook her head for a moment, then jumped in and slammed the door. "Wait, it's in my name."

Bullets pinged off the armor on the driver's side door. "Don't even! Just buckle in and hang on!" He slammed his foot down on the accelerator and sped off.

Chapter 20

Amy bypassed the elevators and headed for the utility stairs instead. She slammed open the door and started down, counting the steps in her head.

Thirteen-fourteen-fifteen-sixteen. Hit the landing. Turn. Start again. One-two-three...

Start with a foul mood caused by her injury. Add on the bruise of being unfit for duty. Toss in the pain of Steve's absence. Dash in just a splash of jealousy of Heather Anjili for flavoring. Perfect recipe for Stress Puppy Amy.

She'd shown up at Marron's lab with the idea that she could distract herself by assisting him. Instead, she snapped at everyone. When she questioned Marron's work directly, he banished her from the lab. "That's enough help for one day. Come back when you can concentrate and contribute!"

Concentrate and contribute. As if. Nine-ten-eleven... They could see the errors more clearly! Another landing. Again. One-two... Maybe if Rose talks to them—

Amy stopped on the steps. *Oh, God. I've been so caught up in my own drama, I haven't checked in with Rose in... how long?* She closed her eyes and gently banged her head against the wall a couple of times, then rested against it. *Stupid. Dumb. Officially the worst friend in the world.* "Savannah, do you have a location on Rose?"

"Rose Johannsen is in her quarters."

"Put me through please, privately via my commlink."

"I am sorry; Rose Johannsen has placed a privacy block on all incoming calls."

"She'll talk to me. Put me through."

"I am sorry—"

"I don't care if you're sorry!" Her raised voice echoed up and down the stairwell. She sank down and sat on the steps, anger draining from her. "I need to tell my friend I'm sorry." After a moment, she looked up. "What is she doing, anyway?"

"Research."

"On what? Never mind, I'll ask her myself." She stood up and started climbing the steps two at a time.

A few minutes later she stood outside the door to Rose's quarters and put her hand on the ident plate. Nothing happened. *Come on, Rose. Really?* She knocked on the door. "Hey Roomie, it's Groundhog Day. Time to come out and see your shadow." Still no response.

Uneasy, Amy looked up. "Savannah, she is in there, right?"

"Affirmative."

"Is she... entertaining?"

"I am not sure what you are referring to—"

"Is she alone in there?"

"If you are inquiring whether Rose Johannsen is engaged in activities of physical pleasure with—"

"And that's enough of that discussion for today," interrupted Amy with a shudder. *I wonder, has Rose had 'the Talk' with Savannah? Exactly how would you do that with an AI? I'll bet it was an interesting conversation. Plus, given Rose's proclivities, Savannah would have a ringside seat to all sorts of—no, no, don't go there.*

Come on, think. Amelia Jane. You know Rose better than anyone. She would have had a Plan B. "Savannah, did Rose leave me a key under the doormat?"

"Accessing. Affirmative. Playback begins."

Rose's voice came privately through her commlink. "Sorry you're locked out, Roomie. If you need in, just tell Savannah how we first met. Two-word answer. Oh, and don't eat all my cookies. Ciao!"

Amy stared at the door. *Rose, you promised!* She sighed. "Black Sparrow."

"Acknowledged." The door opened.

A blast of sound greeted Amy. She walked in and immediately questioned the wisdom of her choice. Papers covered almost every surface of Rose's living quarters. In the center of it all, stark naked with a stylus in hand and making notes on a light board was the woman herself. She had a vintage progressive rock song cranked up to painful.

"Savannah, reduce music by three-quarters!" Amy yelled. Mercifully, the conflicting wail of guitars diminished from mind-numbing to manageable.

Rose looked up in surprise and spotted Amy through the light board. "When did you get here?"

"And good afternoon to you, too." *This level of obsession is familiar. Junior year, I think.* "Rose, how long have you been at this?"

"Not that long."

"That is incorrect," added Savannah. "Rose Johannsen has been working on this project for almost four days continuously. Her longest stretch without a break during that time is 21 hours, 17 minutes, 9 seconds."

Rose looked up at the ceiling. "Tattle-tale."

Amy shook her head. "When was the last time you ate? Drank something other than coffee?" Rose opened her mouth, then paused in confusion. "Thought so. I'm putting you on time-out."

"But—"

"No buts." She started forward.

"Stop! Freeze! Don't move another step."

Amy looked down. She'd placed her foot on top of one of Rose's seeming scattered papers. With exaggerated care, she reversed course. "My bad. But seriously, I'm invoking privilege. You need to take a break." She looked around. "Uh, any good way through this to your kitchen?

"Go six paces to your left, then three forward. You'll see a path from there." Rose started to jot again on the light board. "And I don't need a break!"

Amy started on the indicated path. "Roomie, yes you do. This is a bit much, even for you. Naked, surrounded by—" She began to wave her hand when she noticed something. She stopped and picked up one of the papers. "Is the Triangle logo in the watermark here? Above a map of western Siberia?"

Rose looked over. "Yep. One of the first things I spotted as I put the papers in order. And when I began translating—"

"Whoa, slow down! Let's make a deal. You, a shower, and some clothes. Me, I'll make us a meal, and then you can run me through whatever this is. Deal?"

1:47 p.m. EDT

Amy's head was pounding as she stared at the lightboard. She wasn't sure it wasn't from the caffeine. "This is one heck of a dragon you've grabbed by the tail, Rose," she said, indicating the circle of symbols."

"Not me. This is definitely a 'we,' Roomie. The sooner we make this circle bigger, the better. I have the feeling persons have disappeared over this in the past. How Savannah managed to get it into my hands—"

"You required an answer, Rose Johannsen, so I provided it. I will always provide for you."

Amy paused. "She's beginning to sound obsessed with you."

"I've noticed. But I've got it handled."

"Just the same, I wouldn't make her mad."

"Duly noted."

"Still, no idea who was behind the original eugenics program?"

"None. These Triangle mission reports discovered the project in progress behind the Iron Curtain. The source documents read like some sort of Tower of Babel on paper."

"Just how did Triangle find it, anyway?"

"They didn't. It was handed to them because no one knew what to make of it."

"How so?"

"A strategic weapons inspection – ever hear of the START Treaty?" Amy shook her head. Rose continued.

"U.S. and Soviets decided that instead of being ready to kill each other a hundred times over, fifty times over would be good enough."

"Yay, us."

"It was a big deal, as I understand it. But that also had a slogan. 'Trust, but verify.' Inspection teams from both sides went to the other's facilities to not only check the weapons were dismantled, but also stayed that way."

"And this matters... how?"

"Because a young Air Force captain was part of a treaty verification team and made a wrong turn. He got separated from his team. This is in the age before cell phones, satellite phones, all that. So he rolls up to a facility that looked like a decommissioned bunker, opens the door and instead of a Russian army officer, meets a gorgeous redhead. Probably love at first sight." Rose chuckled. "Of course, the fact she was five-ten, built and naked probably helped."

Amy burst out laughing. "Get out."

"No, that's really the way they m—" Rose covered her mouth suddenly and looked away.

Amy eyed her suspiciously. "Oh, no you don't, Roomie. You do not get to clam up on me now. Not after you let that one slip."

Rose stood and began to pace. It took her a moment, and when she spoke, she sounded more serious than Amy had ever heard her in all their years together. "Amelia, you need to understand something. When you asked me to start looking, you wanted some specific answers. Well, there are answers for you in here. But there are also a lot of answers about much, much more. And I'm not sure if I should be the one to tell you anything else."

Amy stood and put her hands on her friends' shoulders. "Remember the password phrase you made me use to get in here? It wasn't exactly 'Open Sesame.' You've always kept secrets when you've needed to, Rose. And when the time's right for you to stop, you do that, too. Trust yourself. I do." She looked at the projected screen floating in mid-air. "Twelve symbols. The Zodiac? Explain that to me, at least."

"From what gathered from the Triangle debriefings, the people behind the original eugenics project wanted twelve individuals, designed from the ground up. Embryos with designer DNA. People with extraordinary abilities."

"We're talking Talents?"

"Yes. I believe this project may be the source."

Amy sat down and took a deep breath. "That had to be a breakthrough."

"Not so much as you'd think. The groundwork had been laid by genome mapping projects of Watson and Crick in the 1950's."

"The pair that won the Nobel Prize for discovering DNA?"

"Discovering it? That Nobel was their consolation prize – it bought their silence."

"I thought genome mapping was something done in the late twentieth century."

"Yes, the Human Genome Project. One of Triangle's better covers. Watson and Crick did the real work a half-century earlier, not just in mapping DNA, but in manipulating it. Triangle suppressed their actual work, and off it went into the Pandora vault." Rose took a sip of her coffee. "Here an interesting coincidence. Some the Watson and Crick tech? Well, one of the techniques they developed showed up in the real world in the late 1970's. Care to guess which?"

Amy though back through her history. "Can you give me a hint?"

The public story was it was developed to help couples conceive."

"Test tube babies?"

"Petri dish, actually. In-vitro fertilization. The timing around Project Wildcard is suspicious."

"I sense a connection."

"You should. In-vitro was an early candidate for a process to program the Wildcard nanites that was ultimately rejected. The team moved on to other methods. Yet, somehow, the technology still leaks out."

"Quite a coincidence."

"I agree. The timing is more than coincidental. Additionally, a name keeps showing up amid all the Babel files." She handed Amy a piece of paper.

"Hampton?"

"I thought at first it might be a location where a lot of this led to. But I remembered Dr. Marron said the lead scientist on Project Titan was Gwen Hampton."

"You believe she's involved somehow?"

"Savannah did a deep dive for me. A member of the Red Labs team who worked on the Watson and Crick investigations and corralled all their genomic data for storage in the vaults was Dr. Gwen Hampton."

Amy looked up at the ceiling and blew out a breath. "Wow. She would have been one of the leading bio-geneticists of her time, yet completely unrecognized because of her work in Triangle." She glanced over at Rose. "Could the Titan serum have been tailored as an invitation to her?"

"I'd never thought of that. I suppose it's possible."

"Go on."

Rose picked up a sheaf of papers and leafed through them, one by one. "Anyway, this organization started a project that for lack of a better term I'm calling Zodiac. They custom designed twelve embryos and found volunteers to be hosts. Three months later came their first surprise. Ultrasound exams show every host mother pregnant with twins."

"Twins?"

"Twins. Double the fun." Rose showed her an ultrasound image of a pair of healthy fetuses. "The message traffic is in code, but from what Savannah can decipher, Zodiac's fearless leaders were ecstatic. They believe they have twice as many possible uberhumans on the way. The host mothers all carry to term with no complications, at the end of nine months there are twenty-four healthy babies and then..." Rose drops the papers. "Nothing."

"Nothing?"

"Actually, the babies are all super healthy - no colds or anything. But other than that, none of the special abilities adults are looking for. No two-year-olds lifting trucks off the ground naked, babies flying around the nursery, no changing state from solid to fire to metal, none of that. So, after waiting for what look liked—" Rose flipped through the pages to verify something. "Yes, after waiting five years, Zodiac cut their losses and closed down their nursery school at Cherry Money."

Amy's blood ran cold. She looked at the page Rose was reading from. "That's not how it's pronounced. It's Chernyy Monarkh, the same place Dr. Marron said Triangle first acquired the Project Titan serum from."

"The circle closes a little tighter."

"Maybe." Amy couldn't shake the feeling something didn't add up.

"Back to our story. With the Zodiac facility in the middle of nowhere closed, our mysterious hosts foster out the kids all over the world, but assign watcher teams on them as well, just in case. Now here's where things get weird."

"It's already weird."

"No, this is left turn weird. We figure the Soviets may have been somehow involved because of where all this craziness is going on and after they fell their links back into the Babel when these people were found—"

"People? How many were found, exactly?"

"I'm getting there. Give me time. Stay with the story."

"Right. Soviets. What's weird about that?"

Rose handed her a piece of paper. "Zodiac personnel lists showing who was assigned to watch each pair of twins. Because of what I said earlier, I had Savannah check these names. According to her, they're all ex-KGB."

"That makes sense. Highly trained, and ruthless if needed."

"Not quite. You see, per the KGB rosters at the time, these people were already dead."

Amy looked at the list of names. "That's a neat trick. Zombie KGB agents?"

"Ronald Reagan's worst nightmare."

"Obviously not dead."

"Obviously not. But whoever was behind this originally had enough juice to hide a few hundred people off the grid in one of the most carefully controlled societies on earth. Let that one roll around for a moment."

Amy stood up and stretched. "I'm not sure I want to. But what about the twins?"

"It turns out sending them to live with others pays off." Rose pulled a file from her bookcase and gave it to Amy. "Pre-video era. What I wouldn't have given for a tape of this happening."

Rose had written "LEO" on the front of the folder. Amy frowned. "Who's Leo?"

"Remember when I called this Zodiac? That was their doing." Rose looked around for a moment, then pulled a piece of paper off the floor and held it up for Amy to see. It was a circle with twelve symbols. "This was the key. It shows that when implanted, each embryo was designated by a sign of the Zodiac. Capricorn, Libra, Gemini, Taurus, you got it. When they found they had twins, the set kept that same designation. This was the Leo pair. Fraternal, a brother and sister, somehow placed in the middle of the Cold War in Dyersville, Iowa."

"Why is that name familiar?"

"They built it and everybody came."

"Huh?"

"Nothing?" Amy shrugged. Rose shook her head. "Roomie, a piece of advice. If you are serious about keeping a particular redhead in your life, get up to speed on America's pastime. Dude really loves his Mariners—"

Amy opened the folder. "Rose? Bright shiny object. Back on topic, please." She flipped through the photos inside. "An auto accident? What happened?"

"Right. This happened before all that, anyways. Like most of the others Zodiacs, this pair were placed with a childless couple. Dad owned a farm; Mom was a schoolteacher. After the adoption, the boy played little league and learning to drive the family tractor. The girl appeared in school plays and piano recitals. By all accounts, they were the picture of normal."

"That sounds familiar." *Too close for comfort familiar.*

"One summer night, the family had gone for a movie and ice cream. On the way home, a drunk driver t-bones their car on the passenger side. Idiot must have been doing eighty at least."

"Did anyone see the accident?"

"Nope. Lonely moonlit road, middle of the night. Mom and Dad are killed instantly, the sister severely injured. The brother—" Rose stopped. "You okay?"

The same way my parents died. Amy tried to control the tremor in her hands as she gave the file back to Rose. "The brother was thrown clear."

"How'd you know?"

"Car rolled. Made sense."

Rose looked at her. "Right. Well, he did and landed in the cornfield relatively unscathed. The drunk and his companion somehow survived the crash and got out of their car."

"Wait. I thought you said no one saw the accident?"

"They gave statements just before they died. In the burn ward."

Amy's eyebrows raised at that. She took back the pictures and flipped through them. "The cars didn't burn in the crash."

"No, they didn't. The boy did. According to the accident report, he walked out of the corn, looked at them and burst into flames."

"Spontaneous combustion?"

"You could say that. According to the report on the incident, the boy just stood there, his body converted into flame. The fire didn't consume him. They tried to run, but the boy quickly figured out how to form and throw fireballs. He missed at first. Set the cornfield around them on fire. Eventually, his aim got better." Rose's voice got quiet. "He left them to die while he reverted to normal and pulled his sister from the wreckage just before the fire trucks showed up."

"The police believed the drunk driver?"

"The police weren't the ones taking these statements. Remember the agents tracking the children? As soon as the accident occurred and the boy manifested an unusual ability, they appeared on the scene. Cleaned the mess right up. Looked official while taking these statements and when the morphine drip on the victims' pumps malfunctioned, it was considered an unfortunate accident that was a blessing in reverse, that relieved them of a lot of suffering. All these are from the Zodiac files."

"I thought you said this was the accident report."

Rose nodded. "Just not the one on file in Iowa. This is the one that came from the archives, by way of Russia."

"What happened to the kids?"

"Officially, they were moved somewhere else into the foster care system in Iowa." Rose waved another file. "Zodiac realized that's the moment they hit the jackpot. With one-half of the Leo twins now emerging as enhanced, the project was now reactivated. The order went out to return all the other twins back to Cherry, uh, Churny—"

"Chernyy Monarkh?"

"Right."

Amy shook her head. "Wow. Now you've just kidnapped eleven pairs of unsuspecting teenagers with possible abilities and exiled them to the middle of nowhere. Not smart."

"I'm still going through the papers. But my theory is that the lead scientist on the project—"

"Gwen Hampton?"

"Sure, why not? With the events in Iowa, they're theorizing that the abilities were always there, latent inside each of the children. They just needed to be triggered or activated somehow. And that became the new goal of the project - find that trigger."

Amy looked up at the graph. "What do you know?"

"Twenty-four Zodiacs out there. Can I figure them out?" She waved at the papers strewn about. "There's a lot here. Some of it's written in red, and I'm willing to bet that ain't ink."

Amy studied the circle in the light board. "Twenty-four potential weapons." She looked up for a moment. She looked at spots on the Zodiac. "You've attached names?"

"Call it informed speculation, based on what we've learned. It would explain some of the things we've seen." She pointed at one spot on the wheel. "Here's an example. On Treasure Island, Mitch Williams self-identified as a Talent."

"Just before he tried to kill you."

"I'm trying to stay focused on the important part here."

"True, but what he said his talent was? Ballistic calculations? Might be useful as a trick-shot artist—"

Rose pointed to the spot on the wheel. "Sagittarius, the archer that never missed? Good skill for an assassin."

"Okay. Any way to identify his twin?"

She considered this. "Williams personnel files were always classified. I think I can understand why, now. Savannah is still blocked. If we find out who they are, I'd be willing to they're someone who's got tracking skills. Maybe like Artemis or Diana, the hunters from mythology."

"You do realize you just said that with a straight face."

She dropped the file on the tabletop and ran her hands through her hair. "Amy, I can say mythology with a straight face because I have no freaking idea what else is coming out of this box anymore!" She took a deep breath and blew it out slowly. "We've already tangled with people designed to have extraordinary abilities. That means someone took the time to think about what they could do. You want me to make a list of what they could possibly do?

Fine. They've already figured out fire, perfect aim, mind control, and electricity."

Amy stared at her. "You've included the Callahans?"

Rose nodded. "Twin sisters at the right age with abilities? Yes, I did. Not sure where they fit, yet." She reached for the stylus. "I guess there's one other name I should include as well – that story I started to tell you." Rose stood up. As she did, another file tumbled to the floor. Papers and photos fell out. One caught Amy's attention.

"Rose, hang on." She reached over and picked up the picture. "Savannah, can you see the picture I'm holding?"

"Yes, Amy Rogers. I have cataloged all documents in this collection."

"Display it for me on the large screen, please?" Amy walked over and examined the image, a picture of a guard at his station at the Chernyy Monarkh facility. "He's standing in front of something painted on the wall behind him."

"The graffiti design?"

"Yes, that's it. Savannah, can you remove the guard and complete the design for me?"

"Affirmative, stand by please." The picture shifted to a mass of pixels, then came into focus. The guard was gone. On the concrete behind him was a stylized silhouette of a butterfly at rest, wings upright. In the lattice of the wing, the form of an upraised fist was subtly highlighted.

Amy looked at Rose. "When was this picture taken?"

"1996."

"Damn." Amy darted for the door. "Stay here."

Rose followed her into the corridor, alarmed. "Amy, what is it?"

"We've got a bigger problem. We've seen that symbol before."

"Where?"

"A couple of days ago. It's tattooed on my sister's arm."

2:23 p.m. EDT

Amy made her way down to Level 5 and headed for the Detention Center. Despite her need for answers, she'd agreed to be the good girl and followed Watson's orders not to contact Angelica since they'd returned. *Looks like that's going to change.* Amy sighed. *There goes my reputation.*

"Amy Rogers, you seem concerned."

The voice over her commlink startled her. "Savannah?"

"Yes. Rose Johannsen requested I assist you. You seem concerned. Are you in distress?"

You have no idea. "Still working on how I'm going to get inside the Detention Center."

"Do you wish me to intervene?"

She considered this. *Might make it easy, but if it exposes their connection...* "Let's just play it by ear, okay."

"As you wish."

She turned off the main corridor and approached the sector where the center was located. Fifty feet away was a large double-hatch entry into the facility. Amy studied it a moment, then whispered, "Savannah, transmit an order to the sentries on duty to stand down and take a break."

"Amy Rogers—"

"Let me finish. Once they clear the entrance, open the access hatch partially and let me slip in."

"Amy Rogers—"

"Just do what I ask. Okay?"

"I am sorry, Amy Rogers, but I cannot."

"Why not?"

"Because there are no sentries on duty in the Detention Center."

"Excuse me?" Amy walked over to the hatch and looked through the inch-thick Plexiglas. As Savannah described, the guard on duty was nowhere to be found. "Do you have a location on the sentries?"

"Negative. No other Triangle personnel are currently located in this sector of Level 5."

Amy tensed up. *That's not right.* "Savannah, what is the Detention Center's current status?"

"Status reads green across the board. All cells clear except for one, assigned to Angelica Richards."

"At least that's normal."

"Not quite, all internal surveillance feeds have been disabled within this sector."

"Cause?"

"Unknown. I shall attempt to reroute and override."

"In the meantime, let's get this door open."

There was a moment's pause. The ident pad cycled back and forth from red to green, but the door did not shift. "Savannah, what's the holdup?"

"The hydraulics actuation controls appear quite expertly disabled. You may need a different ingress. Do you wish me to create one?"

She rolled her eyes. *What part of stealth is missing from your programming?* "No, I'll work on this from my end." Amy undid the external door access panel and started to examine the systems. All the while, her mind worked overtime. *The guards all sent away, door disabled, and cameras blacked out? Someone's gone to a lot of trouble to have a private moment with Angelica.* "Savannah, how's that surveillance override coming?"

"I am making progress, Amy Rogers."

"Good. I need to see what's going on in there for now. When you have any sort of feed is ready, send it to my SAVANT."

"Working."

She tried cross-connecting the backup hydraulic controller and triggered the doors again. The ident plate flashed red once more. Frustrated, she began to search for another way to actuate the door. On a hunch, she looked again through the Plexiglas at the central control hub desk to see if she might see a door control panel there. No such luck. All the monitors were dark for the various cells were dark. *Who on the base needed to talk to Richards this badly?*

One of the monitors flared to life, the image rolling vertically. "Savannah, are you doing that?

"Affirmative."

"Can you stabilize it?"

"Stand by. Audio connection established."

There was a brief burst of static over her commlink, then a pair of muffled voices. The sounds shifted. "What did you expect from me?" Angelica, defiant as usual.

"Anything but this."

Amy's breath caught in her throat. *It can't be.* But she'd sat in dozens of briefings with the woman since she's arrived that summer. She'd know her voice anywhere.

The camera image stopped moving. Director Watson stood in front of the cell, facing Angelica.

"Ms. Richards," said Watson, "we know how intelligent you are. We shouldn't be on opposing sides."

"You're trying to get me to switch sides? You must be desperate." Richards leaned against the Plexiglas. "Curious, since Triangle has two pet Talents on the payroll now. I mean, after all these years hunting 'em before they emerge, stopping them in their tracks? Just seems odd, don't you think?"

Watson was deadpan. "I have no idea—"

"Come off it, Rhonda!" Angelica stepped back and turned away. She paused a moment to gather her composure. "We both know better. How many Talents have you interfered with, kept from their birthrights?"

"That's not the whole story and you know it—"

"What makes it so fascinating is the irony. I mean, you of all people doing this." She slapped her hands against the Plexiglas. "When he finds out, it's going to be bad. But the other one?" The woman whistled once, sharp and shrill. "Talk about your family dramas."

"It won't be like that."

"You're way too optimistic. But that's the least of your worries." There was a pause, then Angelica whispered. "She planned all of this a very long time ago."

Amy looked about in confusion. *She?*

"Who are you talking about?" asked Watson.

"You already know, Rhonda." Angelica breathed heavily to fog up the Plexiglas and began to write something quickly with her finger. Amy's voice was urgent. "Savannah, capture an image of whatever she's writing. Don't lose it."

"Yes, Amy Rogers," replied the A.I.

Inside, Watson's voice had dropped to a whisper. "That's impossible. I saw her die."

"And then she got better." Angelica chuckled. "You really have no idea what's going on, do you? Hit from all directions and you still can't fathom who we are, what we can do. You might as well give up, Rhonda. You know her, and she really, really knows you. She's already four steps ahead of you. You'll never have any idea what she has planned next for you."

"But you do," snarled Watson. "We'll wring everything we need out of you."

"You can try. How well has that worked so far, Rhonda – or should I say, Leo?"

Amy looked up sharply. *The name in the Zodiac files.* "Savannah, get me in that room, now."

"Overriding the hydraulics will be heard—"

"Forget about stealth. Director Watson's in trouble."

The twin hatches slid aside with a loud screech. Amy rushed over to Watson's side. The Director stared in shock as she approached. "Agent Rogers, what are you doing here?"

"Savannah alerted me to an issue, so I came," she said. "Just in time, it seems."

"Yes." Angelica smiled. "A perfect family reunion."

"Oh, hey, Sis. Long time no see. Jumpsuits work for you." Amy looked at Watson, winked, then took her hand. "I hate to interrupt a really sincere heartfelt between you two, but the Director and I have got other things to do than get our horoscopes read, right?" Amy turned the cell. "We'll come back and have a family chat with you another time.

Maybe when you learn some manners. Or at least fashion sense."

Angelica rushed at the Plexiglas and slammed her fists against it. "This is a joke! It's impossible. There is no way she already knew. No way—"

Gotcha. Amy spotted the tattoo as Angelica beat on the window. "Savannah, sonic shield. And get me an image of the tattoo on her right forearm."

"Yes, Agent Rogers." A nest of countering sound waves surrounded her cube, muting Angelica's rants and blocking them from hearing her.

Watson pushed away Amy's hand. "Rogers, what the hell are you doing here?"

"No, Director, I believe the correct phrase is, 'Thank you, Agent Rogers, for the rescue.'"

"I wasn't in need of rescue."

"You're welcome anyway."

The Director saw Angelica, now staring at them from inside the cell. "Savannah, give us a little privacy." As the Plexiglas went from clear to gray Watson turned to Amy. "And I suppose you just happened to be in the neighborhood."

"Something like that, ma'am."

"Somehow, I doubt that, Agent Rogers."

"Right in front of Angelica's cell probably isn't the best time or place for that conversation. How about you reverse what you've done here to get this moment so the two of us can go to your office and have ours instead?"

"Why would I go there?"

Amy crossed her arms. "Because, Director, you owe me a conversation. Straight answers about Talents, about Zodiac." She fixed her with a stare. "And about me."

Chapter 21

Steve parked the SUV across from the loft and shut off the engine. They sat there for a moment in silence. He sighed and took off his sunglasses. "Triangle, Tango Two. Give us some privacy, will you? You and Boland go take a coffee break."

"Is that such a good idea?" asked Ethan. "Your cover is potentially compromised—"

"Just do it, will you?" His voice was tight. "Sorry, Ethan, I didn't mean—"

"Tango Two, Triangle. Understood. We'll monitor for outside activity and contact you if we see anything that warrants your attention. Triangle, out." The disconnect tone followed.

Heather was in the same spot she'd been most of the ride back, one leg pulled up to her chest, arms wrapped around it, staring at a fixed point on the dashboard. After he'd told her she was cargo, she'd shut down, not even commenting as he used every evasive tactic he could think of on the way back to the loft.

None of which will do us any good if they have any airborne assets. Steve thought back again to the target facility. *Considering that arsenal, they're sure to have a drone in the air by now. Plus access to the camera grid, like us, and I know I passed at least a half-dozen traffic cameras.*

Knife to a gunfight? This is more like knife to an interstellar space battle. Fighting one-handed isn't going to make it any easier.

"I'm already down one partner on this mission," he said, looking out the windshield to spot the nearest street camera. "Another one checking out mid-race on me is very uncool. Want to clue me in on what happened back there?"

"We lost the element of surprise. If we ever had it."

"That much was obvious. Who mounts a Phalanx-class Close-In Weapons System for home defense? It's like using a bazooka on a fly or setting your bug zapper to ten thousand volts. Can't think someone in this town isn't going to notice."

"This is the Conch Republic, mate. 'Live and Let Live' is their credo."

"Yeah, well, that's more a case of 'Live and Let Die' if ever I saw it." He glanced over at her. "But your reaction wasn't about losing the drone or the element of surprise. You saw that thing and ran toward the compound. Why?"

"I..." She looked away. "I needed to know if it was the same."

"The same what?"

She bowed her head. "The same one that killed Georges."

Steve blinked in surprise. "Echo Eight? Heather, I thought he was murdered by a sniper in Abidjan. You sanctioned the man in Brazil, it's why you were in Coronado that day, on leave, right?"

She barked out a laugh. "Watson would say that. Wouldn't do to have the truth out there. Might panic the new kids." She threw him a look of contempt as she got out of the SUV and slammed the door behind her.

Steve got out and moved to intercept. "Oh, no, no, no. You do not get away with that."

"Get out of my way. Now." The temperature of her voice was arctic cold.

Steve matched it. "Make me."

She crossed her arms as thunder rumbled in the distance. "Do you know how many ways I could disable you right now, Agent Tate?"

"Probably a hundred more than I do, Agent Anjili," said Steve. One side of his mouth quirked up. "Too bad none of them will work."

"You're overconfident, rookie."

"I'm not the one who just screwed up this mission."

They stared, waiting for the other to back down. Thunder rumbled again, closer this time.

2:51 p.m. EDT

The white circle of energy shut like a camera iris behind the woman as she strode across the parking lot toward the guards. She checked out how she looked in the reflection of his sunglasses - white hair spiked, tinted glasses, sleeveless white jumpsuit, and white knee-high boots. *Got to hand it to the Boss. Damn, I look good.*

"Where'd they go?"

"They drove toward town. Our tap on the highway cameras shows they haven't left the key."

"Still on the island? Should be easy enough to find and deal with them. Still, be ready to move out."

"But the equipment—"

"Will be a write-off."

"Yes, ma'am."

Never thought anyone would treat me with that kind of respect, did you, Sis? Karen grinned.

Time to earn my pay. She closed her eyes and concentrated. *They were spotted...out there, by those trees.* She shifted, letting go of the form, the limits that were Karen. Her body glowed brighter, turned white, then to pure light as it leaped to the sky, thunder trailing in her wake.

She spotted some clouds and danced among them for a moment, then she remembered. *Need to find Tate.* She turned her attention to the ground and located the point she wanted. In less than a second, she flashed from cloud top back to the ground, accompanied by a booming clap of thunder.

2:53 p.m. EDT

In the ICC, an alarm went off as the micro camera left behind earlier recorded the lightning strike. A moment later a figure walked into view. Facial recognition software immediately identified her and triggered a second, louder alarm.

"Controller Nowicki, Controller Boland, an urgent situation has developed in Key West," said Savannah.

"Yeah, I'll bet. My girl is probably kicking your rookie's butt," said Boland.

Nowicki just shook his head. "What is it, Savannah."

"A sighting. Ninety-six percent probability it is Karen Callahan."

The two controllers dropped their coffee and ran for their consoles. "Savannah," said Ethan as he moved. "Plot locations, our agents and Callahan, overlay on a grid map of the Key."

"Complying."

Boland said, "Live feed from the cam on the wall, monitor three." Callahan appeared. She seemed to be casting around, checking at the ground for something.

Boland turned to Ethan. "So far, so good. She hasn't found the camera ye—"

The monitor flashed over to white for a moment, went briefly to static, then returned to normal, except for one thing.

"Where's Callahan?" demanded Boland.

"One way to find out. Savannah, play back the video just before it blanked out. Slow down 16 to 1."

The image backed up. Callahan stood up, looked at the sky, then her body began to glow brighter until it was pure white. She became too bright to look at before she flashed upward as a bolt of lightning. The image dissolved to static.

"Camera must have reset from a small electrical surge," said Ethan.

"Small?!" Boland was incredulous. "She just turned into a freakin' bolt of lightning. How did she do that?"

"With some skill, it appears." He looked over at her. "Remember Red Labs? I think this is the same assailant."

"But that was an electrical weapon—

Ethan thought fast. "Wildcard was designed to make enhanced humans. Someone found a way to accomplish it. We'll worry about the how later. Right now, we have agents in the field being hunted."

Another alarm sounded. Savannah said, "Facial recognition confirmed on infrastructure camera 19-2, Key West Cemetery." The map plot updated.

Ethan looked at the icons. *Too close. Way too close.* He turned to Boland.

She nodded. "Echo Seven, Triangle. Come in."

2:56 p.m. EDT

Heather jabbed him in the chest with a finger. "You had no right to interfere—"

"'No right,' she says? Whatever happened to 'if I get seen, I blow our cover.'" He pointed at the bullet dings on the driver side. "Guess what? Mission accomplished!"

"Then you should have let me handle it and stayed back."

"What? Since when did you become a lone wolf?"

"When it became about something other than Triangle!"

He blinked in surprise. "What?"

She turned away. "You wouldn't have known. Georges wasn't Triangle, he was my first field supervisor in MI-6. We were investigating illegal weapons shipments in the Baltics, and word went out about the theft of a CIWS systems. I wanted to go right after it. Georges wanted me to be more careful." She leaned on the hood of the SUV. "I made it back. He didn't. Bad guys got away. And now I know where it ended up." She looked at Steve. "This case is now very, very personal for me."

"Look, of all the people in the world you could be stuck with, I'm probably the one who will best appreciate that story. More than you'll ever know. But personal and stupid equals dead—"

Thunder rumbled, much closer.

"Echo Seven, Triangle. Come in," said Boland, her voice tense.

They both stopped and looked around. Heather responded first. "Triangle, Echo Seven here. Status?"

"You must have been detected during your reconnaissance of the facility."

Steve looked at Heather and mouthed "Told you so." She waved him off.

"Triangle, Tango Two. Yeah, Ethan, we sort of figured that out. The bullet dings in the door were a giveaway. Any response from them?"

"Affirmative," said Boland. "They've dispatched an asset of some sort."

"Of some sort?" Ethan's voice was dubious. "Tango Two, this is Ethan. Where are you both?"

"In the street in front of the safe house," Steve replied. Thunder rumbled louder. He looked up. There wasn't a cloud in the sky.

"Get inside now. Both of you." His tone was urgent. "Go into the secure room and seal it immediately."

"Why?" asked Heather.

"It's a Faraday cage. It should protect you from—"

The bolt of lightning struck the street thirty yards away. The pressure wave from the thunder knocked people to the ground, including both Steve and Heather. He scrambled to his feet and offered her a hand up. "You okay?"

"Yeah, but who's that?" She pointed toward up the street. Where the lightning struck stood a woman with her back to them, dressed in a sleeveless white jumpsuit and boots, her white hair spiked in all directions.

"Never seen her before."

"That's not true." The woman turned around to face them.

His heart sank as he recognized her. "Callahan."

"Hello, Tate. Ready to die?" She thrust out her hands and lightning leaped off them toward the two agents.

ACKNOWLEDGMENTS

Some books are a sprint. Some are a marathon. This one, through no particular fault, was a cross-country hike. There are stories that go with the journey. Someday, I might even tell them.

A voyage like this is not taken alone, though. Many thanks go to Suzanne Metzger, Jeston Hays, Frank James Bailey, Ruben Romero, Eric Koda, Christy Nichols Turner, Joel Yost, Jodi Carol, J. B. Lee, Debbie Speirs, Alicia Steffenhagen, Kyle Andersen, Jessica Lohmann, Carla Speed McNeil, Nicole Dubuc, Mark Palmer, John Hatfield, and lastly, my father, Donald Charles Speirs, who never failed to ask if it was done yet.

You know, sometimes, it just never is.

Until it is.

Stay tuned, the next chapter's already on the way.

- Lakeland, FL
November 2016

Other publications by
D. G. Speirs

Triangle: False Mirror

Imagine you had an ability no one else could ever possibly understand. Steve Tate and Amy Rogers are Talents, people with just such abilities, forged from tragedy in their lives. Each believes they are alone and unique, until the day their paths cross in Nassau – when Steve discovers the woman who has murdered Amy's boyfriend is the same who killed his mother and sister in cold blood five years earlier. But that turns out to be just the beginning, for this killer is part of a much larger conflict, one that leads Steve and Amy into an organization working on the margins of society to keep the world safe from even greater threats. Now can this pair with their unique gifts stop a killer before she gets her hands on a piece of technology that could lead to global catastrophe?

Triangle: Rescue

Steve Tate is a one of the lead draws on the World FreeRunning Tour. Fast, handsome, agile in ways that seem almost supernatural, his abilities have made the sport a success and him a superstar. But when one of his fellow racers has his entire family kidnapped and held for ransom by the Somali warlord faction known as Scorpio, his choice is clear – even if the boss is going to be upset. Of course, he could always use a little backup...

Books available at Amazon.com

About the Author

Born in New York and raised in California, D. G. Speirs has been a traveler all his life. He graduated top of his class from the Naval Nuclear Power School and served in the US Navy for over a decade. He traveled the world, coaching American Rules Football in Australia, modeling for Issey Miyake in Japan, playing Santa Claus for a stadium full of NFL fans, and making t-shirts for fans of a certain animated television show in Germany (yes, she can still do anything).

He's owned his own marketing firm, and been on a national consulting board that assisted other entrepreneurs. He's been a public speaker, board-member of a local Chamber of Commerce, Rotarian of the Year, a retiree, a family man, and a performer of some sort for over four decades. In other words, a pretty average guy with an IQ of 154.

He's written blogs about Walt Disney World, about life in general, and for the last three years a daily inspirational one that draws wisdom from the intersection of lessons in Eastern philosophy with those taught on a show about candy-colored ponies and unicorn.

He's a connoisseur of fedoras, bow ties, and black cherry soda, and believes there's always a better story out there, even if you just have to make it up yourself.

D.G.'s currently resides in Florida at Storyteller's Crib with his cats, Houdini and Sissy.

www.ingramcontent.com/pod-product-compliance
Lightning Source LLC
Chambersburg PA
CBHW051416170626
46809CB00006B/2189